ALMOST IN LOVE

KYLIE GILMORE

Copyright

Almost Dating © 2014 by Kylie Gilmore

Almost in Love © 2015 by Kylie Gilmore

Excerpt from *Almost Married* © 2015 by Kylie Gilmore

First Edition: February 2015

Cover design by Rogenna Brewer

Published by: Extra Fancy Books

Originally published under the title *Stud Unleashed: Barry*

ISBN-10: 1942238010

ISBN-13: 978-1-942238-01-0

For every person who dared to be different. Rock on!

Author's Note

I've included a bonus story, *Almost Dating*, a short novella that shows how Barry and Amber meet.

Computer genius and frozen yogurt store owner, Barry Furnukle, hasn't had a girlfriend in fifteen months, two weeks, and three days. Not that he's counting. And even though his new beautiful neighbor, Amber Lewis, is way out of his league and has a beefy, tattooed boyfriend, he can't help but wish she'd notice him. After Barry sees Amber's boyfriend with another woman, he knows she deserves so much better—a guy who will treat her right. But how will he prove he's more than just the nice guy next door?

ALMOST DATING

KYLIE GILMORE

CHAPTER ONE

Barry Furnukle tried never to judge from appearances, but he couldn't help it in this case. He was fascinated with the blond woman with streaks of pink in her hair. She'd just left the apartment across the hall, passing him with her overly muscled, overly tattooed boyfriend without a glance. Was his new neighbor a druggie? Artiste? Punk rocker? The pink streaks told a story he wanted to hear from beginning to end. Not to mention her pink sweater full of lacy holes that gave him a peek at a snug, white tank top.

He set the box of stuff he was carrying on the floor, opened the door of his new apartment, grabbed the box, and turned to get one more enticing look at Pink Hair. Despite her boyfriend's hand stuffed possessively into her back jeans pocket, she tossed him a look over her shoulder and winked. He nearly dropped the box he was carrying.

Vixen, he thought with a grin.

After a few more trips, he was moved in. He put together the king-size bed frame, tossed the box spring and mattress in place, and flopped down. Moving was exhausting, especially when you did it alone. He could've hired a moving company, but with so little stuff, he hadn't seen the point. His new apartment was in Clover Park near the frozen yogurt shop he owned, The Dancing Cow, and only a ten-minute drive to his mom's place in Eastman. It was a temporary situation until he found a house he loved.

He thought again of Pink Hair. She reminded him of an anime character with the long wavy hair, the big blue eyes, the heart-shaped face, the curvy figure. He hoped he'd get to see her again soon. Of course he would, she lived across the hall. His luck was finally going in the right direction. Not that he was counting, but he hadn't had a girlfriend in fifteen months, two weeks, and three days.

That night, after a dinner of take-out Chinese while watching an old episode of *The Twilight Zone*, he went to bed, muscles aching from his big moving day. He was rudely woken from a deep sleep by loud laughter and voices right outside his apartment door. He squinted at his cell phone in the dark. Two a.m. Great. He hoped this wasn't a regular thing with his new neighbors.

He peered through the peephole across the hall. It was Pink Hair and her boyfriend.

Should I introduce myself?

It's two in the morning! They're probably drunk and about to do it.

He shuffled back to bed to the sound of Pink

Hair's giggling. The silence that followed wasn't nearly as welcoming now that he knew the cause—wild monkey sex. Surely that was the kind of sex Pink Hair had.

Don't go there.

Still, he couldn't help thinking about the women that generally found him appealing, other computer geeks he met at his old software engineering job in California, who were into regular man-on-top-hurry-up-already sex. Like Sheila, his last girlfriend, who left him for a job at a new start-up tech company in Boston. He hadn't even known she was looking for a job. He hadn't been heartbroken, just surprised. Theirs had been more like a friends-with-benefits situation. Actually most of his relationships went that way. They'd start out as friends at the office, where they spent most of their waking hours working on networking and systems communications products, then onto a hookup on the weekend, back to work on Monday, no hard feelings.

His computer geek bedroom experience came down to simple arithmetic, really. The women, outnumbered ten to one at work, didn't need to look very far for a date. And every single guy there wanted them. Barry did have the distinction of being chosen frequently over his fellow computer geeks, making him a bit of a rock star to some of the guys. He supposed it was his friendly, nonthreatening demeanor. Also, he was a gem.

His mother said so.

He hadn't had much luck meeting women since moving home to Connecticut a year ago. He mostly only saw his mom and the families that came into his shop.

Something had to give. Self-serve was fine for frozen yogurt, not so great for orgasms.

~ ~ ~

The next day Barry left his apartment happily humming "Sunrise, Sunset" from *Fiddler on the Roof* as he looked forward to a morning at his favorite place in Connecticut, the state park along the Long Island Sound. On one side was the sound, the other side a saltwater marsh, which was one of the best places to go birding in the entire state. Birding was one of his many hobbies, along with app development, watching sci-fi movies from the '60s, and enjoying musical theater.

He walked downstairs, ultra-high-definition binoculars clipped onto his belt loop, and was joined by the muscled, tattooed boyfriend of Pink Hair. Looked like the guy didn't stick around long after the deed was done. Barry always made his lovers breakfast and tried for round two, never sure how long he'd have to wait for his next opportunity for sex.

"Good morning," Barry said.

Tattoo Guy grunted, and they continued down the stairs, awkwardly in step, both long-legged, both tall. Barry was six foot. This guy was an inch shorter, but much wider due to a ridiculous amount of bulky muscle. Tattoo Guy headed for his monstrous chrome and leather motorcycle.

Barry headed for his Honda Accord with the giant Dancing Cow magnets on both sides, a very effective advertisement for his shop. He'd also installed a loudspeaker on top of the car that mooed, though he only used that in town when he saw families walking down the street. Sort of like the cheerful tune of the ice-cream truck he remembered from when he was a kid. You always knew good treats followed that sound.

When he arrived at the beach, he did his usual run on the sand, followed by a more leisurely stroll through the nature trails where he went birding. He found it easier to be still and observant after wearing himself out with a run. He noted a variety of waterfowl—loons, grebes, and ducks—some of the last of the wintering species along the saltwater marsh. He traveled further inland where trees lined the paths and came across a real find for the first weekend in April—a nest of black-capped chickadees. He snapped a picture with his cell. He couldn't wait to add that to his birding spreadsheet.

April in Connecticut meant one thing—mating season. He shifted uncomfortably. He only hoped this time he'd be in on it. With a female of the human variety, of course.

After a very successful morning of birding, he headed back to his apartment and ran into Pink Hair heading out with a basket of laundry.

"Here, let me help you with that," he said.

She eyed him. He self-consciously pushed a hand through his unruly dirty blond hair and hoped he didn't look too rumpled from his run on the beach. He hadn't shaved either, but he suspected someone like Pink Hair wouldn't care about a little stubble. She wore a pink My Little Pony T-shirt that revealed her midriff, where a diamond belly-button stud sparkled at him, and pink jogging pants. Bubble-gum pink toenails peeked out of pink flip-flops. So very pink. Like cotton candy with a splash of hot sauce. He found he really wanted a taste, even at the risk of getting pummeled by Tattoo Guy.

She flashed a quick smile that had his heart picking up speed. "Oh, I remember you. You just moved in, right?"

He grinned. "Yes, I'm Barry." He gestured to his place. "I'm just across the hall. Can I take this for you?"

He held out his hands for the laundry basket. His glance fell to a pink lacy bra right on top of the pile, and he felt his ears burn. Fortunately, she didn't seem to notice.

"Nah, I got it. Nice to meet you, Barry." She padded toward the stairs heading to the basement laundry.

"Hey, Pink Hair, what's your name?"

She barked out a laugh and turned. "It's Pink Hair."

"Do you like birds?" he blurted.

Her brows shot up. "Uh, sure." Then she kept going, out of sight.

Do you like birds? Real smooth, guy. This is exactly why you're still single.

His eye caught on something pink on the stairs. Pink Hair was gone, but she'd dropped something. He went to fetch it—a pink thong. What to do? Should he follow her to the laundry room and hand it to her? He quickly ran the possible outcomes through his mind.

Him: Hey, Pink Hair, I found your panties on the stairs.

Her: A) Thank you! I'm <insert name here>. Let's hang out. (Fantastic results, probability 1%.)

B) Gross! I don't even know you, and you followed me to the basement, holding my most private unmentionables? (Likely results, probability 85%.)

C) Throw them out, weirdo! 'Nuf said. (Worst-case scenario, 14%.)

He didn't like those odds.

Barry stuffed the thong in his pocket and headed back to his apartment. With minimal handling (he wasn't an animal), he tossed the thong in the hamper to be washed and returned at some later date when he hoped they'd look back on this incident like some funny, inside joke between them.

CHAPTER TWO

Barry walked into Garner's Sports Bar & Grill on Thursday night, Ladies' Night, as he always did—with fresh breath and great hope.

He always walked out with a slight buzz and a couple of wrong numbers in his pocket.

Tonight started out no different. He chatted up a couple of pretty ladies sitting on his right, unsure which one to give special attention to, but then it turned out it didn't matter as they moved on to grab some dinner, bidding him goodbye.

He sipped his beer and soldiered on, giving himself a little pep talk. He was a catch if anyone took the time to get to know him. Sure he didn't have movie-star good looks or huge muscles (no fat either), but he owned his own business, had plenty of money socked away in the bank thanks to a hugely successful app he'd sold to one of the big guys, and had a handful of investments. His app, Giggle Snap, was a social media phenomenon focused on sharing sounds— laughter, conversation, and sound effects. Some of the stuff people came up with to share was hilarious. His favorite was a growly, old man reading flowery poetry he wrote himself. With a one-minute limit on the sound, sometimes the old man had to speed up at the end, which was even funnier. (Dewdropsfromyourlips-Idotastemysweet.) Other people were into the fart noises.

He'd made enough money from Giggle Snap to quit his old job. Opening The Dancing Cow had just been for fun. Besides all that great stuff, he always had fresh breath. He huffed into his hand to check. Yup, still had the good stuff. Maybe a little beery now. He popped a breath mint and prepared to regroup.

He did a casual scan of the bar and noticed Tattoo Guy approach a woman with long black hair and lay a big, wet one on her. Barry stiffened. He'd wanted Pink Hair all to himself, but not this way. Not with her getting cheated on. He narrowed his eyes. He should say something. Let Tattoo Guy know he was onto him.

He took a sip of beer for courage. Tattoo Guy did have a lot of muscles.

He'll crush you.

Maybe Tattoo Guy and Pink Hair weren't exclusive. That would work out even better for Barry. He wouldn't have to tell her that her boyfriend was cheating on her *and* she'd still go out with him. Minutes ticked by. He sipped and watched as Tattoo Guy proceeded to run his hand up and down the woman's ass, occasionally stopping to lay another deep-throated kiss on her.

Tattoo Guy suddenly looked up and met Barry's eyes, nearly causing him to topple off his bar stool. Barry quickly averted his gaze and grabbed a handful of pretzels, concentrating on removing every bit of salt from each pretzel. They really should offer pretzels in two varieties—salted and unsalted.

A beefy hand landed on Barry's shoulder, and something approaching a squeak emitted from the depths of his terrified soul. *Cool it! This is a public place. Lots of witnesses to prevent a homicide from occurring.*

Barry cleared his throat. "H-hi, Tat—I mean, h-how are you?"

"I know you," Tattoo Guy said in his face. He had the worst cigarette-beer breath. Barry immediately switched to breathing through his mouth.

"I don't think we've been introduced." Barry held out his hand. "I'm Barry."

Tattoo Guy gripped his hand, crushing his fingers. "You never saw me here."

"No," he gasped out.

Tattoo Guy released his hand and clapped him on the back, nearly sending him into the bar. "Enjoy your beer."

Yeah, like he could enjoy his beer now. He sat there for a few minutes just so Tattoo Moron wouldn't think he was the reason Barry was leaving, and headed home. When he arrived at his door, he glanced across the hall at Pink Hair's door, wishing he had some excuse to talk to her so he could tell her to dump that asshole. He walked over and put his ear up to her door. Sounded like she was watching TV.

Why tell her about her cheating boyfriend? So you can have her?

That stopped him. He wasn't going to hurt the woman just to further his own agenda. With a resigned sigh, he let himself into his quiet apartment. He just wished there was something he could do to alleviate her inevitable, crushing pain when she found out the man she slept with was two-timing her.

Then he had a great idea.

~ ~ ~

Amber Lewis was in the zone. She had her fave TV show, *Zombie Bonanza*, on DVD in the background while she painted with watercolors on a canvas she'd prepared the night before with a swirling, pale blue background. She applied wet paint on wet paint to achieve a suffused color of yellow and red mixing together. Today she painted fire—flames shooting across the canvas, highlighted by the pale blue. She mostly created abstracts and considered herself a watercolor artist first, an elementary school art teacher second. The latter by necessity.

She added a few flaring finishing touches and leaned back to take it in. Not bad. She'd add it to next week's listing on eArt. She hadn't sold a single piece off the independent artists' website, but she was always hopeful that one day her work would be appreciated, and she'd be on her way to financial independence.

She stood and stretched her back, noticing some small papers lying on the floor by the front door. That was odd. She walked over to investigate. They were coupons. Ten percent off frozen yogurt at The Dancing Cow. She'd heard of the fro-yo place at the edge of town though she'd never stopped by. She'd heard it was overpriced, and on her teacher's salary, she contented herself with occasional binges of ice cream at Shane's Scoops. It must've been some sales guy sticking these under everyone's door.

She went to throw them out, and one of the coupons fluttered to the ground. She squatted down and picked it up. There was a picture of a guy in a cow costume, and for some reason he looked familiar. She studied it. What a geek! Dressing up like a cow. Wait a minute. She did know this guy. It was her new neighbor across the hall. She headed across the hall, intending to introduce herself and then explain she didn't appreciate him littering her floor with advertisements.

She knocked on his door, and a moment later it swung open. The man—tall, lean, and wearing a green Hawaiian shirt—beamed at her.

"Pink Hair!" he exclaimed.

She found herself smiling back. With his rumpled, in-need-of-a-haircut, dirty blond hair, brown eyes, stubble, and lopsided smile, he was appealing in a boy-next-door kind of way. Which was perfect since he was literally next door.

"Amber Lewis," she said. "Got the coupons." She held them up.

He nodded and smiled. "Good, good. Stop by anytime. The fro-yo is healthy and full of pro-bee-otics."

"Probiotics, you mean."

"No, no, it's pro-bee-otics."

"Barry, right?"

He smiled again, and laugh lines formed around his eyes. "That's right."

She hated to bust his happy little bubble, but the man couldn't even pronounce what he was advertising. "You're mispronouncing probiotics. Look it up. You'll see."

He cocked his head. "Well, no one's ever said anything before. I've been running the shop for a year now."

She grimaced. "Sorry to bear bad tidings. Speaking of which, don't slip any more coupons under my door. Our building has a no-soliciting policy."

"Oh, I wasn't soliciting. I only gave them to you."

"To me? Why?"

"I thought maybe you'd like some fro-yo."

"I like ice cream."

"But you haven't tried mine yet, have you?" His eyes met hers, warm and friendly. "I definitely would've remembered you coming into the shop."

She slipped into flirty mode easily. "Oh, really? Why is that?"

"Because you're so…I mean—" He gestured to her hair. "Who could miss those pink streaks?"

She tossed her hair over her shoulder, enjoying messing with him. He was flustered and becoming an interesting shade of pink himself. "What do you think of a girl with pink streaks?"

He straightened. "Oh, well…I think she's either an artist or…*mutter, mutter, mutter.*"

"Didn't catch the end of that sentence."

"Er, into some pretty funky stuff."

She jutted out a hip. "Funky as in…"

He stared at her hip, then his gaze traveled to the floor. "Er…"

She was suddenly annoyed. "What?"

"I'd rather not say." He shook his head. "I was wrong. Very wrong."

"What? Prostitute? Druggie?"

He waved his hand. "No, no. Nothing like that." His eyes told a different story.

She lifted her chin. "I'm a watercolor artist."

He nodded. "Yes, I would've guessed that right away about you. Artist. For sure."

She took a step back. "Well, nice to meet you, Barry."

"Wait! Can I see your art?"

She narrowed her eyes. "Is that some kind of pickup line?"

"No, I'm actually very interested. I have a lot of respect for artists."

She stared him down.

He cleared his throat. "Besides, I know you're with Tattoo Guy."

"Rick. His name is Rick."

He nodded gamely.

And because it was very rare for anyone to ever ask about her art, she found herself agreeing.

"Wait here," she said.

She headed back to her place and brought back her favorite canvas, the one that had been on eArt for a year now for the bargain price of a hundred fifty bucks and still hadn't sold. It was a dragon, serpentine and breathing flames, on a hazy lavender background. When she opened her door, he was standing in the hallway waiting.

"Oh, just come in," she said, waving him in. "You're not a serial killer, right?"

"My mother raised me not to be a serial killer, I swear. Right after eat your veggies, it was"—he raised his voice to a falsetto—"don't be a serial killer, Barry." He stepped inside. "I can give you her number if you don't believe me."

She laughed. "We'll skip the parental conversation. Here it is."

She held her breath. It was so hard to share her work. Rick thought it was a cute little hobby. But to her, it was much more important than that. It was her soul—that inner spark needing to express itself on canvas.

He didn't say anything at first, merely held the piece up and peered at it closely. Then he held it at arm's length and stared at it some more. She wanted to snatch it back and tell him to forget it, but then his kind, brown eyes met hers. "It's stunning. Amber, you are so talented. Wow. What else have you got?"

"You want to see more?"

"Yeah, if you've got it."

"Of course. I keep the finished canvases in my bedroom. Oh, just come with me. You look harmless."

"Famous last words." He wiggled his fingers. "Look out, I might mess up the covers."

She snorted. "Like I make my bed."

"I didn't suppose someone with pink hair would."

She laughed as she led him to her bedroom. Her paintings were stacked three deep along one wall. He took his time, stopping in front of each one, studying it from different angles, murmuring responses that she soaked in like a desert parched for one drop of encouragement.

"Nicely done," he murmured. "Angsty," came another response, and he was right. She'd painted it after she broke up with Steve, a six-month relationship that ended when she'd found him in bed, *her* bed, with another woman. "Gorgeous," he said about an abstract that an ex had described as a spiral made on a kids' toy, but was one of her favorite pieces. She felt like hugging this guy.

He went through the rest of them, murmuring soft praise under his breath, and finally turned to her. "Why are you hiding all these? They should be in a gallery in SoHo."

A rare, beaming smile crossed her face, so big it made her cheeks hurt. "Thank you," she said. "I'm not exactly hiding them. They're all for sale on eArt. It's just that no one has bought them."

He raised a brow. "How much?"

"All different prices," she said. "All very reasonable for original art. Nothing above two hundred dollars."

"Why not try a gallery?"

"I sent my portfolio to a few, but no takers."

He nodded. "Well, I'm sure you've heard this *ad infinitum*, but your work is incredible. You should be very proud."

She blinked back tears. "I am." She resisted hugging him. Barely. "Would you like to stay for some coffee?"

His eyes lit up. "I'd love to."

~ ~ ~

Barry knew he'd be up for hours with a cup of coffee, but no way was he turning down this golden opportunity to sit in Pink Hair, er, Amber's apartment and get to know her. Her place was a mirror image of his place, but much cozier. The walls were painted with golden swirls that reminded him of an Italian restaurant, Tuscany style, he thought it was called. The living room was spare, just a purple sofa and coffee table on one side, the other side had an easel with canvases and art supplies nearby. A TV sat in the corner.

He followed her to the kitchen, trying very hard to push his fantasy of a naked Amber lounging among the floral pillows in her queen-size canopy bed out of his head. She'd look so hot there with the floral comforter and the white gauzy canopy framing her in all of her pink glory. He got hard and quickly sat at the round kitchen table with a mosaic top he was sure she'd created herself. He watched her prepare the coffee and racked his brain for conversation that didn't involve asking why she was with a two-timing lunkhead like Rick.

"So who do you know in Clover Park?" Amber asked. "We're all connected by six degrees of separation."

He grinned. "Like Kevin Bacon. I'm not all that well connected. I just moved here a year ago from California."

"What made you move here?"

"My dad died." His throat went tight. "I came home to Eastman for the funeral and stayed for my mom."

He still missed his dad. He was a good man, a hell of a mechanical engineer too. His parents had been close, and his dad's death from a heart attack at seventy had been a shock to them all. His two younger brothers stopped home briefly, but they couldn't stay long. Daniel was in military intelligence, and Ian was a grad student in computer science at M.I.T. He knew some people thought it strange for him to move home at thirty, but for him it was no big deal. He'd been in between gigs since he'd sold his app, and his mom had been in bad shape. It was a hard year of mourning for her, and he'd done what he could to make it better. He knew she was doing okay when she told him to go ahead and find his own place.

Amber cocked her head. "I'm sorry."

He put up a hand. "It's okay. How about you? Who do you know?"

She plopped into the seat next to him. She had blue eyes the color of the sea. "I teach art at Clover Park Elementary, so I know all the teachers, all the kids, K through five, and all the parents. I'm close with Daisy O'Hare. You know her? Her sister, Liz, works with me, but Daisy and I really hit it off."

He brightened. "Sure I know her. I spend a good amount of time at her parents' restaurant."

"Yeah, everyone knows Garner's. So how'd you get into the fro-yo business?"

He shook his head. "Thought it'd be fun. It is. Fro-yo bars were really big in California. I just saw an opportunity here and ran with it. It's definitely more fun than what I used to do—software engineering."

"That does sound more fun."

"I develop apps on the side." He shrugged. "Just a hobby."

"Yeah? Anything I might know?"

"Have you heard of Giggle Snap?"

"I love Giggle Snap! So fun! That was you?"

He beamed. "Yeah, that was me."

"Awesome! What other apps have you made?"

"That was the first. I've been noodling around with another one for bird watchers." He waved that away. "I won't bore you with all the gory details."

"I love gory details."

He raised a brow. "Yeah?"

She nodded encouragingly.

"Well…" He checked in with her again, and she smiled. She was *so* pretty. "It's basically a database with information for a bird, like its relative size, color of plumage, shape of bill. It helps you figure out what bird species it could be from a narrowed-down selection. You know, since so many birds match similar descriptions."

"Sort of like a field guide."

"Yes!" He pointed at her. "Smart lady."

She grinned.

"But then I take it a step further. You can take a picture of the bird with your phone and match it that way, or if it's not in the guide, add it as an alternate match. It would help with conservation efforts to have that kind of shared information at our fingertips. Oh, and you can also tap on a bird picture and hear the bird's song. That, of course, is going to take a while to program. A lot of data points, plus accounting for new data being fed in by end users, but I thought it worthwhile."

"Barry, that is so cool. Is that why you asked me if I liked birds before?"

He nodded, relieved to have his dorkiness for blurting out that bird thing earlier explained. He should stop talking about birds, though. He could go on all night, and he really wanted to get to know more about her.

She stood and poured them both a cup of coffee. "So what do you call your app?"

He shook his head. "It's silly. Just a name I call it. I don't know if I'll keep it."

She set a mug down in front of him. He grinned. It was Cookie Monster with a space on the bottom for cookies. "Nice."

"One of my students gave it to me." She took her seat, with a mug that read Absurd.

He pointed at her mug. "I like that one too."

She flashed a smile, and he fell a little further in lust with her. "I designed this one. So, what's your app called?"

"Bird Bonanza."

"Ha!"

He waved his hand with a grin. "I told you. It's a placeholder."

"I like it."

He smiled and took a sip of his coffee. Her cell vibrated on the counter. She jumped up to check it.

She frowned and returned to her seat.

"Bad news?" he asked.

"Rick cancelled on me. He's already tired from work and just wants to head home after. He's a bouncer at a bar in Norhaven."

Bouncer, that he could believe. And also a big liar. He'd just seen him sucking face with another woman at Garner's, which wasn't work or in Norhaven. Jerk.

"You and Rick been going out a while?" he asked casually.

"Four months." She drank her coffee, still looking upset.

"He cancel on you a lot?"

"I understand. It would've been late by the time he got here. It's fine."

He should let it drop. He really didn't want to hear more about Rick, and he didn't want to let slip what he knew, but he couldn't seem to help himself.

"You and Rick exclusive?" he asked. "Pretty serious?"

She narrowed her eyes. "Are you hitting on me?"

"No, no, no." He shook his head to emphasize it. "Absolutely not. My curiosity got the better of me. Forget I said anything." He took a sip of coffee. "This is good."

She stood abruptly. Damn. He'd overstepped.

"I didn't mean anything by it," he said.

She got out two shot glasses. "You want a drink, Barry? Cuz I could sure use one."

"Uh, sure."

He watched as she slammed around in the cabinets, emerging with a cocktail shaker, a couple of liqueurs, and vodka. Now this was getting interesting. She expertly mixed the drink like one who had a lot of practice.

"Did you used to be a bartender?" he asked, impressed with her quick movements.

She shook it all up. "Smart guy. Yeah, I bartended in college once I was legal." She lined up two shot glasses and poured. It smelled a little like coffee. He checked the labels. Amaretto and coffee liqueur. Sounded tasty.

She handed him a glass and held hers up. He clinked it against hers. She downed the shot, and he quickly followed suit. Yum. He shook his head. Bit of a kick there at the end.

"What was that?" he asked.

"Screaming orgasm."

He sputtered. "Been a while since I had one of those."

She winked. "Been a while since I had the drink kind."

An image flashed through his brain of Amber in full ecstasy, screaming as she came. Sweat broke out on his forehead. He discreetly adjusted himself under the table. She poured them another shot, and they clinked glasses again.

"Down the hatch," he said. They drank at the same time. Warmth spread through him. He rolled his neck, feeling looser already.

She slammed her glass down. "Why do men suck? Just be honest with me."

He was used to women sounding off to him, the nonthreatening friendly guy, so he put it out there, the cold, hard truth. "Because they don't appreciate what a wonderful woman you are."

She blushed. "Stop. You hardly know me." She traced the table with a fingertip. "How am I wonderful?" she asked softly.

"Well, just look around. This place is warm and full of vibrant colors." *Like you.* "That tells me you're a passionate woman who loves life."

He worried for a moment that he shouldn't have said "passionate" even though he knew instinctively she was exactly that, but then she met his eyes and grinned. "I like you."

"Thank you, I like you too." He smiled goofily, a little buzzed. "Plus you're an artist. A very talented one at that. Not many people can do what you do. If I tried to do what you do, it would look like a chimpanzee got into the paints."

She smiled.

He lifted a finger. "And you're smart. You caught on right away to the brilliance of my birding app."

She laughed, and he grinned.

"You're kind," he said, serious now. "Look how you welcomed in your new neighbor. Like you knew I needed a friend."

He really did. It wasn't easy to move into a tight-knit small town, the outsider. Sure, people were friendly, but he didn't hang out with anyone on a regular basis. And it had been fifteen months, three weeks, and one day since he'd had a girlfriend. He really had to stop counting. The numbers racking up were doing a number on his ego.

She took his hand and stared into his eyes. He felt like they were connecting on a deep, deep level. It felt so good to hold hands. He could do this all night.

"You are my friend, Barry…" She paused. "What's your last name?"

"Furnukle."

She wrinkled her cute little button nose. "Really?"

"Why would I make that up?" One side of his mouth quirked up. "My real first name is Barrett, if you like that better."

"Barrett," she repeated. "Barrett Furnukle." She made a face. "Okay if I call you Bare?"

He flexed his fingers like claws and growled. "Like bear?"

"Sure, okay. Bare, you *are* my friend. From this day forward"—she lifted her shot glass dramatically—"oh. It's empty." She poured them both another shot. "Raise your glass, Bare." She waited until he did. Then she touched her glass to his. "From this day forward, you are my friend. Deal?"

He smiled, a smile that didn't feel altogether genuine because he already knew he wanted her as much more than a friend. Yes, she was way out of his league, but he had needs, dammit.

"Deal," he said.

They drank on it. She smiled brilliantly. "I am toast. Come watch TV with me."

He stood, a little wobbly. Three shots was a lot for him. He usually only had a couple of beers once a week. And he'd had a beer earlier.

She waved her hand and veered unsteadily to the side. "Ooh, wait. Let me get some cheese. I love cheese." She grabbed a bowl of cheddar cheese cubes from the fridge and headed for the sofa. He followed.

"You like zombies?" she asked.

He didn't. He liked sci-fi movies, especially old movies with laughable special effects. Zombies gave him nightmares. What was so appealing about dead people walking around with various body parts rotting off them?

"I love zombies," he said.

"Great! I've got seasons one through three of *Zombie Bonanza* on DVD." She hit play on the DVD remote. "Hey, that's like Bird Bonanza." She tapped her head. "Great minds, Bare."

They ate cheese cubes and watched zombies while Barry contemplated doing one of those casual stretch-an-arm-around-her-shoulders moves. An hour later, Barry still hadn't made a move and had more grotesque zombie images burned into his brain than he knew what to do with. Still he wasn't complaining because, without any prompting from him, Amber had just curled up against his side, which allowed him to easily and quite naturally slip an arm around her shoulders.

She smiled up at him, her eyes soft. "You're like a best girl friend," she mumbled before conking out.

Best *girl* friend? She must still be tipsy. He certainly hoped so. He was a red-blooded *man* with a lot to offer. Sure, he didn't have Tattoo Guy's machismo, but he had smarts, he had money, he had…a raging hard-on. He had needs, *dammit*.

He also had moves from his mother's romance novels he was dying to try out.

That's right. In his boredom kicking around her house this past year, he'd picked up a few books his mom had left lying around. No shame in that. *Carnal Werewolf* had been especially interesting.

He let out a breath, enjoying the feel of her cuddled up against him. He'd figure out how to move things to the next level tomorrow.

CHAPTER THREE

The next morning, Barry stepped out of the shower and took a good, hard look at his naked bod in the mirror. He puffed out his chest. Would Amber want this? He was long and lean, sort of a string-bean effect going on here. He struck a pose, arms up, flexing his muscles. He had some muscle definition along his biceps and abs from the pushups and stomach crunches he'd added to his morning routine months ago in an effort to up his hotness factor, but nothing extraordinary. He thought about beefy Rick with muscles and tattoos coming out the wazoo. Did Amber want more of the same, or was she ready for a change?

Last night at three a.m., she'd woken up, mumbled bye, and went to bed. He'd gone home, took care of his bad case of blue balls, and fallen asleep. He'd woken up determined to end his involuntary celibacy ASAP. With Amber. She was so different from the women in his past. She fascinated him. An artist with a sense of humor—she'd laughed at his jokes as so few did—and an innate kindness.

He dressed quickly in his black Dancing Cow T-shirt, rainbow tie-dyed boxers, and black pants, thinking of the romantic heroes in his mom's novels. They all had mouth-watering (according to the heroines, who drooled a lot) pecs, abs, and biceps. Maybe he should up his game, really go for the muscle thing. Couldn't hurt. Might even give him a confidence boost. He'd read in *Cosmo* (he just happened to stumble upon an issue online) that the ladies responded to confidence. He might even unknowingly be giving off an aura of desperation with his single state going on fifteen months, three weeks, and two days.

He grabbed his iPad and did a quick search online for workout DVDs. He'd just see what happened. Expectations set reassuringly low. Ah, this one sounded good with a lot of five-star reviews: *Six-Pack Abs and Two-Pack Butt in 30 Days*. Perfect. Ooh, and it was set to a party song mashup. See, this could be fun. He ordered it with express delivery.

Out of curiosity, he looked up Amber Lewis and art. He found her paintings on eArt. Look at this stuff. Awesome. He bought the most expensive one, a splatter of black, white, and red, somehow made feminine by puffs of pale green behind it. It was unusual, one of a kind, and gorgeous.

Just like Amber.

~ ~ ~

Amber spent the weekend in a rush of creative energy. Her paintings were selling on eArt, and she was so encouraged she dove into a series of paintings detailing her feelings. She called this series Elation. Polka dots exploded on the first canvas, the second bouncing marshmallows, the third a serene sunset, one of the few naturalistic paintings in her collection.

She still couldn't believe her most expensive painting had sold. Two hundred bucks. And then shockingly the next day, she'd sold another painting. And then another. Three paintings in three days! So far the sales had been from the same collector, a woman named Susan Dancy, but she hoped more people would discover her soon too.

She dipped her brush in fire red and made a diffuse line around the sun. Painting all the time was glorious. She felt like she'd finally made it. She was a success.

Over the next two weeks, Amber's creative energy amped up to a frenzy. She was selling paintings nearly as fast as she posted them on eArt. Susan Dancy was her biggest fan ever. She'd made over two thousand dollars in the past couple of weeks. Newfound hope and renewed interest in her craft had her swearing off men and dedicating herself to her art.

She called things off with Rick, who responded with, "Whatever, babe, I've had better." What a jerk. She had no time for people who didn't one hundred percent support her artistic side.

She lost herself in painting her latest, titled

Jubilation, a pink starburst surrounded by beautiful golden light. Hours passed like a blink of an eye, until she finished the painting and looked up, surprised to find it was night. Her back ached, her stomach growled, and she slowly returned to reality. She spotted a slip of paper by her front door and smiled. Bare never wanted to interrupt her artistic flow, so he just slipped her a note now and then to see when it would be good to hang out.

She knocked on his door. He answered, shirtless. *My, my, my. Someone is working out.* He had mouth-watering abs. A dusting of light hair ran down his chest, leading to a happy trail that made her lick her lips. Geez, it hadn't been that long since she was with a man. She forced her gaze back to his eyes.

He smiled—big time.

"You forgot your shirt, Bare."

"I was just changing." He turned and reached for a clean white T-shirt from a pile of laundry in a nearby basket. "I like to leave work at work, you know?"

His work shirt was also a T-shirt but whatever.

"You want to see what I'm working on?" she asked.

"Love to."

He followed her to her apartment, where she showed him her work-in-progress. She planned to let it dry and return to it with another layer of paint tomorrow.

He studied it, then turned to her. "What do you call this one?"

"Jubilation."

He nodded. "It fits. So things are going well, then, huh?"

She put her hands on her hips and looked around at the newly completed canvases lining the wall of her living room. "Amazingly, they are. Hey, you want to get some takeout? I forgot to eat lunch."

"Sure."

"Great. Thai okay?" She headed for the kitchen drawer full of take-out menus.

"Works for me."

A few minutes later, she'd placed the order, and they sat on the sofa with a couple of beers. Bare was so easy to be with. He was always so cheerful and agreeable, quick with a joke, and he liked her art. Friends didn't get any better than that. Sure, she had Daisy and Steph, another teacher friend, but Bare was right across the hall and available at a moment's notice. It was nice having a friend so close by that could just stop by whenever. She hadn't felt lonely ever since he'd moved in.

"Guess what?" she said.

He smiled. "What?"

"My art's selling really well. I mean, really well." She couldn't help her ridiculously happy smile. "I'm selling my paintings almost as fast as I put them up on the website."

He straightened. "That's great!"

She took a sip of beer. "I know!"

Bare grabbed the remote. "Feel like watching more

Zombie Bonanza?"

"Sure. So far it's just one collector buying, but it's a start."

"Mmm…yeah, a start." He pressed a few buttons on the remote. "Do you know who it is?"

"Yeah, I've got the name and address. I'm the one shipping them."

"Anyone you know?" He still wasn't looking at her.

"No. Why?"

He shook his head. "Nothing. Ah, here we are. Lots of zombies eating brains."

Bare was acting a little stranger than usual.

"Why would you ask if I know them?" she asked. "Don't you think it's possible someone I don't know actually likes my art?"

"Of course. Forget I said that. Sometimes my mouth moves without clearance from my brain."

He held out his arm in invitation. She hesitated, then gave in, cuddling up against his side as she always did when they watched TV.

As soon as she had more buyers, she was quitting her job. If she could dedicate herself full-time to painting, well, it would be a dream come true. She could live frugally if it meant she could create art for a living.

"Bare?"

"Hmm?"

"You ever think I could make a living as a painter?"

"I think you can do whatever you put your mind to."

She gave him a little squeeze around the middle and met hard, toned muscle. She sat up quickly, startled by the rush of heat that ran through her and her sudden urge to explore that muscle with her fingers and tongue.

"Thanks," she said.

He smiled at her. She felt a rush of love for him just for being so supportive. Was she that starved for encouragement?

He turned back to the TV, holding his arm out for her to return to her spot against his side. She thought maybe a little space was a good thing. Her brain was getting crossed signals, mixing up friendly affection with love. She stayed where she was, and he dropped his arm.

They both took a long drink of beer. She considered how uber-supportive Bare was compared to her family, who considered art a waste of time. Her father was a physics professor, her stepmother also, and her younger half-sister Kate was working on the same. Kate would soon graduate a year early from college and head to grad school for her doctorate in physics. The only way Amber had been able to major in art, and have her dad help with the tuition, was if she also majored in education. Her dad said he wasn't flushing his money down the toilet on a degree that made her unemployable.

So she was an elementary school art teacher by

default. She loved kids, but the hard truth was, except for the occasional student, most kids didn't care about art. They considered art class a chance to run around and throw markers.

Bare gave her hair a playful tug. "Hey, Pink Hair, why so down?"

"I'm fine. Just thinking." She blew out a breath and tried to think positive. "In two months I'll have the whole summer to paint."

"Sounds like an artist's dream."

She nodded and cuddled up against his side again. He wrapped his arm around her, and she was enveloped in warmth. She breathed in his clean scent. He always smelled like the ocean. His arm tightened around her, and she felt suddenly like she was in a loving embrace. Was it just her desperate need for approval of her art that made her feel this way, or was something building between them? She didn't know, but cuddling with Bare, watching her favorite show just felt right.

CHAPTER FOUR

It had been thirty days, and the DVD delivered on its promise. Barry was now the proud owner of six-pack abs and a two-pack butt. He had to show off to Amber. He'd given her a teaser a couple of weeks ago when he was starting to show six-pack abs, but now he had the real deal—a full six-pack. He considered how to properly show off his tight, two-pack butt and finally decided it might be too soon for this stage in their relationship. He peeled off his T-shirt and threw it on top of his laundry basket, where he also stashed her pink thong, finally feeling comfortable in safely returning it without her thinking he was a perv.

He knew she was home. She was still in a painting frenzy, working hard every day as soon as she got home from work and working through the weekend. The only breaks she took were to hang out with him. He made sure to regularly stop by with crackers and cheese, her favorite snack, or she'd completely forget to eat.

Guilt weighed him down. He was still the only one

buying her paintings. He had ordered the first one and sent it to his mother as a gift. And then, well, he couldn't seem to stop himself from checking the website every day and buying one more. He'd hoped the sales might trigger some website algorithm that pushed her work in front of more customers, but so far it was just him. He'd told his mom to store them in her guest room, promising to claim them once he had a house to hang them in. His mom had kept her maiden name, so at least the connection back to him wasn't obvious. He'd bought the paintings to help Amber out, but he also really liked them and believed in her talent. If he told her he was her buyer, he risked dashing her newfound confidence.

She seemed so happy creating art all the time. He couldn't interfere with her happiness.

He knocked on her door, bare-chested, the laundry basket at his feet.

"Oh, hi, Bare." She blinked and rubbed her forehead, leaving a black mark there from leftover paint on her hand. He left it there. She looked adorable. "What time is it?"

"Thursday night, seven o'clock, otherwise known as laundry time." He shifted closer so she could get an up-close look at his new muscle definition and breathe in the Ocean Love cologne that promised pheromones that women couldn't resist. He needed all the help he could get. "Have any laundry you'd like me to do with mine?"

"Sure." She padded into the apartment in her bare

feet.

He was a little miffed. She didn't seem to notice all the work he'd put in on the *Six-Pack Abs and Two-Pack Butt in 30 Days* DVD. He did the workout every damn morning. He'd even given up sugar to move things along. And that wasn't easy when you owned a frozen-yogurt store with a toppings bar full of delicious candy. Thirty days of hard work and no sugar to get totally ripped and nothing? Not even a *Hey, did you get a haircut? Something's different about you.*

He struck a pose, leaning an arm over the doorjamb, the other hand tucked into a jeans pocket.

"Here you go, thanks," she mumbled, handing over the basket. She turned and went right back to her painting.

Clearly he had to be more obvious if he wanted to compete with her art. He pulled a T-shirt on and headed for the basement laundry, thinking hard.

~ ~ ~

Amber finished up her painting with a start. She never knew exactly when it would be finished, but with her habit of painting every day now, she'd actually found a rhythm that told her, *yes, that's it, done.* She stepped back. It was her finest work, if she did say so herself. Ever since Bare had moved in and she'd kicked Rick out of her life, she'd been so driven, so creative, so satisfied. It was like it only took one person to believe in her to help her believe in herself.

She grabbed some dryer sheets and went to meet Bare in the laundry room. The man was always there for her, bringing her dinner, doing her laundry, taking away the mundane in her life so she could focus on her art. She had to find a way to thank him.

She found him sitting on a plastic chair staring blankly at the front-loading washing machine. Only one machine was running. She saw a flash of something pink, then something blue.

"Hey, look, our laundry's having a party in there," she said.

He startled. "Oh, hey. Yeah, I didn't have a full load, so I put our stuff in together. Easy enough to sort it out after. Mine's so much bigger."

She laughed. "I wasn't worried about that. I brought the dryer sheets."

"Cool."

She sat in the plastic chair next to him. "Thanks so much for helping me out while I paint."

"No problem at all." He grinned. "Just consider me a patron of your arts."

She elbowed him. "You're a funny guy. And a good friend."

He stopped smiling. "Yeah. So I'm told."

"What's wrong?"

He hesitated. "Truth?"

"Always."

"Well…" He stared at his hands. "The truth is it's…" He shook his head. "I can't believe I'm telling you this—"

"Spit it out," she sang.

He met her eyes and immediately looked to the floor. "It's been a long time since I've had a girlfriend and...I'm trying to figure out how to change that. Weighs on a guy, you know."

Oh, that was so adorable. Bare wanted woman advice. "You've come to the right place. I'll help you meet women. Let's practice."

He met her eyes warily. "Practice," he echoed.

"Yeah, you say what you normally say when you're interested in a woman, and we'll practice conversations that go from friendly to a date."

He swallowed. "Okay."

She hopped up on the washing machine and kicked her legs. "Pretend I'm sitting here at a bar. What do you say?"

He stood and crossed to her. She smiled at him encouragingly. They were nearly eye to eye.

"Happy *Star Wars* day," he said.

"I don't get it."

"May the fourth be with you. It's May fourth."

She thought about that. "Okay, yes, it is May fourth, but maybe not a *Star Wars* reference for a convo opener. Maybe something less..."

"Geeky?"

"Yes."

He walked away, turned, and crossed back to her. "Hi, I'm Barry. Bare, you can call me Bare."

She smiled. "I'm Amber."

"Come here a lot?"

"Only when my clothes are dirty."

He laughed. "Buy you a drink?"

"I'd love one."

They pretended to drink.

He pulled a coupon from his jeans pocket. "You like fro-yo?"

She held up a hand. "Stop."

"What?"

"Put the coupon away. Don't bring up your work. Keep the focus on her."

He shoved the coupon back in his pocket, walked away, turned, and crossed back to her. The machine changed to the spin cycle, and the vibrations ran through her, kicking up her sex drive. Or maybe it was the look on Bare's face, because this time when he came for her, that good-natured smiley look was gone, and in its place was what she could only call a fierce determination.

"Bare?" Her voice came out in a near squeak.

He stopped right in front of her, between her legs, grabbed her head, and kissed her. His hand slid into her hair, gripping it, while his mouth devoured hers. He tasted delicious, minty and fresh. She wrapped her arms around his neck while he rocked her world, and the machine's vibrations pushed her further over the edge.

He slowly pulled back. She stared at him, dazed by the unexpected kiss.

"Go out with me," he said.

"Yes."

He stroked her hair. "I don't mean as friends." He looked in her eyes. "I mean a date."

"I know, I know. Kiss me again."

And he did. And it was like the freaking *Star Wars'* Death Star in her body. Unbelievably, shockingly explosive.

~THE END~

Turn the page to read *Almost in Love* (how Barry & Amber fall in love)

ALMOST IN LOVE

KYLIE GILMORE

CHAPTER ONE

"You rock my world, Bare."

A little pre-date pep talk couldn't hurt. Positive thinking and all that.

Barry Furnukle grinned at his reflection in the mirror, standing in his cow-print boxers that read *Milk Me* and white tube socks before the biggest date of his life. Amber Lewis, the beautiful woman in the apartment across the hall, with funky pink streaks in her wavy blond hair, had agreed to go out with him.

How did a guy like him get so lucky? Four weeks of careful, nonthreatening friendship and one mind-blowing kiss. That was how.

It hadn't been his usual gentle kiss. He'd purposely been aggressive like the guy in *Carnal Werewolf*, one of the romances his mom had left lying around the house. And Amber had liked it.

He did a one-two punch with some fancy footwork. "Lookin' good. You been working out?"

He turned for the rear view. *There's that two-pack butt.* He turned back and posed arms up, flexing his biceps to show off his six-pack abs. "That's the stuff."

That *Six-Pack Abs and Two-Pack Butt in 30 Days* DVD had paid for itself.

He dropped his arms and loosened up his neck. *You got this.* He had the date all planned out perfectly. First, a trip to the wildlife preserve at the beach, where he'd share his favorite hobby with her—birding. Amber was a watercolor artist, so he figured she'd appreciate the beauty of nature. Maybe she'd be so inspired, she'd want a return trip (with him) to paint some birds. After that, he'd take her to his successful frozen yogurt shop, The Dancing Cow, for some fro-yo and a special entertaining surprise.

He pulled on a gray T-shirt that was a size too small so it would cling to his newly formed six-pack abs. Unfortunately, Barry, at thirty-one, didn't have a ton of dating experience. Mostly he just had casual hookups with women from his old software engineering job, who chose him for their occasional needs. He would've liked a relationship that moved beyond takeout and hookup, but once the weekend was over, the women always went right back to work without a second glance.

He really wanted things to be different with Amber—much more than a one-time thing—so he'd planned the exact opposite of his normal date. It was a morning date, not evening. No takeout or dinner even. Just nature and fro-yo. He was pretty sure they wouldn't hookup right away either, since they were still getting to know each other. His previous hookups had happened after months of friendship. He and Amber had only shared one month of friendship.

He wanted her more than he'd ever wanted any of the women in his past. She was an amazing woman— beautiful, talented, kind. And so-oo-oo sexy.

He blew out a breath. *Don't think about that.* He didn't want to go through their first date sporting a woody. He'd already taken care of business in the shower to avoid such an event.

He pulled on jeans that were tight enough to show off the rear view. Yes, things would be different with Amber. She was already very different from the computer geeks he normally hooked up with, both in looks and profession, and he'd made a big effort to look more like the kind of guy she'd want.

He wouldn't screw this one up. He slipped into his sneakers. He'd be smooth, moving them from friends to lovers with a future. He liked the sound of that— lovers with a future.

He huffed into his hand, popped the third breath mint of the morning, and headed out the door.

~ ~ ~

Amber dressed in one of her favorite pink halter tops with a white skirt and pink leather sandals with high heels that made her feel sexy and less like a shrimp (she was five foot two). She had no idea how to dress for a morning date, but she thought the outfit was perfect for a beautiful spring May day in Connecticut.

She brushed out her long hair, musing over the fact that she was actually going on a date with Bare. She usually went for hot, edgy guys. Guys who knew how to have a good time, for however long that lasted. Usually not long once they'd slept together. Whatever. She never really expected anyone to stick around for the long haul. She'd had a few relationships that lasted a while—six months was the longest—but the thing about hot, edgy guys was they sucked at relationships. Most of them cheated on her. Hell, probably all of them.

She applied a little mascara and thought of Bare with his rumpled dirty blond hair and loud Hawaiian shirts. He was…sweet, a little geeky, a nice guy. And a good friend.

The only reason she'd agreed to a date was that mind-blowing kiss they'd shared in the laundry room while she sat on top of the washing machine during the spin cycle. Bare had shocked the hell out of her with that move. They'd been role-playing how to pick up a woman in a bar when he grabbed her head and went for it. *Bold move, Bare.*

So, here she was about to go on a date with her good friend. She felt oddly calm, no first date jitters at all, on account of she already knew Bare very well. They'd hung out plenty since he'd moved in across the hall a month ago. And she'd cuddled up with him on the sofa many nights while they watched their favorite TV show *Zombie Bonanza*. She felt safe with him.

This could be a very boring date.

She hoped if things didn't work out, they could still be friends. She'd really miss hanging out with him.

~ ~ ~

Barry knocked on Amber's door. It swung open, and his jaw dropped. Amber wore a pink half top with a short white skirt and high heels. He took in the golden skin of her midriff, where a sexy, tiny diamond belly-button stud glinted at him. Her slender legs were shown off to perfection in the heels. His erection pushed painfully against his tight jeans, reminding him it had been sixteen months, three weeks, and three days since he'd last had a girlfriend. These jeans were a hazard when Amber was around.

"I have to change," he said, forcing his voice to a deeper register to hide the fact that the jeans were squeezing him into soprano range.

She cocked her head. "Yeah? I think you look nice."

"And you look incredible," he said. "Come in. It'll only take a minute." He walked back to his apartment, careful to keep a step ahead of her so at least she could appreciate his two-pack rear view before it disappeared in jeans with some room for his Amber problem.

He quickly changed, made an attempt to tame his unruly hair, gave up, and they were on their way. He offered his arm when they got outside, she took it, and he walked her to his Honda Accord.

"So I've never been on a morning date," she said.

"What's the plan? Breakfast?"

He shook his head. "Something much better than that. It's a surprise."

"Ooh, I love surprises."

He unlocked the car and opened the door for her. She stared at the loudspeaker mounted on the roof.

"What is *that* for?" she asked.

"Don't worry about that. It moos, but I only press the button when families are around who might want some fro-yo."

"It…moos." She cringed and slid into the car.

He shut the door gently, whistling "Summer Nights" from the musical *Grease*. It was spring, the same time of year he'd played Danny Zuko in his high school's production of *Grease*. The girls had been all over him then.

He got in and smiled at her. It was so hard not to tell her where they were going. He couldn't wait to share one of his favorite hobbies with Amber. He just knew she'd love it.

She regarded him somberly. "Bare, promise me you won't make it moo when I'm in the car."

He laughed. "Are you sure? The kids love it."

"I'm sure."

"Okay, but you're missing out."

He started the car. She put a hand on his arm, and he warmed on the spot. "Any chance the giant Dancing Cow stickers on the doors come off?"

"Be right back."

He peeled off the two giant magnets that were

advertisements for his shop, slid them into the trunk, and got back in the car.

"Anything else?" he asked.

"I'm good."

"Okay, then." He pulled out of the lot and headed for the beach.

"What're these for?" Amber asked, holding up his binoculars.

"The better to see you with," he said wolfishly.

"No, really."

"It's part of the surprise."

"Are all of your dates surprises?"

"Well, there haven't been that many dates per se. I used to just meet someone at work and, you know, hang out for a bit." He glanced over. "I'm a little rusty, but if you'll bear with me, I think you'll like it."

"I'm entirely in your hands."

He grinned. "I like the sound of that."

A short while later, he pulled into the state park he loved to visit along the Long Island Sound. "Here we are."

"Ooh, the beach! How romantic! Are we going to walk barefoot on the beach and have a picnic?"

He grabbed the binoculars. "Much better than that. Come on!"

He led her to the nature trails along the saltwater marsh. He stopped at the base of the trail. "You'll need to move quietly, and don't make any loud noises—"

"Like this? Ooh, Bare, yeah, right there!"

He went rock hard. All coherent thought left him as he pictured Amber riding him, his name on her lips.

She smacked his arm. "Kidding! I won't make a sound."

"Good," he croaked.

Binoculars in hand, he led her to where he'd spotted the nest of black-capped chickadees the last time he was there. He peered at them through the high-resolution lenses and handed the binoculars to her.

She held them up to her eyes, one eye squinted closed. "What am I looking at?"

"Don't squint. Just look normally. It's a nest of black-capped chickadees. A little early this year. An amazing find, really."

She peered again. "Oh. Yeah, there they are." She handed back the binoculars. "Got it."

"That's it? Don't you think it's special?"

"Well...aren't they supposed to make a nest?"

"Yes, but it's rare to see one this early and so close to the trail. It's a fantastic view."

She nodded, lips drawn in. Barry tamped down his irritation. He thought someone like Amber with an artist's soul would appreciate the beauty of nature.

"Let's keep going." He led her further down the trail. The sunbeams peeked through the tree branches. Birdsong was in the air. A light, salty breeze rustled through the leaves. It was breathtaking, amazing, the best kind of morning for birding.

He stopped suddenly and put a finger to his lips.

He peered through the binoculars and smiled. "Look, a red-tailed hawk," he whispered, handing her the binoculars.

She looked. "Cool." Only she sounded really bored.

"Do you not like birding?" he asked.

"Birding?" She laughed. "That's what we're doing? I didn't know there was a name for it."

"It's a very popular hobby," he said defensively. "I thought you liked birds."

She'd said she liked birds. He'd asked her that when he'd first met her in the prequel.

"I like them okay, just not like…as a hobby."

"Should we go?"

"No, no. I accepted your date. Bring it on."

"All right," he said gamely.

They spent the next hour birding, and while Barry was thrilled with some of the birds returning to the area, and especially excited over the rare sighting of a bay-breasted warbler, he sensed Amber wasn't having any fun. He really thought Amber would be inspired by the beauty of birds. He gave up when he caught her texting just when he turned to her, excited about a bobolink.

"Ready to go?" he asked.

"If you are," she said.

He nodded, putting the binoculars back on the clip on his belt loop. "I'm ready."

She took his hand, and his hopes soared. Maybe the date wasn't going so badly.

"Let's walk along the beach for a bit," she said.

"Sure."

When they reached the sand, she slipped off her heels. She lost four inches without the shoes, reaching the middle of his chest. He was six foot, so most women were shorter than him, but Amber was so petite he just wanted to scoop her up and spin her around for the hell of it. He forced himself to keep his hands in his pockets. He knew he could get carried away sometimes.

He grinned. "You're a tiny thing without your heels."

"I'm five foot two."

"That's below average for a woman," he said.

"Gee, thanks. I love being below average. Would you also like to comment on my age or my weight?"

He squinted at her. "Twenty-five and one hundred pounds?"

She shook her head. "Twenty-eight and, yeah, let's go with that weight."

"I wasn't supposed to answer that, was I?"

She laughed. "I forgive you because you guessed in a complimentary direction."

He wiped his brow dramatically. "Close one. I've got you beat by three years and a lot of heavy muscle." He flexed his biceps, which were nothing to write home about.

She giggled. He loved that she laughed at his jokes. So few did.

They walked along the beach in comfortable

silence. Amber stopped, facing the water, and took a deep breath in and out. He watched her more than the sea because she was infinitely more beautiful.

She turned to him suddenly and smiled. "Thanks for bringing me here. It was nice."

"I wasn't sure…" He trailed off as she stood on tiptoe and kissed him on the cheek.

She smiled up at him. "What's next?"

A kiss on the lips was the next natural progression, but did she want a warning before he went for it or—

"You're thinking awfully hard," she said with a grin. "Is there more to this date or just the beach?"

He shook his head. "Oh, I thought…yes, there's more." He nodded once. "Ready to go?"

"I'm ready."

He held out his arm and led her back to where he parked, thinking he could get used to the feel of Amber on his arm. Next stop—The Dancing Cow!

~ ~ ~

Amber was nothing if not open-minded. So, okay, the birding thing was a little unusual for a date, but she could roll with it. Still, when Bare brought her to The Dancing Cow, she began to wonder why she'd agreed to this date. She was okay with the lime green melamine tables, pink cushioned chairs, and long counter with bright yellow stools, even though it was a little glaring on the neon end of the color wheel. Farm scenes of green hills with cows on the walls—also okay.

Serving herself a bowl of peach yogurt covered in Oreos for a late breakfast—cool.

Bare ditching her in the middle of his busy shop full of cheerful families with little kids—not cool.

It was near noon, and since she still hadn't eaten, she settled at the long counter with her fro-yo and wondered what kind of guy brings a date to his fro-yo shop and then leaves her to eat alone with a quick, "I have to take care of something in the back."

Was he ever coming back? She was halfway through her fro-yo. She waved to a family she knew from Clover Park Elementary, where she taught art. If Bare wanted to work, she could just go home. But then she found out why he'd disappeared. And it was much worse than sitting alone eating fro-yo surrounded by cheerful families.

The lights started flashing, and a disco ball spun. And then, hand to God, Bare appeared doing an Irish jig in a cow costume right there in the center of the store. She nearly fell off her stool laughing.

He handed her a pair of black-rimmed glasses with huge blue eyes on the lenses that blinked when you moved them. "Hope you're having a moo-tastic date," he said with a smile.

"Uh…"

He didn't wait around for her response. This was by far the weirdest date she'd ever been on. He danced around the shop, giving out glasses to all the kids. She set the glasses on the table. Several parents looked over at her with a nod and a smile. What was he saying about her? Her cheeks heated. She had to see some of these parents at school events.

This was getting truly embarrassing, and she wasn't even the one dancing in a cow costume.

And then suddenly he grabbed her hand and pulled her to the center of the shop, doing a fast tango with her from side to side, his giant cow udder pushing between them. She went from embarrassed to mortified at the titters and whispers from the parents she knew she'd have to see at school. She was about to pull away when he grabbed her by the waist, lifted her, and twirled her around.

She smacked his arm. "Put me down," she hissed.

He set her down with a grin. "My lady."

She slowly backed away and watched in horror as a large boy got overly excited and belly-bumped the dancing cow when Bare's attention was still on her. Bare lost his balance, knocking into a table full of preschoolers. Fro-yo and candy spilled everywhere. The kids started crying. Bare kept slipping on the fro-yo.

"Little help here?" Bare called.

One of the dads helped him up. Amber rushed over. "Are you okay?" She took in his formerly white with black spots costume now covered in pink, orange, and brown. "Your costume is ruined."

Bare looked down at himself. "No problem. I'm sure the dry cleaner can get it out." He grimaced at the crying kids and told the parents, "They can get whatever they want no charge. I'll get this cleaned up in a jif."

He walked behind the counter and sent a teenage employee out to clean the floor. Amber joined him behind the counter, grabbing some napkins to help him clean up the sopping mess on his costume as best she could.

Bare's mouth formed a flat line as he also worked to sop up the mess. "No need. You just go back and enjoy your treat."

"Let's get you out of this," she said.

He hung his head and shuffled to a back room. She unzipped the costume in the back and helped him step out of it with minimal damage to his clothes underneath.

"My mother made that costume special for me," he said quietly. "She was so proud when I opened my own shop. It was the first thing I ever did that she could enjoy. She's a technophobe."

Amber's heart squeezed. Bare was a software engineer and had made a really cool app too. His app, Giggle Snap, was hugely popular. People all over the world used it to share sounds. She knew very well what it was like to be good at something your family just didn't understand. She grew up in a family of physicists—her dad, stepmom, and half-sister—who thought her painting was a complete waste of time. Her mom, an artist, had dropped her off with her father's new family when Amber was thirteen so her mom could take a trip to Paris to find herself. Amber figured she never did find herself because she hadn't seen her since.

"We'll fix it," she said. "Let's soak it so the stains don't set."

Bare took the costume over to the sink, put the stopper in, and filled it with water. He dumped some dish soap in. His always rumpled hair fell over his forehead as he stared down at his ruined costume.

"Not much of a date, huh?" he asked.

"It's been…memorable." She searched for something nice to say. "Unique."

He turned to her. "I guess we should just…I dunno. Stop."

She nodded. "I think we've done plenty. That was a lot of date you packed into one morning."

"Come on, I'll take you home."

She didn't protest, merely followed him to the parking lot. She never wanted to hurt Bare's feelings, but she was starting to think maybe the spin cycle of the washing machine had more to do with that amazing kiss than Bare. They were just so…different. I mean, sure they both liked to watch *Zombie Bonanza*, but beyond that…not much in common. She was a watercolor artist/art teacher, and he was a brilliant computer guy with a fro-yo shop on the side. Artists and techies didn't mix all that well. Just look at her and her family.

Bare was uncharacteristically quiet on the drive back to their apartment building. She tried to get him talking about their favorite show, but his one-word answers told her he was still upset about his costume getting ruined.

He walked her to her door. "Can I kiss you goodbye?"

It was sweet he asked, but…she just didn't think this was going to work out between them. "I think maybe we're better off as friends."

His shoulders slumped. "Oh. Yeah." He took a step back. "Sure, I understand."

She blew out a breath of relief. "You do? Great. Because I would hate to not be friends."

"Yeah, me too."

She smiled and was glad to see he smiled back. "All right. I'll see you later."

She unlocked the door to her apartment. He turned and went into his apartment. That went better than she'd hoped. Good. They'd tried, it didn't work out, no permanent damage done.

CHAPTER TWO

Amber went back to her normal routine of teaching rowdy kids art by day and painting with watercolors nights and weekends. Bare hadn't stopped by for a chat or takeout like he usually did. It had been a week since their date, and she was starting to worry she wasn't going to see him again. It had been so nice having a friend right across the hall who stopped by almost every night. She'd gone into the date expecting boring and safe and came out embarrassed, but also at peace with her decision that they were better off as friends.

She missed him a lot.

And what about that kiss? Slutty Amber asked. It had been a really amazing kiss.

She confided in her friend Steph Moore, a fifth grade teacher, over lunch in the Clover Park Elementary School teachers' lounge. "Do you think Bare's upset? He said friends was okay with him, but I haven't seen him at all since then. Usually he'd stop by, like, almost every night if he wasn't working the late shift at his shop."

Steph considered this while chomping on a baby carrot. "Maybe he just needs a little time. He took you on a date, and you rejected him."

Amber thought about when he'd asked if he could kiss her goodbye. Maybe she should've said yes. Maybe it wasn't the spin cycle that made their previous kiss so great. Just because they had nothing in common didn't mean they couldn't have a physical relationship. No, she didn't want to be like that with Bare. He deserved better than a fling. She hoped he found someone that really appreciated what a great guy he was. Someone that really enjoyed birds and dancing cows.

Liz O'Hare, a third grade teacher, waddled over and eased herself into a chair. Her friend looked about to pop, nearly eight months pregnant with twin girls. "Are you going to eat that?" she asked Amber, eyeing her small wheel of Babybel cheese.

Amber handed it over. The woman was eating for three.

"Thanks." Liz emptied her lunch onto the table—chicken sandwich with lettuce and tomato, salad with chopped egg whites on top, strawberries, thermos of milk, and Amber's cheese.

Steph and Amber exchanged an amused look. Liz used to be such a calorie counter she could barely enjoy a salad with crackers for lunch. It was good to see her enjoy food.

"What'd I miss?" Liz asked around a mouthful of sandwich.

"Amber's hung up on the guy she *claims* she's not interested in," Steph said.

"Barry?" Liz asked. "He's nice."

"Exactly," Amber said. "He deserves someone nice that will appreciate him."

"You're nice enough," Steph said.

"Gee, thanks," Amber replied.

"I don't see the problem," Steph said. "He's nice, you get along, so what if he likes birds and cows." She pressed her lips together and added with the voice of hard experience, "That's better than what some guys are into."

Liz dabbed at her milk mustache daintily with a napkin. "I kinda know what Amber means about someone special appreciating him. You haven't met Barry, Steph, but he's a little...unusual."

"Exactly!" Amber said.

"He means well," Liz went on. "But he's definitely not who you might dream of as a boyfriend." She took a bite of her sandwich and chewed. "Not the kind of guy you might crush on for a while and fall head over heels for." She smiled dreamily, probably thinking of her own dream guy, her husband Ryan.

Amber was willing to admit Bare wasn't in the same class of hot guy as Ryan, but he did have good qualities, and she didn't appreciate Liz talking about her friend like that.

"You just have to get to know him," Amber said. "He's a nice guy. Smart too."

"So bang him," Steph said with a smirk.

"Stephanie!" Liz said. "You're so crude."

Steph shrugged one shoulder. "Either she wants to or she doesn't. If she doesn't, then it's friends all the way. It's not rocket science."

Amber took a sip of her iced tea and thought about that. "There was one amazing kiss…"

Liz giggled.

Amber's eyes snapped to hers. "What's so funny about that?"

"It's just hard to imagine," Liz said. "You know, Barry dancing in his cow costume…" She giggled. "Kissing."

Amber thought back to that kiss. "Well, it was nice," she said defensively. "Of course, I was sitting on the washing machine on the spin cycle."

Liz cracked up, one hand on her ginormous belly.

"Shhh!" Amber hissed.

Liz looked contrite and bit her lip in an attempt to stop smiling. "I shouldn't have laughed. Sorry."

"We've talked about this guy long enough," Steph said. "Kiss him again without the spin cycle. *Boom*. Simple as that. Now who wants to share a room with me at the Connecticut Core Standards teacher conference in August?"

"I'll be on maternity leave," Liz said.

"I don't have to go," Amber said. "Art doesn't change all that much."

"I hate rooming alone," Steph said.

"So pick up a hot guy teacher and have a conference fling," Amber said.

They all laughed at the idea of a hot guy teacher. They were like unicorns. They'd heard they existed, but none of them had ever seen one.

Amber went home after work that day, still unsure what to do about Bare. If she kissed him and it wasn't great, wasn't that like encouraging him further? And then she'd have to reject him again and further hurt his feelings. No, better to wait him out. He'd warm up to her again. Soon, she hoped.

She reached her front door and let out a gasp. There was a picnic basket with a bouquet on top in a vase. But the bouquet wasn't flowers, it was paintbrushes. She bent down. Sable brushes, the highest quality, a dozen of them in different sizes. Omigod. She carefully put the vase to the side and opened up the picnic basket. A bottle of merlot, crackers, and cheeses. All her favorite cheeses—cheddar, Monterey jack, gouda, havarti, baby Swiss. She loved cheese.

She closed the basket with a smile. There was only one person in the entire world that would give her something so thoughtful. She knocked on Bare's door, holding up the block of Monterey jack. The door swung open. "I got the cheese."

He smiled and nodded. He wore a loud red Hawaiian shirt, and she tried not to get distracted by it.

"And the paintbrushes," she said. "I can't believe you remembered about the sable brushes. And the wine, oh, everything!" She shook her head at him. "What am I going to do with you?"

His voice dropped to a low tone, almost a growl, that made all her good parts start to party. "As much as possible, I hope."

Look out, Slutty Amber in charge.

She licked her lips and considered testing the no-spin-cycle kiss theory. Her gaze dropped to his mouth. He did have nice lips, smooth and full, perpetually curved into a smile. Like now.

"You want to try again?" he asked.

She met his warm brown eyes. "I was thinking about it," she admitted.

If the next kiss was anything like the first one, she'd gladly go birding every weekend just to get more.

"How about Saturday night?" he asked. "This time you plan the date. Whatever you like to do."

Oh. He meant a date. *Get your mind out of the gutter.*

"Yeah, okay, sure." She glanced at his mouth again. Maybe they should kiss now just to see if it was really worth the hassle of another date. "I was wondering," she ventured, "if maybe we should try—"

"The cheeses?" he asked. "I had a feeling you'd say that. I skipped dinner, so I'm good to go."

"Yes, okay," she quickly said.

They shared a picnic on her living room coffee table while watching their favorite show *Zombie Bonanza.* After a while, from the wine and the warmth of his body next to hers, Amber got sleepy and curled up against his side as she often did when they watched TV together. He slipped an arm around her, holding her close. She breathed in his fresh ocean scent. She didn't know if it was his deodorant or cologne or just all of his visits to the beach, but she loved that scent.

She was glad to have Bare back, even if she didn't know how long he'd end up staying in her life. It all depended, she supposed, on how well their next date went. She yawned. He'd asked her to plan the date. She'd have to show him what was really fun. Maybe that was what went wrong with their first date. Maybe Bare just didn't know what made a good, non-embarrassing date. He'd said he was rusty. She'd take him to a club. They'd have a few drinks and let loose on the dance floor. A dance club date would be so kickass.

CHAPTER THREE

The dance club date was not kickass. Well, actually, it almost was.

It started out with great promise. The pounding bass beat felt like home to Amber as she walked into her favorite club, The Bohemian, in South Norfolk. There was a huge dance floor, a bar done up with a purple gauzy canopy over it, and, instead of chairs, there were giant beanbags to lounge in.

"Kind of a '60s vibe going on here," Bare commented. "I like it. Of course, if I'd known it was '60s themed, I would've worn my tie-dye shirt and my dad's old bellbottoms."

She tried to cover her look of abject horror with a quick smile. "You look great just like you are."

Like someone that just stepped out of work on business-casual Friday—button-down blue shirt and khakis. She *had* given him advance warning about the club. When she'd suggested he change, he'd said, "But this is my nicest outfit."

She hadn't had the heart to argue.

Now he beamed at her. "You look great too. I like the thigh-high boots and the, uh, half top."

"Halter top. Thanks." She figured why get a belly-button piercing if you weren't going to show it off. "Want a drink?"

"Sure."

They pushed through the throng of people and made their way to the bar.

"Screaming orgasm?" he asked when they reached the bar.

"Yes, please," she said with a straight face. It was the drink they'd shared the first night they'd hung out together. Bare brought it up frequently in his joking way.

His lips twitched. "I'll have the same."

After they got their drinks, they stayed at the bar for a while sitting side by side on bar stools. Bare peppered her with questions about her latest watercolor paintings. She'd recently had a slew of sales on the eArt website and had been painting a lot more as a result. She loved that he actually cared about her art—he was her biggest cheerleader when she started selling for the first time—but it was difficult to have a conversation with the loud club music.

She finished her drink and turned to him. "Ready?"

He straightened. "We're leaving already? Just one drink and then"—he gestured toward the exit—"out the door."

"No, silly. I meant are you ready to dance?"

He glanced over at the dance floor, where a lot of women and a few brave guys were dancing. The women writhed; the men slid their hands all over their partners. Amber loved that. Bare's head bobbled around, like he couldn't decide if he was going to nod or shake his head no.

She grabbed his hand. "Come on."

"All right."

She pulled him to the center of the crowd, where he could lose himself in the pulsing beat and the rhythm of the other bodies pressing close. She threw her arms in the air and danced freely, giving herself over to it, moving in a sensuous wave.

Bare stood there, staring at her. She danced closer to him, so close she occasionally bumped into his chest. He settled his hands on her hips, his fingers gripping her tight.

She grabbed his hands. "Loosen your grip. I gotta move."

He released her, and she danced a sexy circle around him. He stayed stock-still, but his eyes never left her. She reached his front again and looked up at him. "Come on, Bare, dance with me."

He did a few head bobs. She kept dancing, waiting for him to catch up. Suddenly he burst into an Irish jig. One hand waving in the air, the other behind his back, his feet moved in a quick shuffle-tap motion. She slowed her dance, almost afraid to see what he'd do next. He kicked up his heels to one side, then the other. He was graceful, in time to some mysterious

Irish song in his head, perfect for The Dancing Cow but…not at all right for The Bohemian.

People stopped dancing to watch him. He took that as encouragement and kept going. She stopped dancing and watched in growing horror. Should she tell him to stop? People closed in around him in a circle, clapping in time to his jig. She lost sight of him as more people pushed in to watch the strange dance.

She felt a hand on her back, and then someone spun her around. She smiled at her frequent dance partner Carlos. "Hey, stranger."

"Hey, *chica bonita.*"

"I've got a date," she said, quickly sidestepping him, trying to find Bare. She went up on tiptoe. There were so many people. She still couldn't see him, and then Carlos grabbed her, pulling her back to him. He danced in front of her, face to face, pelvis to pelvis, as they did every time they found each other at the club. It never went further than that. They danced, he moved on to the next woman, just fun. Her friend Steph used to dance with him too—the two of them on either side of him.

She tried to see around Carlos, but he was moving side to side now, all in her space. She kept dancing, hoping Bare would show up sooner or later. Finally, the crowd around Bare dispersed. She shifted, turning away from Carlos, searching the sea of people. Still no Bare. Carlos moved behind her, a hand on her stomach, grinding into her from behind, not hard, just enough for her to know he was there. She lifted her hair up, cooling the back of her neck, rocking her hips in time to the music as she kept an eye out for Bare. Carlos' hands went to her hips as he moved with her.

She danced, scanning the sea of people, and was about to leave the dance floor when Carlos pulled away suddenly and a sprinkle of cold water hit her back. She turned. Omigod. Carlos was absolutely soaked, mostly through the crotch of his black leather pants. He turned, furious, looking for the aggressor.

"You two need to cool off," Bare said, holding an empty plastic cup.

Carlos dove for him, knocking the cup out of his hand and throwing Bare to the ground. Amber leaped into the fray, hanging onto Carlos' arm before he could smash his fist into Bare's face.

"Stop!" she cried. "Don't hurt him."

"These are leather!" Carlos exclaimed. "He ruined them."

"He'll pay for it," she said.

"Like hell," Bare snapped. He took advantage of Carlos' distraction and rolled away from him. He stood and leaned into Carlos' face. "You stay away from her. Hear me?"

Amber jumped in before Carlos had a chance to beat the crap out of Bare. She didn't know how Bare would do in a fight, but she'd seen Carlos before. He was a black belt. "Very sorry, Carlos, I'll make it up to you."

She pulled at Bare until he finally followed her out the door.

The night air was cool, and she tried to focus on deep breathing so she wouldn't yell at him. What was he thinking picking a fight with Carlos of all people! The man was a lean, muscled super-ninja fighter. And Bare...she glanced over at his scowling face, his wrinkled shirt, and khakis. Bare was an Irish-jig-dancing cow.

"Bare, I don't think this is going to work out between us," she said gently. "We're too different. We should just stay—"

"Friends," he bit out. "I know."

"I mean, we just don't fit in each other's lives."

His jaw clenched. "I couldn't agree more."

Okay, then. They walked down the street to where the cow car was parked. Tension radiated off her usually good-natured friend. She couldn't take the silent treatment.

"Are you mad?" she asked.

He stopped and pinned her with a hard look. "No, Amber, I love watching you have sex on the dance floor in front of me."

She jolted at the harsh words. "I wasn't having sex with Carlos."

"You did everything you could with your clothes on," he sneered. "What do you call it?"

"I call it dancing, you jerk! And I would've danced like that with you if you weren't so busy doing that crazy Irish jig."

He laughed mirthlessly. "Well, I'm real glad you got to *dance* with Carlos. Really made my night."

"Don't talk to me like that you judgmental, uptight…bird-cow man."

"Amber…" His voice came out in a deep growl that had her heart thumping like crazy. "I won't share you."

She recovered fast. "*Share me?* I'm not *with* him. I'm not with you either!"

"Obviously not, or we wouldn't have had a scene like that."

He strode toward the car and opened her door for her. She got in and slammed it closed herself.

They drove home in silence.

CHAPTER FOUR

Three weeks later...

Barry was still stuck in involuntary celibacy and missing Amber like crazy. Sure, he'd known he wasn't Amber's usual type, but he'd made an effort. Did he or did he not have six-pack abs and a two-pack butt now? And they always had fun hanging out together. At least they did before they'd gone out on a date. She'd hated his date, and he'd hated hers. Any red-blooded guy would've hated watching their date all over another guy. She couldn't blame him for that. He still didn't know what went wrong with his idea for a date. Okay, she wasn't crazy about birds, but she'd liked the beach. And then later at his shop, well, he'd wanted her to see his successful business and see him with all the kids. The kids loved the cow. He had to admit his spectacular fall with fro-yo splashed all over him hadn't helped his cause. That didn't exactly scream sexy.

He blew out a breath. Maybe he just wasn't cool enough for her. She'd called him a bird-cow man. Birds weren't cool, he supposed. Neither was dancing in a cow costume, no matter how much the kids loved it. He probably shouldn't have done that. Sometimes he went overboard, not realizing it until it was too late. Still, there was that amazing kiss in the laundry room. The way she'd made little moaning sounds in her throat had him about to lose it right there. How could he make things right?

He fiddled around with his new Bird Bonanza app on his laptop, trying to fix a glitch in the program that kept mixing up the plumage of the birds. Maybe he should've just stuck to hanging out with Amber, watching that nightmare-inducing show *Zombie Bonanza*; then he would've gotten the chance to kiss her again. He hated zombies, but he loved cuddling with Amber on her sofa.

But now Amber seemed to have moved on. He'd stopped by her place twice, and she'd said she was too busy with end-of-the-school-year stuff to hang out with him. He knew that wasn't it. The problem was him. He should've kissed her when he had a chance, all those nights when she'd curled up against his side watching TV. He'd been afraid she'd kick him out if he did. He shoved a hand through his shaggy hair. What was wrong with him? Why could he not seem to get his footing with Amber?

Someone knocked on his door. He jumped up. Amber! She was the only one who popped by unannounced. He swung open the door, a smile on his face.

"Hey, bro, can I crash here for a while?" his younger brother Ian asked.

He lost his smile. "Sure, come in."

Ian dropped a duffel bag next to the sofa. His youngest brother, at twenty-four, was halfway to a doctorate in computer science at M.I.T. But Ian was notably different from Barry in one very important way. Somehow his computer nerd brother was a ladies' man. And not just with computer science geeks, he'd even made inroads in the engineering and physics departments.

"So what's up? Why the visit?" Barry asked, flopping down on the sofa next to his brother.

"Semester ended and campus cleared out." Ian lifted his brows. "Translation: lack of babes."

"Ah. So do you have a job this summer?" Barry asked.

"Nah. I thought I'd just hang."

Barry nodded, wondering how long Ian would "just hang" at his apartment. He'd never ask. He could never kick his little brother out. And he knew Ian found it hard to stay at their mom's house with the memories of their dad there. Their dad had died a year ago, but it was still too painful for Ian.

"What's new with you?" Ian asked, tossing his messy, wavy brown hair out of his eyes. His brother always looked a little messy. His hair was much more unruly than Barry's, not to mention the fact that Ian couldn't be bothered to shave every day and had a thick layer of stubble.

"Not much," Barry said. "Working on a new app. Still working at The Dancing Cow."

"Cool. What's the app about?"

Barry explained his birding app that he hoped would help with conservation efforts and showed him the error he kept running into.

"Let me see." Ian took the laptop and dove into the coding. Ten minutes later, he handed it back. "Fixed."

"Really?" Barry took another look.

"Your recursive loop was calling back to a variable that wasn't even named. Are you feeling all right?"

It was a stupid mistake. He just didn't have the single-minded focus for app development like he did when he wasn't spending all his time wondering how to get Amber back in his arms.

"Actually, no." Barry exhaled sharply. "I haven't had a girlfriend in an *unspeakable* amount of time, and the one woman I really like, who lives across the hall, by the way, wants nothing to do with me."

Ian nodded. "You need to get laid. Got it. We'll get you a woman."

"I want Amber."

"Sure, sure. You want my advice?"

Barry just knew he was going to regret this, but his own ideas for making Amber his girlfriend had flopped. "Yes."

Ian rubbed his hands together. "C cubed is the

solution. Can you guess what the three Cs are?"

Barry thought hard. "Candy, carats, climax? Hers, I mean."

Ian threw back his head and laughed. "It's not about her, it's about you. And what are you giving her carrots for? Women hate when you act like they need to lose weight. Man, you really do need my help."

"Not carrots, carats, like diamonds—"

"Women want an alpha."

Barry stared at his brother, who was also a long, lean string bean with zero muscles. At least Barry had some muscles now thanks to his *Six-Pack Abs and Two-Pack Butt in 30 Days* workout DVD, but still...no woman.

"Alphas are the confident leaders," Ian went on. "C cubed is contacts"—he pointed to his eyes— "confidence, and condoms."

"I don't wear glasses."

"Yeah, those are my three Cs. Yours might be different." He pushed the hair out of his eyes. "But definitely the confidence one you need to get. Buy some condoms too. It's one of those act-like-you're-gonna-get-some-and-then-you-do kind of things."

Hmm...he did have some condoms, but he could always buy more. He'd like to have lots and lots of sex with Amber. Morning sex, shower sex, nooners, afternoon delights, romantic night sex. All-the-time sex, basically. He had a lot of time to make up for in his celibate state, and he'd had a perpetual hard-on for Amber since the day they met.

He thought about the other C, confidence. They had mentioned confidence in *Cosmo* when he stumbled upon an issue online. He'd tried that with the whole looking-good thing, though, and it hadn't helped.

Barry's shoulders slumped. "It's hard to have confidence when you keep getting shot down." *Or when you watch an alpha have clothes-on sex with your date on the dance floor*, he added silently.

Ian got up and helped himself to a glass of water. "You gotta act like you're all that. Then they'll want some. Got any chips?"

"There's pretzels in the cabinet next to the fridge."

Ian made a face, but grabbed the bag of pretzels anyway. "Wait, I got it. Remember how you had those girls all over you senior year when you starred in *Grease*?"

"Yeah."

Ah, memories. It wasn't just The Pink Ladies and Sandy all over him. Half the girls in the senior class had a crush on him when he played Danny. He was that good. Of course, once the show was over, he was back to being regular old computer-nerd Barry. His girlfriend, Becky, who'd played Sandy, dumped him right after the cast party on the last night of the show. He'd been in love with her, and she'd been in love with Danny. Heartbroken, he'd moped around the house for a month.

Ian spoke around a mouthful of pretzels. "Do something like that."

He shoved a hand through his hair. "I haven't

done any theater since high school. I'm too rusty."

"You've got the chops. Just find some community theater, rehearse a bit, and audition." Ian snapped his fingers. "Women galore. Especially if it's *Grease*."

"Maybe," Barry allowed.

"You got any better ideas?"

"Nope."

"All right, then, we've got a plan. Theater equals confidence. I'm starving. Let's go grab a bite."

"Sure."

They headed out the door and passed Amber and Daisy O'Hare on their way in.

"Hi, Barry, how are you?" Daisy asked. She wore a tank top that showed her pregnant belly and a flowing skirt that ended at her ankles.

"Good. How are you?" He glanced at Amber, who immediately turned away. First step, get the woman to look at you.

"Who is this pretty lady?" Ian asked with a charming smile as he got up close and personal with Daisy.

"Daisy," Barry said, "meet my brother Ian. And this is Amber."

Ian only had eyes for Daisy. He lifted her hand and kissed it. "I hope to see a lot more of you, beautiful."

Daisy raised a brow. Barry pulled his brother away from Daisy. "She's married and pregnant. Move on."

Daisy shook her head and smiled. "Thanks anyway, cutie."

"How are you?" Barry asked Amber.

"Fine." Amber's expression was hard to read, not angry, but not friendly either.

Ian turned his attention to Amber, his eyes lingering on her bare midriff. "You are smokin'. Woo!"

Amber's eyes flashed. "Get lost, twerp."

"Feisty, I like it," Ian said with a grin.

A smile tugged at her lips. "Shut up," she said with no real force behind it.

Barry pulled his brother down the hall toward the stairs. "We'll see you later."

Ian stopped and turned. "Hey, you ladies want to grab a bite?"

Daisy giggled. "No, thanks. Bye!"

The brothers headed downstairs and out to the parking lot. Barry waited until they were in the car to ream his brother out.

"Didn't I tell you Amber was the one I was interested in?" he barked.

"Yeah, so?"

"So that was Amber you were flirting with!"

He pulled out of the lot and headed to Eastman for dinner. He wouldn't stand a chance with Amber if Ian was going for her too.

"That was *the* Amber?" Ian asked. "She's hot."

"No kidding."

"No offense, bro, but she's way out of your league."

"Thanks."

"She lives across the hall?"

"Yes."

"Okay if I hit that?"

Barry did a double take. "No, it's not okay if you hit that. She's the one I'm crazy about. Don't you dare make a move on her, Ian, or I swear I'll kick you out. You'll have to stay with Mom or go back to campus with no babes whatsoever."

A beat passed.

"What about Daisy?" Ian asked.

Barry groaned. "What part of married and pregnant did you not understand?"

"She's super hot."

"Is this gonna be a problem?"

"I can't help it, bro, I love women. And the women in this town are fine."

"Just"—he unclenched his jaw with great effort—"leave Amber to me."

"No prob. I'll be your wingman."

"I don't need—"

"Yeah, you do. 'How are you?' is not gonna get you laid."

Barry ground his teeth.

"Just sayin'." Ian pulled out his cell and started texting.

Barry took a deep breath.

"And ditch the Hawaiian shirts," Ian said. "That's only cool in Hawaii."

"I thought they were fun."

Ian glanced up, taking in the green Hawaiian shirt

with surfers. "Fine. Wear them. Your deprivation."

Okay, fine, no Hawaiian shirts. That left T-shirts. Sure, they were comfortable, but there wasn't much flair to them. Barry drove to Ernie's diner in Eastman because he was afraid if they ate at Garner's in Clover Park, Ian would hit on more married women that were also Barry's customers. Geez, his brother was much worse since the last time they'd hung out together. Ian's success with the ladies on campus had really inflated his ego.

After dinner, Ian searched for community theater info on his cell while Barry drove.

"I got it, bro. Eastman has a summer production of *The Pirates of Penzance*. Women love pirates. You're gonna be set."

"Playing a pirate sounds fun. Yeah, I could do that."

"Not just a pirate. You, my friend, will be the Pirate King!"

He cocked a brow. "Yeah?"

"Oh, yeah. King is the top dog. I'll pull up a song on YouTube so you can rehearse. Audition is next week."

Nerves ran through Barry. It had been years since he'd been on stage. He'd been too busy in college and then too busy with work. He did like to perform. He performed every day at The Dancing Cow, entertaining the kids. He supposed it was like riding a bike. And if it gave him a much-needed confidence boost, maybe he could find some way to make that translate into getting Amber back into his arms.

~ ~ ~

Amber smoothed another coat of black paint onto a wooden pirate ship cutout for the Eastman community theater's summer production of *The Pirates of Penzance*, with help from her friend Steph. She painted scenery for all of their summer shows ever since Steph had started singing in the chorus five years ago. They were at Eastman High School in the large band room just across the hall from the auditorium.

"So what part are you playing this summer?" Amber asked.

Steph had just auditioned a few minutes ago. Her friend said teaching fifth graders made it easy to get up on stage in front of an audience. She was prepared for anything.

"I'm one of the Major-General's daughters," Steph said. "I don't know which one yet. They haven't posted the cast list. Any of them is fine. I doubt I'll get Mabel. Zoe Davis auditioned again this year. Her voice is amazing."

"Cool."

Amber knew Zoe through Daisy. They'd hung out a few times at Daisy's parties.

"You should try out this year," Steph said, slapping paint on in a way that Amber knew would leave lines. She'd smooth it out for her in a minute. "It's not too late. It would be so fun to do the show together."

Steph was always trying to get Amber to join the show. Amber usually just volunteered to paint scenery, which took about a week, then left. Amber dipped her brush in more black paint and smoothed the lines Steph had left. No matter how many times she'd told her friend how to paint smoothly in layers, she never did.

"I wouldn't like being on stage," Amber said.

"Try out for the Major-General's daughters. Then I'd be right next to you."

Amber shook her head. "That's okay."

"Aren't you even curious what it's like to be in the cast? It's so fun, all the rehearsals over the summer, and we go out after rehearsal a lot, plus the show, and the cast party. It becomes like a family by the end."

Amber brushed back and forth. The black would need another coat after this one. "I'm good with just painting."

Steph put her brush down and stood. "Come on. Just watch some of the auditions. I really want you to do this with me."

She stopped painting and looked up. "Why?"

"Because you've been moping around, and I know you're just going to spend the whole summer holed up in your apartment, painting."

"I'll go out sometimes."

"With who? I'll be busy here, and Daze is up to her eyeballs teaching infant massage classes and chasing Bryce around. Come on, hang out with me here this summer. It'll be a blast."

Amber heaved a sigh. "You're not gonna stop bugging me about this, are you?"

Steph grinned. "No. I really want you to give it a try this year." She held out her hand and pulled a reluctant Amber to her feet. "Obviously you like the shows, or you wouldn't help out every year."

"I just like to paint. I'm only here because of you, my friend."

Steph stomped her foot in mock outrage. "Get your ass out to that auditorium."

Amber laughed. "Fine, Miss Bossy. I'll watch a bit, but no promises."

She capped the paint cans and followed her friend to the auditorium. She slipped into a seat next to Steph near the front. The director, Toby, the stage manager, Edith, and the choreographer, Jasmine, sat in the row in front of them, evaluating each person. Right now, a guy with a huge beer belly was giving a version of "I am a Pirate King" that was nearing the high range of a soprano singer. His T-shirt didn't quite meet the waistband of his sagging jeans, and he kept hitching up his pants.

Steph cringed as the man's voice cracked. She and Steph exchanged a look.

"That's how I would sound," Amber whispered.

"How does a big guy like that have such a girly voice?" Steph whispered back.

The song mercifully ended. No one clapped.

"Thank you," Toby said. "Cast list will be posted

this evening at five p.m. Next!"

A tall man bounded on stage in full pirate regalia—white, puffy shirt unbuttoned to show off lots of muscular chest, a black bandana tied rakishly around his shaggy hair, a thick black belt with a sword on one side, tight black breeches, and knee-high black leather boots.

"Wow," Steph breathed.

"Yeah," Amber said. She leaned forward, straining to see his face. Something about him was familiar.

"Ahoy, landlubbers!" he called into the audience. "I am the Pirate King!"

Amber leaned so far forward she nearly fell out of her seat. She knew that voice. Bare. Was it really him?

The man nodded to the pianist, the music started, and he launched into "I am a Pirate King" with a booming baritone that filled the auditorium. He sang, he strutted, he swaggered, even brandished his sword a few times. He finished with a dramatic bow.

Everyone clapped.

Bare slid his sword back into its sheath and inclined his head. "Thank ye, ye scurvy lot."

Toby stood. "Who are you?"

"I am the Pirate King."

Toby grinned. "You are now. I'm the director, Toby Whalen. We're so glad you stopped by today. Rehearsals start Monday night."

Bare nodded once and exited stage right.

"I'll be right back," Amber told Steph before slipping out of the auditorium. She hoped to catch

Bare before he left. She caught sight of his back as he was heading down the hallway to the exit.

"Bare?" she called.

He turned. "Amber?"

"What are you doing here?" they asked at the same time.

"I'm auditioning," he said at the same time as she said, "I'm painting."

He crossed to her, and she felt herself flush. The white shirt, open to the waist, gave her an eyeful of chest and abs. Wow. She forced her eyes up to meet his, which were sparkling with mischief.

"Speak again, m'lady, if you dare," he growled. "Explain what ye do here."

A thrill ran through her. She almost forgot it was Bare for a moment there. She licked her lips. "I paint the scenery."

"Ah. Had me an audition for the Pirate King."

"I know. You were amazing! I didn't know you could sing."

"Arrr, matey, sing, loot, pillage, fight with me sword."

Sword. Her eyes dropped to his crotch hugged snugly by the breeches. She felt her face flame. What was wrong with her? He hadn't meant that kind of sword!

She met his warm brown eyes again. "You don't have to talk like a pirate."

It was confusing her. Friendly and sexy were getting crossed. And wasn't she mad at him for something?

He grinned devilishly. "Aye aye, me beauty."

"Oh." She giggled. "Have you done a lot of theater?"

"Aye, wench, but it's been a while." His voice, low and scraping, registered on a deep, throbbing level.

"Too long?" she asked. Only they weren't talking about theater anymore.

He leered at her, letting his eyes trail up and down her body. "Saucy wench."

She shook her head. "I can't believe the way you just belted that song out."

"Believe. Aye, truth is, me singing is a regular thing." He stepped closer, and his voice rumbled close to her ear. "Me shower knows the tale."

Her throat went dry as she pictured him naked in the shower. *Stop that, you dirty brain.* This was her friend and neighbor Bare. Regular old Bare. Good ole…Bare.

"So…okay," she said, suddenly tongue-tied as their gazes collided. She had the strangest urge to step right into his arms and let him carry her off to his pirate ship and have his wicked way with her.

She cleared her throat. "I'd better get back to painting." She gestured in the direction of the band room. "The pirate ship is huge. It's going to need at least two coats of black."

He gave her a rakish salute with a wink that left her speechless.

"Will ye be at rehearsal on Monday night, wench?" he asked.

"Absolutely," she breathed. "I'll be there."

He gave her a slow smile, and it was like the sun had suddenly come out and shone its sexy good looks all over her body. "That be good news."

He turned and strutted out the back door. *Look at that ass. You could bounce a quarter off it.* She quickly averted her eyes and moved back to the band room in a daze.

A short while later, Steph joined her. "There you are! I was wondering if you were ever coming back. So show business isn't for you, huh?"

Amber looked over. "Need anyone on stage crew?"

Steph clapped. "We'd love to have you! Yay!" She picked up her brush and resumed painting. "Wasn't that Pirate King amazing?"

"I know him." She got a jolt remembering his sexy smile in the hallway. "It's that guy I told you about—Bare. He lives across the hall."

Steph's jaw dropped. "That's Barry? The way you described him I pictured a total geek. I mean, the Hawaiian shirts, the dancing cow thing—"

"I know. He surprised me."

Steph shook her head. "It's a good thing you're sticking around. The women in the cast are gonna be all over him. Maybe some of the guys too."

Amber couldn't blame them. She hummed to herself as she painted. Nope, couldn't blame them one bit.

CHAPTER FIVE

Barry had to admit his brother's advice had worked. He got the part and already had a very sexy talk with Amber as a result. He hoped he'd have the same effect on her at tonight's rehearsal out of costume. On his brother's advice, he'd traded his Hawaiian shirts for some new solid-colored T-shirts. He couldn't resist dressing all in black for his first rehearsal. He was a pirate, after all. He wore a black T-shirt with black pants. Then, because he couldn't be a dashing pirate without it, he tied on the black bandana and the belt with the sword.

He arrived early to find a few of the cast hanging out, sitting on the edge of the stage. The director wasn't there yet.

"Ahoy, me hearties," he boomed before sitting next to them.

"Who are you?" a smooth voice asked. It was the guy next to him.

"I'm the Pirate King."

"I'm Frederic," the guy cooed.

"Then we will cross swords," Barry replied. Frederic and the Pirate King had several scenes and a sword fight together.

The guy raised his brows. "I hope so." He held out a hand. "Zac."

"Barrett." What the hell, he could be anyone he wanted to be when it came to theater. He was tired of being shlubby old Barry. "You can call me Bare." He loved it when Amber called him that.

"Barrett! I love it!" This from an overly excited Zac.

Barry wasn't sure what Zac was so excited about.

Another guy leaned over to say, "My last name is Barrett. Kevin Barrett."

"Oh. Okay, nice to meet you."

"I'm your understudy. I'm Samuel, the Pirate King's lieutenant."

Barry saluted. "Aye aye, lieutenant."

"Ooh!" Zac squealed.

"Hi, Bare," a group of women sitting nearby sang.

He waved and walked over. "And who are ye lovely ladies?"

"I'm Zoe," a pretty woman with curly black hair said. "I play Mabel, one of the Major-General's daughters, in love with the dashing Frederic." She batted her eyes at Zac, who blew her a kiss.

"Pleasure be mine," Barry said.

The women smiled dreamily. It was the pirate effect. He met Lauren and Meg, who also played the Major-General's daughters, and then he spotted

Amber walking down the aisle of the auditorium with another woman, and he forgot about everyone else. Amber wore another halter top, white with pink polka dots, with a black skirt that ended just above her adorable bare knees. He exited the stage and met Amber halfway.

"Ahoy, wench," he said, "welcome to the great ship Eastman High School."

Amber laughed. "Hey, Bare. This is my friend Steph. She's one of the Major-General's daughters."

"Nice to meet you," Steph said. "You were amazing at the audition."

"That's because I am the Pirate King!" he boomed with a fist in the air. He smiled and winked. "Thank ye by the way."

Steph laughed. The three of them headed to the stage. Toby, the director, arrived, along with a few other people Barry didn't know yet.

"Okay, people," Toby called, scripts in hand. "Gather 'round. We've got six weeks to pull this together. That means rehearsal every night except Sunday for two shows Friday and Saturday night. If you miss more than two rehearsals in a row, you're out. Anyone that can't handle that, door's right there." He gestured to the exit.

Nobody moved.

"Good. Let's get started. I'm Toby Whalen, your director, as many of you know. I've been doing this a hell of a long time, so you're in good hands. I'll let the rest of the staff introduce themselves." He nodded to the young woman in a leotard and shorts on his right.

"Hi, I'm Jasmine Davis. I recognize a lot of you." She smiled. "I'm the choreographer."

"That's my sister!" Zoe hollered.

"And I'm Zoe's older sister," Jasmine said with a smile.

A petite older woman sitting next to Toby stood up and waved. "Hello, everyone, I'm Edith, Toby's mother." She smiled. "And also the stage manager."

"She'll keep everything running smoothly," Toby said. He pointed toward the piano. "Will Levi on piano."

Will stood and waved. "Hey."

Toby turned to them. "Will's dad, Brian, will *not* be joining us this year because he's on a booze cruise to celebrate his retirement followed by a month at the beach. What a bum! All right, let's get started. Edith will pass out the scripts; then we'll start with the first song. That's 'Pour, oh pour, the pirate sherry.' I want all of the pirates on stage. When it's not your turn, take the time to study your lines. We'll be going without scripts in two weeks. Any questions?"

"Where's our Major-General?" Zac asked.

It must've been a cue because just then the auditorium doors burst open, and a middle-aged man with a pith helmet started marching down the aisle. On his arm was a middle-aged woman with hair teased to a giant black halo around her head.

"I am the very model of a modern Major-General," the man boomed. "And this young beauty"—a few people snickered—"Delilah is the lovely nursemaid Ruth."

The woman curtsied.

"Very nice, you divas," Toby said. "Now go get your scripts."

The Major-General saluted, and the pair strolled down the aisle to the stage. Barry smiled. This was going to be fun.

~ ~ ~

Amber continued painting the pirate ship in the band room while the cast rehearsed in the auditorium. She added some gold decorative swirls and highlights that would pick up the light on stage. A short while later, Bare and the rest of the pirates came into the band room to practice the Pirate King song. She listened while the pianist Will played the song over and over. Will never corrected them, merely cringed when something was off-key, played the note alone, and waited for them to catch on.

Bare held his own in the song, but she noticed Kevin Barrett kept belting out the words loud enough to block out Bare's lead voice. Will kept lowering his hand at Kevin. The chorus shouldn't overtake the lead. She knew Kevin. He'd played the lead last year in *Joseph and the Amazing Technicolor Dreamcoat*. He was talented, but he didn't dominate the stage the way Bare did.

A few times she'd felt someone staring at her, and

she'd look up. Bare would wink at her even as he sang. There was something different about pirate Bare. It wasn't just the silly pirate talk. There was something tender that came through on stage, along with the swagger, that pulled at her. Something more than just the friendly, good-natured guy she'd gotten to know.

Will finally called a halt and gestured for the group to follow him back to the stage.

Bare stopped in front of her. "Ahoy, me beauty."

She set her brush down and stood. "You don't have to talk pirate to me. You can just be yourself."

"But ye like the pirate in me."

Then he turned her and dipped her over one arm. She let out a squeak. He slowly pulled her upright and stayed close enough she could feel his heat. His eyes dropped to her mouth.

Yes, she thought. *Let's try this again.*

"Anyone see Bare?" a voice called. "We need him on stage."

Bare took a step back from her. "To be continued, wench."

"Tease."

"Tease?" he said in mock indignation. Then he called toward the hallway. "Be right there." His eyes narrowed in on her, and her heart pounded in anticipation. "I'll show you tease."

Then he yanked her up against him and plundered her mouth. There was nothing gentle about the kiss; no, it was a hot, deep, take-no-prisoners kiss that left her deliciously breathless. She clung to him as he kissed her into a puddle of need. He slowly pulled away, gazing at her lips. She couldn't seem to let go of her grip on his shirt. She wanted more.

He groaned. "I wish I didn't have to go. I wish—"

"Me too."

He cupped her cheek. "Until later, me buxom beauty."

She glanced down at her not-so-buxom chest. "Buxom?"

"Curvy?"

"Where's our Pirate King?" Toby demanded, sounding extremely irritated.

Amber loosened her grip on him. "They need you."

"Bye," Bare said before making a fast exit.

"Bye," she said to no one. She smiled as she heard Bare declare on stage a moment later, "Gangway! The Pirate King has arrived!"

~ ~ ~

Amber joined the cast and crew on stage for a quick meeting after rehearsal. She sat next to Steph, who was gesturing wildly for her to join her.

"I'm so happy you're here," Steph said.

"Me too." She glanced at Bare, on the other side of the stage, still looking every bit the pirate, and found herself smiling. He suddenly looked up and returned the smile, and she went warm all over.

"Okay, people, we've got a long way to go," Toby

said. "Will tells me half of you are off-key. This is a musical. Everyone has to be in tune. Please practice at home. And, Kevin, you must blend your voice in."

"I can't help how I sing," Kevin retorted.

"He's a star," Zac sang, tossing his hair, which was so short it barely moved.

Kevin shot Zac a dark look that had Zac simmering down quickly.

"You can help it," Toby said. "And, people, I know we're reading the script at this point, but that doesn't mean you aren't acting. I want some expression, some emotion coming through. Especially between Frederic and Mabel. The audience has to believe you're in love." He paused and took a moment to look them all over. The cast squirmed, probably wondering who he was going to call out next. "Now I know you all like to go out after rehearsal, but I ask you to keep the drinking to a minimum. We need you here at one hundred percent every night if we're going to put on the kind of show we're known for. We have an audience who expects a high level of professionalism. That means you know your lines, you hit your marks, you sing on-key. Any questions? No? Good."

A few people had their hands raised, but Toby ignored them. He clapped once, dismissing them. "See you all tomorrow, seven p.m. Don't be late."

Everyone stood and started talking amongst themselves.

"And study your lines tonight!" Toby added before

leaving.

His mother, Edith, smiled at them all. "You did a good job for your first rehearsal. That's my ride." She followed him out the door.

After Toby and Edith left, Zac said, "The torture begins. Toby was brutal tonight. I need a drink. Who's in?"

Everyone agreed and, on Bare's suggestion, they all headed to Garner's Sports Bar & Grill. The place wasn't crowded on a Monday night, and they all found seats at the bar. Bare gestured for Amber to sit on a stool next to him and slid his arm around her waist. Before long, Bare was telling stories with the enthralled cast gathered around him. All except Richard, the Major-General, who was hitting on some young, pretty women at the other end of the bar.

Bare's warm fingers stroked lazily on the bare skin of her lower back while he shared tales of his old job at a software engineering firm in California and the crazy people that used to work there. The wrestling matches they had with *Lord of the Rings* figures late at night when they needed to blow off some steam. The challenge to see who could build the most complex polygon out of office supplies. The way they decided who would get to ask out the new single female in the office first—hand over hand up a light saber, hand on top won.

"It didn't matter who got to ask her out first anyway," Bare went on. "The answer was always no."

Everyone laughed.

"If you were smart, you worked your way up from friendship." Bare smiled at Amber, including her in his tale. "Which I quickly learned. Some of these guys were too desperate to slow it down like that."

"Slow it down," Lauren, one of the Major-General's daughters, said. "I like a guy who takes his time."

Steph rolled her eyes. "Tell us about The Dancing Cow."

"Not much to tell," Bare replied. "That's my frozen yogurt shop. You're all invited anytime with ten percent off."

"Cool," Lauren said, smiling at Bare like she wanted to lick his cone. Amber rested her hand on Bare's thigh, who responded by resting his hand on hers and squeezing.

"I'll be there," Zac said.

"I heard you dance there," Steph said.

Amber shook her head at Steph. She did not want Bare to demonstrate his Irish jig at the bar. No matter how good he was at it.

"Yeah," Bare said. "That's just for the kids. They love it. Sometimes they bring presents for the cow."

Amber turned. That was so sweet. "Like what?"

"I've got crazy straws, cow figures, bouncy balls, little parachute—"

"What theater have you done?" Kevin interrupted.

"Let's see," Bare said. "Now this was all in high school, mind you—"

"High school?" Zoe, who played Mabel,

exclaimed. "I can't believe that. You're so good."

"Well," Bare said modestly. "It's not hard to play a pirate. Just a few yo-ho-hos thrown in there."

The chorus of Major-General's daughters—Zoe, Steph, Lauren, and Meg—quickly protested this modest claim.

"You're such a good singer," Steph said. Everyone agreed heartily.

"I really believe you're a pirate," Lauren said.

"You shine on stage," Zoe said, stars in her eyes.

"Well, ladies, thank you," Bare said.

"Are you single?" Lauren asked. The girl couldn't have been more than twenty-one.

Steph turned to Lauren. "One, he's too old for you—"

"I don't mind an older man," Lauren pouted.

"I'm thirty-one," Bare protested.

"And two, he's holding hands with Amber," Steph said. "Come on!"

"Are you two together?" Lauren asked.

"Yes," Amber said.

Bare turned to her in surprise. He grinned. "Yes, we are."

"So," Kevin said flatly. "What's on your"—he wrinkled his nose distastefully—"*high school* résumé."

Amber squeezed Bare's hand. He glanced at her, giving her a quick smile. "I was Danny in *Grease*, Linus in *You're a Good Man, Charlie Brown*, the prince in *Shrek the Musical*, and part of the chorus in *Anything Goes*."

"Not much of a résumé," Kevin muttered.

"Don't mind Kevin," Delilah drawled. She played Frederic's plain nursemaid Ruth. "He's a wannabe. Not everyone has *it*." She took a sip of her martini. "I've been doing this for twenty-three years. Believe me, I know *it* when I see it. And Bare here has *it*."

"Well, thank you, Delilah," Bare said. "You're also quite good." He turned to his audience. "She has it too. We all do. Hey, we wouldn't be here if we didn't." He raised his beer in a toast. "To us. The few, the proud, the its."

Everyone laughed. They hung out for a while more, until Bare announced he had to get home. The party broke up. Amber walked out of the restaurant, hand in hand with her Pirate King.

He stopped at her car. "Still think I'm a judgmental bird-cow man?"

She cringed. She'd said that in anger, but, in retrospect, his reaction to her dancing with another guy wasn't that far off the mark. Most guys would've balked at that.

"I think you're a chameleon," she said, thinking of his transformation from friendly neighbor to dancing cow to swashbuckling pirate to fabulous kisser.

"That's better than the other thing." He tapped the roof of her car and saluted her smartly. "Godspeed!"

She watched him get into his Honda and got into her little Toyota. There was no question he was geeky, but he was also a hell of a lot more fun than the usual hot guys she typically went for.

When she got back to her apartment, she found

Bare standing by her front door.

He gave her a quick smile. "We forgot to kiss goodnight. Now that we're, you know, together. I mean, you said we were…"

He just stood there, looking at her. Gone was the pirate swagger and in its place an uncertain, almost shy man.

She stood on tiptoe, wrapped her arms around his neck, and kissed him. Soft and tender, not at all her usual style, but she was starting to feel tender for him. His hands went around her waist. He didn't push for more just kissed her back soft and gentle. She traced his lips with her tongue and sucked his lower lip into her mouth. Next thing she knew he had her pinned against her door, his mouth hard on hers, his tongue delving in, his hands stroking up and down her sides. The fire ignited between them as he took from her hungrily and she gave, raising her arms to give him better access to her body while she tunneled her fingers through his hair. His hands stroked lower, over her hips, one hand sliding under her skirt—

Someone wolf-whistled, and they broke apart. It was Ian passing down the hall.

"Hey, sexy," Ian threw over his shoulder at her.

Bare rested his forehead against hers. "Fucking younger brothers."

She laughed. "I know. I've got a younger sister."

"She can't be nearly as annoying as my brother."

"Hey, I heard that," Ian said from where he was standing outside Bare's apartment door. "I forgot my key."

Bare turned and tossed him the key. He turned back to her. "Now where were we, wench?"

She put a hand on his chest. "You should go." She'd been about to drag him to bed when his brother's interruption gave her a nice bout of sanity. Sleeping with a guy just meant they'd leave soon. And she wasn't keen on things ending between her and Bare yet.

"Sure." He shoved his hands in his pockets. "Yeah. Okay. Well, goodnight."

The door shut behind Ian. Bare bent to give her a quick peck on the lips, and Amber couldn't help wanting a little more of that heat. She kissed him passionately and grabbed his firm ass that she'd been admiring ever since he'd worn those pirate breeches. His mouth fused to hers while his erection pressed hard into her belly. She went up on tiptoe. If she was only taller, they would fit. She lifted one leg, wrapped it around his, straining to meet him, throbbing pelvis to pelvis.

He set her away from him. "What are you doing to me, you saucy wench!"

She smiled. "I wanted you to think of me tonight." She turned to unlock her door and jolted as he smacked her butt. "Ow!"

"Tease," he said, throwing her word back at her.

She laughed and went inside. She'd certainly be thinking of him tonight.

CHAPTER SIX

Barry was enjoying the hell out of play rehearsals. It had been a week of fun, and he couldn't believe he'd stayed away for so long. Sure, his true performer nature had leaked out here and there—office parties where he'd led conga lines, karaoke nights he'd organized, playing the dancing cow at his store. But here, walking the boards, this was where he was meant to be. He'd learned his lines within a couple of days, leaving the rest of the cast scrambling to keep up, and he listened to the musical's soundtrack at work, at home, and in the car until he had that memorized too. He loved working with this group, loved having his moment in the spotlight, loved the camaraderie backstage and after hours. Most of all, he loved having Amber by his side through it all.

She'd finished painting scenery and now hung around backstage, helping out where she could, calling people when they were needed on stage, rehearsing lines with them, calling out a line for those who forgot. She also helped with gathering just the right props and costume accessories. He was glad she was backstage today watching. He'd rehearsed his big song, "I am a Pirate King," solo with Will the pianist—hell of a nice guy—and it was time to do a full run-through on stage for the first time with the rest of the cast. This scene had his pirate crew, Ruth, the Major-General, and his daughters.

He wore the eye patch to help him get in character. He waited on his mark on stage and winked stage right, where he could see Amber watching. She didn't react. Probably the eye patch made it look like he was blinking. He smiled instead. She smiled back, and he felt a surge of love. Lust too. Just one look from her, one smile could do that to him. He had to look away and cool himself down. Some part of him, some little niggling voice in the back of his mind kept reminding him of his past experience with Becky, totally in love with him during *Grease*, dumping his sorry ass once the play was over.

That was high school, he reminded himself. Everyone was an immature jerk in high school. Amber was better than that.

Yeah, but she wasn't into you before you became the Pirate King, the voice said.

The music started, and Barry pushed everything else from his mind. He belted out the lyrics, moving around the stage, hitting his marks perfectly as he sang certain lines with the pirate crew backing him up, some lines with the Major-General, others with the daughters, stealing kisses as he moved among the women.

Though he wasn't quite stealing kisses, not with Amber watching. He was dipping each daughter, putting a hand over their mouth, and kissing the back of his hand. He didn't think anyone in the audience would notice. He did it out of respect for Amber. He sure as hell wouldn't want to watch while she kissed four men on stage. He kept going as the song built to the big finish. Swaggering to center stage, he finished with a flourish of an imaginary sword.

The room went quiet as they all waited to hear Toby's verdict.

Toby bounded onto the stage. "What the hell is this?" he asked, leaning over and kissing the back of his own hand.

Barry felt his cheeks flame. He didn't think you could see that from the audience. He raised his palms. "Just being respectful."

"Well, knock it off!" Toby said. "You're the Pirate King. The Pirate King is not *shy*. He's not *respectful*. He *takes*. Do it again the right way."

Toby returned to the audience. Barry glanced over at Amber. She lifted one shoulder up and down.

The music started again.

"Don't be a pansy," Toby hollered over the music.

Barry stiffened. He took a deep breath and sang. He moved through the song as he had the first time, the timing working perfectly as he moved among the other actors. He stopped at the first daughter, Steph, dipped her, and came very close without quite kissing her.

She giggled.

"Cut!" Toby hollered.

The music stopped. Toby stood and approached the stage. "It's not just a dip. It's dip and kiss. Do we have a problem here, Bare?"

"No, sir."

"These ladies don't mind if you kiss them," Toby said. "Do you, ladies?"

"No," Zoe and Meg said in unison.

"Not at all," Steph said.

"Please do," Lauren purred.

"I'll kiss him," Zac said.

Kevin socked him on the arm. They were, apparently, a couple.

Barry took off his eye patch and turned to look at the four pretty young women, all eager for his kiss; then he looked at Amber, but she had left. Dammit. He turned and scanned the seats in the auditorium, but she wasn't there either. Was she upset? He'd make it up to her. He'd give her the longest, hottest kiss of her life. Just as soon as he finished kissing these four.

How had his life turned into this? Crazy theater people.

Toby returned to the front row of the audience. "Let's do this, people!"

Barry nodded over to Will at the piano, who looked highly amused. The music started again. He launched once more into "I am a Pirate King," forcing the blustering arrogance and swagger into his performance because without Amber there it was a hell of a lot less fun. He gave each woman a quick peck on the lips, which worked well, except Lauren slipped him the tongue, but he kept going because he was nothing if not professional. The song ended, and Toby must've been satisfied because they moved on.

Amber finally came back. They moved to the next scene, and he mouthed "sorry" to her, but she just waved it off like it was no big deal. Finally rehearsal ended, and he caught up with her.

"Hey, I didn't really want to kiss those other women," he told her as they headed to the parking lot.

She glanced at him and quickly faced forward. "Bare, don't worry about it. I'm fine. It's just a show."

"Exactly. It's just a show." She wasn't looking at him, and it was making him nervous. "So you're okay with it?"

"I better be. We've got five more weeks of rehearsals and two shows to get through."

He smiled. "So I'll see you at the diner?" They were all headed out for a late-night snack.

"You know, I'm kind of tired. I think I'm going to head home."

"You are upset."

They reached her car, and she unlocked it. "I'm fine. Goodnight."

He leaned in to kiss her, and she turned so his kiss hit her cheek. "Amber."

She looked at his mouth, and her gaze quickly flicked up to his eyes. "I just need time. You've still got lipstick all over your mouth."

"Oh." He scrubbed at his mouth.

She got in her car and powered down the window. "Bye, you scurvy dog."

He wasn't sure if he should be glad she was speaking pirate to him or worried she was calling him a scurvy dog. "Bye, me beauty."

She inclined her head and drove away. Maybe flowers were in order. But that would be like admitting he'd done something wrong. He'd just done what he was supposed to do. He was acting. It was just acting. She had to get used to that.

"Hey, Bare," Lauren called, hips swinging, saucy as all hell in her short shorts. "Can I hitch a ride with you? Meg bailed."

He swallowed hard. Lauren was the one who asked if he was single. The one who said she liked older men. The one who had her tongue in his mouth.

"Sure," he croaked. He really, really hoped this didn't get back to Amber. It was a car ride and nothing more. Nothing would happen if he had anything to say about it. Which he most certainly did. He was the king, after all. He could handle a young, twenty-something flirt. Right?

She got in his car. He turned the ignition and startled when she pushed the button that made the loudspeaker moo on top of the car. She laughed. He'd nearly forgotten about the loudspeaker. He hadn't used it in so long because Amber didn't like it.

"What was that?" she asked.

"It's for my shop. It lets the kiddies know fro-yo is nearby."

"Cool."

Really? That was cool? Amber told him never to play it when she was in the car. Lauren pressed the button again and again, making the car moo the entire drive to the diner. Even Barry was getting tired of it.

He parked, and they headed to the diner's entrance.

Lauren put her hand on his arm, stopping him a short distance from the door. "Bare, can I ask you something?"

He turned. "Sure."

"Do you think I'm pretty?"

"Yes."

He turned to go, but her hand tightened around his arm, anchoring him in place. He turned back to her. She bit her lip and gave him these big soulful eyes that made him feel like she might be hitting on him.

"Did you like our kiss?" she asked.

"Now, Lauren," he said in his best I'm-thirty-one-years-old-and-I-know-better-than-you voice. "That was just acting. You know I'm with Amber."

She stuck out her lower lip. "You didn't answer my question."

It wasn't that he didn't like it. It was just that it felt wrong. He really didn't want to encourage her.

"Sorry," he said. "Just didn't do it for me."

"Well," she huffed. Then she marched ahead of him into the diner. He followed her to the big table in the back, where the rest of the cast was already seated. "I'll get a ride home with someone else," she hissed before taking a seat next to Zac.

He stayed for a little while, eating some mozzarella sticks, before making an excuse to head home. He wanted to kiss Amber again. He wanted her to know he only had lips for her.

~ ~ ~

Amber drove around for a bit, blasting the radio, reminding herself Bare was a great guy who would never fool around on her. He'd done nothing wrong. Nothing sneaky or behind her back. Hell, he'd been hesitant to even kiss those girls in the first place, until Toby threw a fit about it. That's why she'd made herself scarce. She had a feeling he was holding back because of her. And that was sweet. This was so not a big deal.

You'll have to watch every night.

Don't remind me.

Finally, she headed home. It was Friday night after a long week of work and rehearsals. She just wanted to zone out on the sofa with a glass of wine and *Zombie Bonanza*. She stopped short at her door, where someone was sitting, knees drawn up, leaning against it. She got closer. Oh, hell in a handbasket. She did not have the energy to deal with this tonight.

"Hi, Kate," she said, stopping in front of her half-sister.

Her sister was twenty-one going on fifty—conservative, obsessed with equations, not men, and into comfort before fashion. She even drove a station wagon, chosen for its safety record. Though they resembled each other in coloring and size, the rest of them was absolutely different. Kate was her usual mess—blond hair half wrapped in a bun, half down in a weird half tail, her baggy T-shirt had a stain on it, her jeans faded to the point of fraying, but not in a cool way, more like a thrift-shop-reject way.

Kate looked up through her huge tortoiseshell glasses. "Hi," she mumbled.

She stood, and that's when Amber noticed the wheeled suitcase her sister had been leaning against. *Oh, no.*

"Planning on staying a while?" Amber asked with a sinking feeling as she unlocked the door.

"I can't deal with the mothership," Kate said, wheeling in her suitcase. Knowing Kate, she'd probably packed one pair of ancient jeans, a dozen T-shirts, and her laptop.

Amber sighed. "Your mother doesn't hover."

Maxine was, in fact, a brilliant physicist with an absentminded, benignly neglectful way about her. Still, she was *there*, at home every day by five thirty, which was more than Amber had ever gotten from her own mother. Even when she'd lived with her mom, her mom had spent all of her time painting in their sunroom, barely noticing her young daughter painting nearby, trying to reach her mom in the only way she knew how. Since moving to Paris, her mom sent Amber hand-painted cards on her birthday and whenever the hell else she got around to it, but she never visited, never called, never even emailed. She was the kind of artist that was so wrapped up in her art she didn't have the energy for anyone else. Amber vowed long ago to always keep a balance between her art and the people in her life that mattered.

Kate interrupted her unhappy memories when she exclaimed, "Mom bugs me all the time! She wants me to spend the summer studying ahead of time for grad school. Isn't it enough I did a double major in math and physics in three years? I've been taking college classes since high school. Don't I deserve a break?"

Amber's head spun, thinking about cramming all those equations into such a short time. "Of course you do."

"I've only got the summer, and then it's grad school here I come."

Kate wheeled her suitcase into Amber's room.

"Uh, Kate. You've got the sofa."

"Oh." She wheeled her suitcase back to the living room and flopped down on the sofa. "So what's on the agenda tonight?"

Amber flopped down on the sofa next to her. "I just got home from a long day. I had work, then play rehearsal. I just want to crash."

"Great! I'll crash too."

They sat side by side on the sofa. "Kate?"

"Yes."

"Next time can you call?"

"I emailed you yesterday. Don't you check your email?"

"Oh, yeah. I guess I haven't checked it in a couple of days."

Kate shook her head.

"How long are you staying?" Amber asked.

"The whole summer," Kate said.

"The whole—now wait a minute." The doorbell rang. Amber headed to the door and said over her shoulder, "We need to talk about this."

She peeked through the peephole. Bare. This was the never-ending night. It was nearly ten o'clock. Just put her out of her misery. A long sleep to end this day.

She opened the door. "Hi, Bare."

"Hey, wench. Just wanted to make sure—"

"Who is this?" Kate asked, appearing at Amber's side.

"This is Bare." She turned to her sister, who had the strangest look of awe on her face. "This is my sister, Kate."

"I know you," Kate said, pointing at him. "I read about you in *The Journal of Computing Science and Society*. You're Giggle Snap. I mean, Barry Furnukle."

Bare grinned. "Oh, well. Yeah, that's me."

"You're brilliant," Kate breathed. "The compression algorithm you developed for sound recordings was groundbreaking."

Bare smiled and shuffled his feet. "Thank you. It was nothing. There's much better on the market now."

"I'm Kate," she said, holding out her hand.

He shook it. "Yes. Nice to meet you, Kate."

Kate pulled the rubber band out of her hair and shook her hair loose. "You want to come in for a drink?"

Amber stared at her sister. Really? Now she was interested in a man? She'd been starting to wonder if her sister was into women.

"Actually I came by just to k—" Bare shook his head with a smile. "I just wanted to talk to your sister."

"Come on," Kate coaxed, hand on her hip. "One drink. I'll tell you the latest in operations research for databases in apps like yours."

"I am working on a birding app that's database dependent," Bare said.

Kate pushed up her glasses. "Excellent!"

Amber stifled a groan as they settled in the living room with glasses of iced tea. Kate waxed on enthusiastically to Bare's eager ears, both of them completely forgetting about the drinks. After an hour of computing and higher mathematics talk that went way over Amber's head, she slipped away and went to bed.

A few moments later, the door creaked open.

"Amber?" Bare called.

"What?" she mumbled.

"I'm going to kiss you goodnight."

"Don't."

He'd kissed enough women tonight, and then he'd kissed up to her sister.

"Come on, wench. Ouch!" The bed shook. He must've bumped into it.

She bit back a laugh. "Don't call me wench."

"Give us a kiss, me love."

She threw the covers over her head. "I'm not your love."

He yanked the covers down. "I say you are."

His hands found her hair, then her cheek, and he turned her toward him. His lips came down over hers, soft and gentle. She relaxed into it, forgetting about her worshipful sister and the worshipful Major-General's daughters.

He kissed the tip of her nose. "Good night, Amber."

"Night."

He kissed her forehead. "I hope one day to say good morning."

"Don't push it."

"Where's me buried treasure?" He felt all over the bed, then all over her, his hands patting over the covers, making her giggle; then he slid into the bed with her.

She shoved at his chest, trying not to laugh. "Your treasure's not here."

"Aye, but 'tis." He pulled her up against him, so they were both on their sides, chest to chest. She wore a tank top with pajama shorts, and he felt deliciously warm through the thin fabric. She snuggled closer. His hand cupped the back of her head, and he kissed her again. This time was a hard, claiming kiss, his tongue thrusting inside, his leg wedging between hers. Then he was kissing along her jawline, down her neck, while his hands roamed up and down her body, never lingering at any of her good spots, just an allover stroking that left her fully awake, fully aroused, and wanting more.

"Amber?" Kate knocked on her door. "I forgot my toothbrush. Do you have an extra one?"

Bare nuzzled along her collarbone while his hand worked its way up her shirt, caressing her breast.

"Yes," she gasped as his finger rasped over the sensitive tip. "Take it. There's extra."

"Is Barry sleeping over tonight?" Kate asked through the door. "I forgot my pajamas too. Is he going to see me without my pants?"

Bare laughed into her neck. Amber stifled a laugh.

Kate went on. "It's okay if he does. But…can I borrow a few things? My underwear's plain white and *mumble, mumble…*"

Amber didn't catch the rest of that sentence. Kate was probably looking down at herself and talking, but seriously, was she supposed to share Bare *and* her underwear with her sister?

"I'm not spending the night," Bare called.

They heard Kate move on.

"I think she wants me," he said.

She shoved him out of bed. "Everyone wants you."

He leaned back over her, hands on either side of her shoulders. "Does that mean you too?"

"You're going to get a big head."

"You'll keep me humble." His lips brushed hers. She tangled her hand in his hair, keeping him there for more. He obliged, kissing her long and hard until they heard Kate's footsteps stop right outside the door again on her way back from the bathroom.

"Soon, love," he whispered.

"You wish," she said, because she didn't want him to leave yet, even with her sister hovering nearby.

Kate's footsteps moved on to the living room.

He pressed a finger to her lower lip. "I know."

She took his finger into her mouth and sucked.

He groaned. "Vixen."

She released his finger and smiled.

"You're pushing me control, wench."

"Night, Bare." She rolled onto her side away from him, wondering if he would slide in next to her again or just go. His hand cupped her bottom, slid lower still, and pressed into her heat. She gasped.

His voice was a throaty growl. "Night, Amber."

He released her and left. She tossed and turned after that, wishing Bare was there to ease the ache or that she hadn't teased, because she needed now in a way she hadn't needed before. Sleep was a long way off.

CHAPTER SEVEN

Amber was watching backstage on Monday night, script in hand, while Mabel and the Major-General's daughters sang their song when boisterous voices and the sound of something clashing together carried through from the hallway. She went to the stage door and poked her head out. Bare and Zac were having a sword fight with wooden swords in the hallway.

"Really?" she asked. "Do you have to do that here?"

"Don't interrupt when men are crossing swords," Zac said, slamming his sword into Bare's.

Bare parried and grinned at her. "We were told to stay nearby in case we're needed."

"I'll call you," she said. "Go fight like big boys in the cafeteria."

Zac turned and held his sword out from his crotch. "Excuse me, we are men."

Bare gave her his lopsided smile. He raised his sword high in the air. "Yes, men."

Amber shook her head and returned to the

backstage area. The sound of swordplay quieted.

A short while later, Edith stopped by. "We need Zac on stage. Could you fetch him? Then if you have a minute, help me out by the storage closet with costumes."

"Sure, no problem."

Amber went to the cafeteria, where Zac was sitting on top of a cafeteria table talking to Bare. She watched as Zac kept touching Bare's arm while Bare good-naturedly chatted away. Did Bare even realize Zac was into him?

"Zac," she called. "They need you on stage."

Zac jumped up and turned to Bare. "Until we cross swords again, my good man."

Bare inclined his head, and Zac left.

Bare crossed to her. "Hello, me buxom beauty."

She snort-laughed. "Okay, you're really pushing it with the buxom. I am not buxom."

His eyes dropped to her chest and looked back in her eyes. "Hello, me beauty."

She smacked his chest.

"Ow!" He rubbed his chest.

"Now you're insulting me."

"How is that insulting? You're the one that said you're not buxom. I thought I wasn't supposed to say that."

He looked so genuinely perplexed that she forgave him. She kissed his chest where she'd smacked him. "Sorry I smacked your chest."

He wrapped his hand in her hair. "You can smack

me in a few more places if you're gonna kiss them after."

"You do not want that," she said cheekily.

He leaned down, brushing his lips over hers. "Maybe I do." He nipped her bottom lip. "Maybe I'll return the favor." He smacked her bottom, and she tipped forward into him.

"Fresh," she said, but she was smiling.

His arm wrapped around her waist. "Amber," he growled before his mouth crashed down over hers. She threw her arms around him, running her fingers through the silky hair at the nape of his neck. His hand gripped her hair, the other tucked firmly over her ass. The kiss went on and on, hot and heavy, and she roamed her hands everywhere she could reach, up to his cheek with its pirate stubble, under his soft T-shirt, over his jeans and that firm ass. He was moving her now, kissing her and backing her up behind the vending machines, pressing her back into the wall, out of sight of the cafeteria doors.

And then his hands roamed everywhere as he kissed her, under her tunic and over the thin cotton of her leggings, drawing a moan from her, then he was lifting her, and she wrapped her legs around his waist, and sweet glory, they fit. The throbbing between her legs intensified as his erection pushed against her through the leggings.

The cafeteria door opened, and they froze.

"Amber?" a voice called.

It was Edith. She'd forgotten she was supposed to

help her out with the costumes. She looked at Bare, eyes wide, and he shook his head. He wasn't putting her down. She was afraid Edith was going to walk all the way in and catch her in this position.

She wiggled, and Bare pressed harder into her, sending a jolt of sensation through her core. His eyes burned into hers, and she barely breathed.

They heard footsteps, and then the door opened and closed again. She let out a breath. "That was a close one. I have to go. I was supposed to help her."

He eased off her and let her slide slowly down his front. "I could use some help too."

"What kind of—"

They both glanced down to where his jeans were bulging.

"Oh," she said.

"Yeah."

She gave him a small impish smile. "Sorry."

She started to walk away, but he grabbed her and pulled her back flush against his body. "I'm not."

He kissed her again, and the rush of sensation made her forget why in the world she was trying to leave. His tongue thrust in her mouth, and she responded with needy mewls asking for more. Her hands smoothed over his chest, feeling the hard planes. His hands were everywhere at once, overwhelming her, making her want to climb back up his body and wrap her legs around him again. Suddenly she found herself set a foot away from him.

"Why did you stop?" she asked. Her lips still

tingled, her body still ached.

He closed his eyes. "You make me want. Too much. You'd better go."

"Aren't you going to look at me?"

"Amber, please. This isn't where I want our first time."

She bit her lip. His eyes were still closed. Did he actually think she wanted to sleep with him here? Then it hit her, what he'd said before about pushing his control, he was trying to control himself. He wanted her that much.

With that heady knowledge lodged deep in her heart, she turned on her heel and headed for the door. She stopped and looked over her shoulder. He'd turned away from her.

"I'm shaking my booty," she called.

"You mean my booty," he answered.

A hot rush ran through her. She headed resolutely out the door, her lips curved into a small smile.

~ ~ ~

Barry headed to the restroom to splash cold water on his face before returning to the stage. He'd been this close to taking Amber right there in the cafeteria. He'd never felt anything like that overwhelming urge to drive into her. Geez, he had to slow things down. Had to be satisfied with a few kisses. He was going to scare her off. Or, worse, push her too hard, too fast. He had a whole week of rehearsal to get through before he'd

have her to himself again. She'd agreed to go out with
him on Saturday to a matinee and dinner before
rehearsal. Dating first, then sex, he reminded himself.
That was the order of things.

He returned to the stage in time to rehearse with
the pirates, Frederic, and the Major-General's
daughters. He glanced backstage as the music began.
Amber wasn't there. Must be off helping Edith. It was
better that way. He didn't want the entire cast to see
him busting his pants because he was in such a sorry
state of hard-core lust.

Jasmine was working with him and the pirates,
having them dance with the Major-General's
daughters, spinning them around, holding hands and
tugging them along, moving in circles around them.
He was distracted, his mind on Amber, so when
Lauren pinched his ass on one go-round, he yelped in
surprise.

The women giggled. Lauren wiggled her fingers at
him. He shook his finger at her and tried to look stern
as the song continued. He didn't want to disrupt
rehearsal for something so silly. He kept singing, trying
to remember his marks, ignoring the sultry looks
Lauren was tossing his way.

The song ended, and Jasmine held up her hand for
them to take five.

"Lauren, can I see you?" Jasmine called as she
moved to the far left of the stage away from them.

Lauren sauntered over. Jasmine spoke in a low,
serious tone that he didn't quite catch. Lauren glanced

over at him, raised her chin, and started to walk away, but Jasmine grabbed her arm and said a few more things.

He looked away. Zac appeared at his side. "That girl is too much. She had her hands all over me last summer."

Bare glanced at him. It was fairly obvious that Zac was gay and into Kevin.

"Yeah?" Bare asked.

"No means no, am I right?" Zac asked.

"Sure."

Bare turned as a hand rested on his arm. Lauren looked up at him, her eyes wide and innocent. "Sorry, Bare. That was unprofessional. It won't happen again."

"Okay, no problem."

She leaned up on tiptoe and whispered, "I'm not too young. I turned twenty-one last month."

He stepped back. "Well...happy birthday."

She pursed her lips. "Thank you."

"Get back to your spot, flirt," Steph called.

Lauren tossed her hair and returned to Steph's side.

"Just say no, Bare," Zac sang.

"No problem," Bare said. His eye caught backstage. Amber was back. He really hoped Lauren didn't do anything else crazy in front of her.

Jasmine raised a hand. "From the top. Ladies, some ad libbing is okay. I encourage that, but no inappropriate touching. You wouldn't like it if the reverse happened."

"Speak for yourself," Lauren muttered.

Jasmine shot her a stern look and signaled to Will to start the music. Barry amped up his performance. He loved when Amber watched him. It gave him an extra jolt of energy that had him soaring through the music.

The song ended, and Amber walked on stage with four parasols. "Look what I found."

"Nice," Jasmine said. "Let's run through it again. We can have a lot of fun with these. Let me see."

Amber handed her a parasol. Jasmine opened it and played around with it—twirling, walking with it, moving it from shoulder to shoulder.

"Let's start with the twirl," Jasmine said. "In front like this. Then, over your shoulder, and work with it as you sing. See what feels natural."

Amber walked by him on her way off stage. Her hand slid across his belly in a warm stroke as she passed. "See what feels natural," she whispered.

"Wench," he said, turning to watch the rear view. Mistake. Her hips swayed, the oversize shirt moving side to side, giving glimpses of her curves encased in the thin cotton leggings. He looked to the ceiling, taking a slow, deep breath, thinking of ice cold fro-yo. Nothing sexy about ice cold fro-yo in your pants.

They ran through the song again. He was careful not to look over at Amber. Who knew what she'd do next to entice him?

Jasmine dismissed the pirates so she could work further with the ladies and their parasols. He went in search of Amber. She wasn't backstage. He just needed to feel her in his arms one more time. He could satisfy himself with a kiss.

He found her half inside the band room closet, on her hands and knees, her curvy ass facing him, taunting him. He stifled a groan.

"What are you doing?" he asked. His voice came out harsh as he strained not to reach out and touch.

She startled and rose to her knees. "Hey. I was just digging through some of the boxes back here. Edith said there might be some more props we could use."

She went back on all fours. He couldn't take it.

"I'll get the boxes," he barked.

She looked at him over her shoulder. "I've got it."

He grabbed her by the hips and pulled her out of the way. Then he delivered three boxes to her feet. "There."

She stared at him strangely as she settled cross-legged in front of them. "Thank you?"

He grunted. "We have a date on Saturday."

And then it would be perfectly acceptable for him to move forward with these urges that were driving him insane.

She pulled open the flaps of the box. "I remember. *All I Want* and sushi."

She'd picked the movie, but now he was starting to think watching a chick flick with her was a bad idea. He wouldn't be into it, and that would leave him free to fantasize how quickly he could get her into bed and whether or not they really needed to eat dinner at all.

He could hear the plink of the piano running through the song in the auditorium nearby and considered how long he had before he had to go back on stage.

She pulled out a few hats—a cowboy hat and a Native American headdress—and a feather boa. "Not much here," she muttered, tossing them back in the box. She shoved the box aside and opened the next box. "Lookee here."

She held up a gold genie bottle and rubbed it. "Three wishes. What will it be?"

He settled himself on the floor next to her, placing his hands on the bottle, on top of hers. "Wish number one, to be with you."

"Aww," she said. "You are. Wish one granted."

"Wish number two, to kiss you."

She gave him a quick peck and grinned. "Wish two granted."

"Wish number three…" He stopped himself. Not all women liked dirty talk. And they still hadn't had that date yet.

"Wish number three?" she prompted.

He stroked her cheek and ran his fingers down her neck to her collarbone. Her breathing quickened. Her skin was so soft. And she smelled like roses. He cradled her face and kissed her. This had to be enough. Just kissing and tasting. He buried his hand in her long hair, but his body was already urging him for more. He wasn't sure who moved first, but the genie bottle hit the floor with a clatter, and then their arms were wrapped around each other, and he was pulling her into his lap.

He could feel her hot through her leggings. He shifted her, so she was cradled in his arms, not riding him like he desperately wanted. Not yet. He couldn't stop kissing her, couldn't stop touching her. The music stopped next door, and she tore her mouth away from his.

They were both breathing hard.

"I know what wish number three is," she said.

"And?"

"Granted."

He groaned and reached for her again, but she slipped out of his grasp.

She scooped up the genie bottle and stood. "You didn't hear my three wishes."

"They're all granted."

She tilted her head to the side and smiled at him. "No questions, just granted?"

"Yes, yes, and yes." He stood. "Wish number three gives you an all-access, no-questions-asked pass."

"We need the pirates on stage!" Toby hollered.

"I like your style," she said.

He really had to go, but he just couldn't resist asking, "When does my third wish come true?"

"Soon enough, matey," she said jauntily.

Soon enough sounded like very, very soon.

"Soon enough, me beauty." Then he turned and strutted back on stage.

~ ~ ~

Amber would be the first to admit things were moving fast with Bare. Once he got into that pirate swagger, she wanted to rip his clothes off. For the rest of that week, every night at rehearsal, she teased and flirted with him relentlessly. She loved watching his gaze heat up, loved having him corner her whenever he got the chance, loved his hands on her, even loved getting him riled up just before he went on stage because he always paid her back for it in hot kisses and whispered promises for more.

"Soon," he'd whisper. "Soon."

It was the hottest week of foreplay of her life. And then, finally, it was time for their date on Saturday. She had a feeling the date was what he was waiting for. Like they had to do things right with a date that didn't end in disaster after their first two dates went so badly. She really hoped this one went smoothly. They were having an afternoon date since they still had rehearsal that night.

He showed up at her door right after lunch on Saturday and handed her a small wrapped gift.

"Bare, you didn't have to get me anything," she said even as she opened it eagerly. It was a box of chocolates. "Mmm, chocolate. I love it." She took one and popped it in her mouth. It was chocolate with coconut. She loved coconut.

She held the box up to him. "You want one?"

"I'll take one," Kate called from her permanent

spot on the sofa. Her sister was glued to her laptop, working on whatever mathematical or sciencey thing grabbed her interest.

"Hi, Kate," Bare called.

"I'm reading a fascinating paper on using lasers to cool a nanowire probe to an incredible level of sensitivity," Kate responded. "You can imagine the implications for the resolution on atomic-force micro—"

"Bye, Kate!" Amber stepped into the hallway and shut the door behind her.

Bare smiled. Then he reached into his pocket and handed her a small Tiffany blue box. She nearly choked on the half-chewed candy in her mouth. She swallowed it down and wiped her mouth with the back of her hand. She stared at the box. Stared at him.

"Open it," he said.

She did. Diamond stud earrings glittered back at her.

"They match your piercing," he said.

She pulled an earring out of the box and examined it closely. "Omigod! Bare! Are these real?"

"Yes. Less than a carat, but real."

She stared at him in wonder. "You really didn't have to do that."

"I wanted to."

She handed him the candy and slipped the dangling black and silver posy earrings from her ears, replacing them with the studs. "Thank you."

Ian poked his head out the door. "You like it?" he

called. "The three Cs?"

She turned to Bare in confusion. "Three Cs?"

"Mind your business," Bare told his brother. He offered his arm. "Shall we go?"

She took his arm. "We shall."

~ ~ ~

Barry headed to the movie theater, working hard to tamp down his irritation at his brother. He just had to stick his nose out and mention those three Cs. Barry was trying to be smooth. He'd like to get through one date with Amber without making a royal mess of it.

Amber pulled the visor mirror down and admired her earrings. "So, spill. What are the three Cs, and does every woman get them?"

"Fucking Ian," he muttered.

"Chocolate," she said. "Right?"

It was candy. Whatever.

"Right?" she prompted.

"Ian made up the three Cs. I've never done them. Forget he opened his big mouth."

He glanced over. She was smiling, and he could just tell she wasn't going to let this go. He wasn't going to help. Geez. He pressed play on the iPod he had hooked into his car, hoping *The Pirates of Penzance* soundtrack would distract her. That lasted two songs when she suddenly shouted, "Carats!"

He groaned.

"I'm right!" she crowed. "Chocolate, carats, what

else?" She tapped her finger against her lips, thinking.

"Actually, it was two Cs."

"No, Ian said *three* Cs. Cage?"

He sputtered. "Cage? No, it's not a cage."

"Cake!"

"Yes, it's cake."

"You're such a bad liar."

"No, it's cake. You like chocolate cake?"

"Well, yeah, but I already had candy and chocolate cake doesn't exactly go with sushi."

"Another time."

Shwoo. Got a little dodgy there, but at least they were off that topic. He was about to ask her what she was working on in her latest painting when she went right back to the Cs like a starving dog on a bone.

"Ah, I know," she said. He bit back a groan. "Candlelight. It's very romantic. It goes with chocolate and carats. Did I get it?"

"Yes."

She pointed at him. "I'm not giving up, Bare. I'll get it out of you."

God, he hoped so. It was candy, carats, climax (hers) in that order.

~ ~ ~

The movie was romantic and funny, and Amber really appreciated that Bare was man enough to sit through a chick flick. He'd held her hand in the dark and laughed right along with her. Some guys suffered through chick flicks. He seemed to like it. She still couldn't believe he'd given her diamond earrings. He either had money to burn, or he really, really liked her. Maybe both.

When they got to the sushi restaurant, they decided to share a large assorted sashimi platter with yellowtail, tuna, sea urchin, and salmon. The fish was fresh and tender. So far this date was going much better than the other two. She loved the movie and the sushi. So did he. At least she thought he did.

"Did you really like the movie?" she asked.

He nodded once. "I really did. It was funnier than I thought it would be."

She grinned. "Chick flick. That's the other C."

"Yes."

"Now why don't I believe you?"

He raised his palms. "You have a very suspicious nature."

"Hmmm…"

"So tell me what you're working on." He picked up a piece of tuna with his chopsticks and dipped it in soy sauce. "What's the latest Amber Lewis original painting?"

"I've barely had any time to paint between work and rehearsals," she said. "I hope to start again tomorrow. And a lot more after that too now that school ended."

"I can't wait to see it."

She smiled and snagged another piece of the salmon. He'd always been so encouraging about her work. She hadn't sold anything in a couple of weeks, but she hoped sales would pick up again soon.

"Tell me about your family," he said.

She stared at the platter. "Why do you want to hear about them?"

Talking about her family was one of her least favorite topics.

He took her hand across the table. "I want to know everything about you."

"I don't want to talk about them." She forced a smile. "Tell me about your family."

"Not much to tell. I told you my dad died, then there's my mom, really sweet lady, and you met Ian. Daniel works for the military. Not in the field. He's behind the scenes. Intelligence work. That's everyone."

"Cool."

"Why don't you want to talk about your family?" he asked.

She set down her chopsticks and blew out a breath. "Fine. Dad is a physicist at Princeton, my stepmother same deal, you've met Kate. That's it."

"And your mother?"

She forced her jaw to unclench. "She's an artist living in Paris."

She left out the worst part. The part where her mother had planned a solo trip to Paris and never looked back. The part where her mother had left a surly teenage Amber, pissed to be missing out on a trip to Paris and stuck at her father's house away from her friends for what she thought was a whole two weeks. The part where her mother had hugged her and whispered, "I love you, Amber. Goodbye."

Amber hadn't hugged her back. Worse, she'd said only one word in reply: "Whatever."

"We don't have to talk about her," he said, gently squeezing her hand.

She relaxed a little. She appreciated his understanding about a topic that still jabbed painfully in her heart. She met his eyes. He was studying her.

"So how long until you give me the third C?" she asked.

She watched as his gaze heated. Knew instinctively she had him now. Knew where he was going with this.

"When do you want it?" he asked, his voice a near growl.

Her heart kicked up. "Now."

His grip on her hand tightened. "Not now."

She smiled. She'd guessed correctly. He was off that horrible topic, and she'd get her third C soon. They finished dinner and headed back to the apartment building. They still had an hour and a half before they had to get to rehearsal. That was plenty of time.

They rushed up the stairs, hand in hand. "My place or yours?" she asked.

"Ian's at my place. Yours."

"Kate's at mine."

"She's easier to move. Tell her I have the latest

issue of *Information Technology & You* at my place."

"That's a real thing?" she asked as she unlocked her door.

"Yes. She'll love it." His hand cupped her bottom, giving her a jolt. She grabbed his hand and pulled him inside.

CHAPTER EIGHT

"My mother's here," Kate said miserably from the sofa. Amber's hopes for her date did a spectacular crash and burn.

"Hello, Amber," Maxine said, her voice tight and clipped. Her stepmother was petite, her gray hair in a severe short cut that emphasized her sharp, elf-like features. She wore a tailored pant suit like she'd just left work, though more likely she'd absentmindedly put it on this weekend because it was hanging in her closet.

Amber let go of Bare's hand. "Hi, Maxine. What are you doing here?"

She'd driven up from Princeton, New Jersey. More than a two-hour drive. With no advance warning.

"I'm here to collect Kate. She only has eight weeks to prepare for graduate school. There are no slackers at M.I.T."

Bare snorted.

Maxine turned. "Who are you?"

"Oh, sorry." Bare crossed to her, holding out his

hand. "Barry. Nice to meet you. My brother's at M.I.T. He's sort of a slacker. But a very smart one."

"Your brother's at M.I.T.?" Kate asked.

"Yup."

"Katherine," Maxine said sharply, "pack your things."

Kate turned pleading eyes to Amber. "Amber said I could stay. Right?"

Amber couldn't make her little sister study physics all summer. But wait. Wasn't that what Kate was doing all on her own?

"Kate's been studying physics on her laptop," Amber offered.

"See, Mom?" Kate said. "I can study remotely. I have access to the university's library online. I can keep up with all the latest journals. Please."

"Amber, may I speak with you privately," Maxine said.

"Sure." She gestured for her to follow her to the kitchen. She could hear Kate happily talking Bare's ear off.

Maxine stared at Amber stone-faced across the table. "Kate has expressed interest in changing her virginal status before graduate school."

Amber grimaced.

"I suspect that's why she's come to you," Maxine went on. "She's hoping you'll guide her in meeting an appropriate man."

"I-I didn't know. I would never—"

Maxine held up a hand. "She looks up to you.

Always has. Can I count on you to keep her from getting into trouble?"

"You mean birth control?"

"No, we've had that talk with her every year since she first got her period. And we don't have a problem with sex per se."

We, Amber supposed, meant her father and Maxine. Geez. All she'd gotten was a book tossed in her room. Of course, she hadn't been all smiles and sunshine as a teenager. Her dad probably didn't have a clue where to begin that talk.

Maxine went on. "We just don't want Kate throwing herself at some guy who's going to…"

A few moments passed in silence. Amber waited, used to Maxine's halting conversations. Her stepmother's brain was whirring a mile a minute though nothing was coming out of her mouth.

Finally Maxine stood. "I'm glad we had this talk."

Amber's head spun. What exactly had they decided? She followed Maxine into the living room.

Kate stood. "Can I stay?"

Maxine nodded. "You may stay if you send me weekly progress reports on your studies. Amber will take care of the other thing."

"You will?" Kate asked, her eyes lighting up.

Amber had no idea what she was supposed to do. Was she supposed to pimp her sister out to some guy? Buy her birth control? Have heart-to-heart talks with her?

"Sure," Amber said.

"I will stay for dinner," Maxine announced.

Both Kate and Maxine turned to Amber.

"I'll call for takeout," Amber said. She went for the Chinese take-out menu, knowing that's what her family always ordered on Saturday night.

"Excellent," Maxine said. "Barry, what do you do?"

Bare grinned. "I'm a pirate."

Kate laughed. "Isn't he funny? That's just a part in a play. Mom, this is Barry Furnukle. The guy behind Giggle Snap."

Maxine raised a brow. "Have you heard the latest with the sparse Fourier transform and its impact on audio recordings?"

"Yes, actually," Bare replied.

The three of them settled into a deep discussion. Amber called for takeout, on the outside of the science nerds once again. Her heart sank. She'd never wanted to be in that brainy circle as badly as she did now.

And, dammit, she still hadn't gotten her third C.

~ ~ ~

"So did you have a good time talking to Kate and Maxine?" Amber asked as Bare drove them to rehearsal later that night.

"Sure, they're good people."

She went quiet. She felt stupid around her family, and now Bare was right there with them. Not that they excluded her. At least not on purpose. She just didn't

have any idea what they were talking about half the
time.

"That was a good date this time, wasn't it?" he
asked.

"Did you ever think you should be dating
someone more like Kate?" she asked, hating herself
for even mentioning it.

"Now why would you say that?" He stopped at a
stop sign and looked at her with his kind eyes.

She felt all kinds of petty for even bringing it up.
"Nothing."

He hit the accelerator. "You think I want a
physics-obsessed girlfriend?"

"Well, she is more like you. And you seem to have
lots to talk about."

"And what about you? Should you only date other
artists with pink hair?"

She snorted. She'd never seen any guys with pink
hair. She got quiet.

"You want a list of reasons why I want to be with
you?" he asked.

That was ridiculous. Insane. She was *not* that
needy.

"Sure," she said.

"Do you have a list of reasons why you want to be
with me?" he asked.

"No, not right now, but I could make one."

"Okay, I'll make a list and you make a list, and
then we'll compare."

"That sounds like the rational, brainy thing to do,"

she said, biting back a smile.

"Mine will have a few equations."

"Mine will be illustrated."

"I look forward to it."

"As do I."

They took one look at each other and cracked up.

Amber changed the subject, embarrassed she'd ever brought up such a ridiculous topic. She wasn't in competition with her sister. She didn't need Bare to tell her why she was special. She asked him about working with Delilah, the older actress who played Ruth. Lately Delilah had spent a lot of time bitching and moaning to Amber backstage about some of the younger actresses.

Bare, being Bare, had no complaints. He seemed to always see the good in people. Seeing her stepmother again, hearing the three of them talk, had put her back in that awful place where she was the outsider. That stuff shouldn't matter now. She lived on her own, supported herself. She was living the life she was meant to be living.

Bare parked the car at the high school and turned to her. "Look, I could write down equations for you. Compose a few equivalencies to prove the sum of us together is greater than the sum of our parts, but you and I both know the shortest distance between two points is a straight line."

She did. But what did that mean exactly?

He cradled her face with one hand, and she waited for the kiss, the physical expression of why he wanted to be with her. It was why all men wanted her—her looks, her body. She closed her eyes.

His voice came out in a husky growl. "The short answer is I'm falling for you, not Kate."

Her eyes flew open. She met his warm brown eyes and saw love shining back at her. She blinked away stinging hot tears, couldn't even speak past the lump in her throat. She nodded.

"Now you know," he said softly. His thumb brushed her cheek where a tear had leaked out. "I'd ask what you'd put in an illustration, but I'm afraid to know."

She found her voice again. "Your big heart."

He smiled. "My mother always says I'm a gem."

"You are."

His thumb stroked down her cheek. "I can't wait to make you mine."

"You already have," she choked out.

He kissed her then, a tender kiss that she fell into slowly, inevitably, where she belonged. All of her insecurities faded because this was not just physical between them. There were feelings here. Real emotion.

He pulled back. They could hear voices nearby as more of the cast arrived for rehearsal.

"We should go," he said.

She walked to the auditorium with him, hand in hand, their fingers entwined. There was something about Bare. He was so solid, so steady, so unlike any of her ex-boyfriends, who she always hoped would stick around, but never did. She knew she had abandonment issues because of her mother. Two years of forced therapy as a teen had taught her that it wasn't her fault her mother left, and that she had every right to be angry and sad, all of which did nothing to soothe her pain. She didn't fall in love quickly or easily, had only been in love once before with a guy that ultimately didn't love her back, but somehow, Bare, with his easygoing, smiling way, had worked his way into her heart. It scared her. Some part of her kept waiting for the other shoe to drop.

~ ~ ~

After a long rehearsal, where Delilah threatened to walk out twice because as she said in a shrill, dramatic voice, "I cannot work this way," Amber joined the cast and crew at Garner's bar for a drink.

"Here's our girl," Zac said, appearing at Amber's side and giving her a smacking kiss on the cheek. "I know you're in love with me, but I'm in love with the fair Mabel."

She giggled. Zoe called over from a few stools away. "Is that my fair Frederic?"

The two did an exaggerated slow-motion run toward each other, holding hands, and turning in a slow, happy circle.

Amber laughed.

"Come here," Bare said, pulling her close and giving her a kiss on the lips.

She smiled against his lips. He responded by

pulling her onto his lap. His arm wrapped around her waist, holding her securely in place.

Steph stopped by for a refill on her mojito. "Didn't I tell you theater was fun?" She elbowed Amber. "Admit it."

"It is fun," Amber said.

"Ha!" Steph said triumphantly.

"As long as I'm back stage," Amber finished.

"We're doing *Grease* next year," Toby said. "Think about it."

"I played Danny in *Grease* back in high school," Bare offered.

"Of course you did," Kevin muttered, tossing back a shot.

"I'll be Sandy," Lauren said, blowing him a kiss.

Amber wiggled on Bare's lap to distract him. His hands clamped on her hips, stilling her.

"Wench," he growled in her ear.

She giggled.

"You're going to be a Pink Lady with me next summer," Steph told Amber.

"I'll be one of the T-birds," Bare said.

"You'll be Danny," Steph said. "Don't kid yourself. As long as you want to be in Eastman Community Theater, you'll be the lead. Right, Toby?"

Toby turned and droned in the tone of someone who repeated the line often, "Everyone has to audition each season and wait for the cast list." He did a slow nod at the same time.

"He'll have to fight me for the role!" Zac said,

raising his finger in mock swordplay, clashing it against Bare's hand. Bare crooked his finger around Zac's.

"May the best greaser win!" Bare said.

"Fuck you all," Kevin said before slamming his drink on the bar and marching out the door.

"Drama queen," Zac muttered.

"I'm surrounded by divas," Toby moaned.

Temperamental artists, one and all, Amber thought. She understood these people. She poured all of her artistic, creative energy onto the canvas, drawing from deep inside. They poured all of their artistic, creative energy outwards, drawing from each other.

She turned and looked up at Bare over her shoulder. "I want to paint you tomorrow."

"Me?"

She smiled. "Yes, you."

"Careful," Zac warned. "She might want to show you her etchings. You know what that means."

They both stared at him in confusion.

Zac did an exaggerated eye roll. "Etchings? Come up for a cup of coffee? It's all the same deal."

"I don't have any etchings," Amber said.

"Forget it," Zac said. "If I have to spell it out for you"—his voice dropped to an exaggerated stage whisper—"S-E-X, then you're too ignorant to be allowed to go there."

Zac grinned and finished his piña colada with a loud slurp.

"You're so bad," Bare said. "Go find Kevin and look at his etchings."

"Maybe I will," Zac said. He turned to go, then swiveled back, hitting Bare with a saucy look. "You don't know what you're missing."

Bare's voice rumbled in her ear. "I think I do."

She laughed.

"You two are a hot mess," Zac huffed before making a dramatic exit.

They laughed. A short while later, they headed home.

Bare dropped her off at her door. "Get some sleep. You'll need your energy tomorrow to paint all this." He gestured to his body with a grin.

She wrapped her arms around his neck and kissed him goodnight. He pulled away quickly, leaving her wanting more.

"Where are you going?" she pouted.

The distance between them kept increasing as he was slowly backing away.

"A man can only take so much," he said.

"You want me," she said, hoping to get him back, hoping to pull him inside her apartment and have her way with him despite feeling kind of droopy and tired. She'd been looking forward to it all day.

"Aye," he said. "Night, Amber."

Then he was gone. Disappointed, she went inside, past a sleeping Kate on the sofa, and crashed into bed. She was asleep instantly.

CHAPTER NINE

The next day Amber slept in. It was Sunday, which meant no rehearsal, and she was eager to get back to painting. Bare would be by in the afternoon for his portrait, so she first worked on an abstract. She added a blaze of deep purple on top of the black and red already there, watching the way the colors merged and blurred at the edges. She'd missed painting tremendously, not having the energy between work and the play's intense rehearsal schedule. Now she had the whole summer open before her. For a while there, she'd been selling a lot of paintings to this one collector, Susan Dancy, which had sent her into a painting frenzy, trying to keep up. That had dried up. She'd been so giddy about it and reported to Bare daily about her sales. He was so happy for her too.

Kate was absorbed in whatever she did on her laptop and was quiet as a physicist all morning. After she finished her painting and lunch, Amber went to fetch Bare and decided she wanted to paint him as the Pirate King. She wanted to capture what he brought to the character. As the Pirate King, he had swagger and confidence wrapped around a tender heart. The combination was immensely appealing. She set up a chair next to her easel for him and stopped across the hall to see if he was game.

Ian answered the door. "Hey, gorgeous. 'Sup?"

"Hey. Is your brother home?"

Ian leaned one arm against the door frame above her head. "Just you and me. Want some company?"

"Who is it?" Bare called.

Amber gave Ian a look.

Ian winked. "Can't blame a guy for trying." He turned and told his brother. "It's some delusional girl who thinks you're all that."

"Lauren?" Bare asked.

Amber froze. He was expecting Lauren to stop by?

Bare appeared in front of her. "Oh, it's you."

"Yeah, it's me. Disappointed?"

Bare shoved his brother out of the way, who seemed to be enjoying the little scene. "Of course not. Come in."

She stepped inside.

"Ian, get lost," Bare said.

"Where am I supposed to go?" Ian moaned.

"You don't have to go," Amber said.

Ian inclined his head, gave her a quick up and down, and wandered into the kitchen.

She turned to Bare. "I just wanted to see if you'd sit for your portrait as the Pirate King. I thought it would be cool."

He looked wary.

"What?"

"You only like me for my pirate side."

She cocked her head. "Does it really matter?"

He thought for a moment. "No. Be right back."

A short time later, he returned in his pirate costume complete with snug breeches and black leather boots. And an eye patch. She went hot all over. What was it about Bare the Pirate King that was such a turn-on? It was ridiculous. But he just had so much more swagger. Like any minute he was about to toss her over his shoulder and have his wicked way with her.

"See? I knew it was the costume," Bare accused. "You've got that look in your eyes."

She tried for innocent. "What look?"

Ian returned to check it out. "Yup. She wants you. Hit that while you can."

"Ian!" they said in unison.

Ian shrugged. "What? You know you want to."

"Don't mind him," Bare said, grabbing Ian by the shoulders and turning him away. "Let's go."

They got back to her apartment. Kate tore herself away from her laptop for the first time that day, took one look at the Pirate King, and whimpered. Amber rolled her eyes.

"Wow," Kate breathed. "Hi, Barry, I was just researching a new method to calculate extremely large prime numbers."

"Cool."

"Yeah." Kate sighed. "Did you know I always use prime numbers less than a hundred when I program the microwave?"

Amber stared at her.

"That could work," Bare said. "Seventeen, forty-three—"

"Fifty-seven," Kate finished for him with a dreamy smile.

Amber grabbed Bare's arm. "Okay, sit here and try not to move."

Bare sat. Kate stared at him with unwavering lust from her perch on the sofa. Amber picked up her brush. Bare looked self-conscious as her sister's eyes burned a hole in his chest.

Amber turned. "Kate, could you do something else? It's hard to focus with an audience."

Kate never took her eyes off Bare. "What should I do?"

He adjusted his eye patch and sat up straighter.

"Could you do more of that prime number stuff?" Amber asked.

"Yeah, sure." Kate opened her laptop and went back to staring at Bare.

"Would you like to meet my brother Ian?" Bare asked Kate.

"Is he anything like you?" Kate asked.

"Sure," Bare said. "We both like computers. We're both six foot. He's the one at M.I.T."

Kate leaped off the sofa. "Take me to him."

Amber looked from Kate to Bare. "I'm not sure

that's such a good idea."

Kate turned on Amber. "Why?" she demanded. "I want a Barry too." She clapped her hand over her mouth and promptly turned red.

Bare waved that away. "I'll tell Ian to be on his best behavior. Come on, Kate." He offered his arm, and she rushed over to take it. Kate turned to give Amber an amazed smile on her way out. Amber smiled tightly.

Ian would eat her sister for breakfast.

A few minutes later, Bare returned. "Alone, at last."

"How did it go?"

"Great. I told Ian that Kate was heading to M.I.T. for grad school. She wanted the inside scoop on campus life, and Ian was happy to tell her all about it."

"Just talking."

"He's not an animal."

She hmphed. "Okay, sit."

"How about this?" He stood with one hand crossing his chest like he was at the helm of a ship.

"Can you hold that position?"

"Absolutely. I am the Pirate King, and this is my ship, the H.M.S. *Amber is Hot.*"

She laughed and started painting. "Okay, stop talking. I need to capture your face in a commanding position."

"So you like when I'm in command?"

She glanced up. His brows were raised in question. "No," she said even as she heated at the idea.

He gave her a slow, sexy smile. "You do."

She clamped her mouth shut, but couldn't help the blush she felt creeping up her neck as she suddenly realized why she liked him so much as a pirate. The same reason she liked edgy guys. She liked a guy who took charge.

He tapped his head. "Filing that info away. I'm an excellent role player. I can be anything you want."

Anything? He was a very good actor. *Cool it. Focus. We're not going* 50 Shades of Grey *here.*

"Stop talking." She stared unseeing at the canvas. What would he be like in bed? Sweet and gentle or playing the commanding pirate to her wench, or something in between?

"Do I get something for being a good model?" She could hear the smile in his voice.

She shook her head, giving up on painting his face and switching to a light outline of the breeches and boots in black. "Sure. What do you want?"

"You."

She put her brush down. "Are you saying you want to trade sex for a modeling job?"

One side of his mouth quirked up. "No?"

She laughed.

"What would you trade sex for?" he asked.

"Bare! I wouldn't trade sex for anything. Now be quiet."

He got quiet, and she painted. It was something about the way he held his body as the pirate. He stood taller somehow, shoulders back, and his expression lost that goofy smile. Yet, even serious, his eyes with their laugh lines spoke of a gentle playfulness.

"Unbutton your shirt more," she said.

He unbuttoned slowly. "Now this is getting interesting."

"Mmm-hmmm," she said as she took in his rippling abs.

"You like my six-pack abs?"

"Are there six?" She walked over to see for herself.

She placed a palm over his ribs and slowly moved down, counting to herself, trying to act casual like she wasn't getting hot and incredibly turned on. They were spectacular. She wanted this pirate to ravish her.

"There better be," he said, "or I'm sending a very harshly written letter to the creator of the *Six-Pack Abs and Two-Pack Butt in 30 Days* DVD."

She was so startled she dropped her hand. She'd seen the infomercial for that DVD with its ripped men and women exercising like crazy to top 40 songs. "You work out to that DVD?"

He crossed his arms. "Damn right I do."

She couldn't help it. She laughed. And laughed and laughed. She crossed her arms over her stomach and bent over with it.

He turned and said over his shoulder, "Do I still have a two-pack butt at least?"

That set her off again.

He grabbed her and swung her up in his arms. "I'll teach you to mock the Pirate King."

He carried her to the sofa. She wiped her eyes and

settled down. "Bare, my paints are gonna dry. I'm not done."

"Tax for the mocking. One kiss."

Then his mouth crashed down over hers, like a pirate who took what he wanted, and she reveled in it, clutching his shirt and forgetting all about her painting.

Finally he pulled back. His eyes were dark with desire. "Amber," he said, his voice a near growl that had her insides clenching with need, "finish the painting before I take you right here, right now."

Heat rushed through her. *Yes. Let's do that* right here, right now *thing*.

"You're kidding, right?" she asked unsteadily.

He set her off his lap, stood, and adjusted his breeches. "No, I'm not kidding. I can't help wanting you the way I do." He didn't look at her, merely went back to pose by her easel. "It's not every day a painting is created in my honor. I know you'll do an amazing job."

She went back to the painting because of his faith in her abilities mostly, but she was thinking she would've liked more kissing. And what he'd said about taking her, wanting her. He spoke so plainly. So openly. So…erotically. It was a little unnerving. Still her artist's eye was intrigued, and she quickly got back into the groove. His expression held a sexy intensity that was distracting. She focused on his chest with its interesting planes and grooves, felt herself growing warmer, but kept going. She had to finish this painting. He wouldn't always be a Pirate King. She wanted to capture that.

When she'd finished, she let him see it.

"That's what I look like?" he asked.

She looked at it again. "Yeah. Pretty close."

He stared at it. "And you didn't embellish it or, you know, Photoshop it."

She stared at him. "How could I Photoshop it? It's a painting."

"I mean gloss over flaws."

"What flaws?"

He turned to her with a slow smile. "Amber, Amber, Amber. You're way into pirate me."

She put a hand on her hip. "So what if I am?"

"Then I should take advantage of that."

"Please do," she said right before he swept her up in his arms in a ravishing pirate kiss. When he let her up for air, he wrapped an arm around her waist, holding her close while he whispered what he'd like to do to her in intimate detail. She throbbed at the words.

"Bare, I didn't know you were a dirty talker."

"Does that bother you?"

She shook her head.

"There's so many things I want to do with you." He nuzzled her neck. "Things I read about—"

"Where did you read them?"

He nibbled along her earlobe. She pushed at his chest because she needed to know. What kind of things? Where had he read them? His tongue traced the shell of her ear. Her knees went weak, and she sank against him.

"Bare?" she said weakly.

"*Hunt and Get Fit* magazine. Very manly."

She pulled back. "You hunt?" she asked, horrified.

"I only read it for the sex tips."

She relaxed and took off his eye patch. "Okay. Let's go. I want my third C."

She took his hand and led him to the bedroom. She'd barely turned and locked the door before he lifted her and tossed her on the bed. She bounced a little, laughing, and then he was on her, and her laugh died in her throat. His mouth claimed hers, and she wrapped her arms around his neck. They rolled together, kissing, pulling at each other's clothes, getting tangled in the blankets of the bed she never made.

She pulled free long enough to gasp out, "Your sword!"

"I know. I can't help it."

"No, take it off!"

"Take it…oh!" He stood, undid the belt and sword, dropped them to the floor, and returned to her.

He kissed her again, and their limbs tangled together as the kiss went on and on. His hands were everywhere at once, touching and stroking, and she let her hands roam freely. He was sleek, with intriguing cut muscles and broad shoulders. He pushed her to her back and settled between her legs, kissing along her jaw, down the side of her neck.

"I should warn you," he said between kisses. "I've been told I have the stamina of a racehorse." He nipped her neck, and her nails dug into his back. "Not in a good way."

She tried to look at him, but he was kissing his way down the column of her throat. She swallowed. "There's a bad way?"

He stopped and looked up at her. "You know, like 'you're taking too long, finish already.'" He frowned. "Some women have complained about it."

"That you take too long."

He nodded. His hands were moving again, touching and stroking her everywhere at once, watching her responses.

"There's no bad way about that," she said, arching into his hand where he'd just managed to free her breast from her bra. "What kind of women have you been with?"

"No one worth mentioning," he muttered before claiming her mouth again. Her bra sprang free, and his fingers rolled her nipples, tugging on them, and she felt an answering throbbing between her legs. He lifted his head. "So you don't mind?"

She sat up and peeled off her top. He did the same. "Hell no," she said.

He stared at her breasts, then slowly dragged his gaze back to her face. "You are so beautiful. I have to have you."

He tossed her flat on her back, suckled her breast, his teeth scraping, while his other hand slid down her belly, dipping into her bellybutton, tracing her piercing. She wanted her jeans off, him naked, but she couldn't form the words as his mouth and hands worked her. His mouth moved to her other breast, his teeth teasing, while his hand slipped lower, cupping her sex, pressing on her, making her arch into his hand. Finally he worked off her jeans, and she grabbed for him frantically, yanking his breeches down.

"I want you," she said, grabbing a condom from the nightstand and handing it to him. "Now. I can't wait."

He dropped his breeches and boxers and rolled on the condom. "Please tell me you're not just man on top."

"I'm anything. Whatever. Just hurry."

He flashed a quick smile, crashed down on the bed next to her, and pulled her on top of him. "Ride me hard."

His words rolled through her, stoking her desire. She immediately settled herself over him, feeling the surge and the stretch as her body adjusted to his. Oh, yeah, this was good. He grabbed her hips, already moving her in the rhythm he wanted, hard and fast. Her breath quickened, thrilled he had some of that take-charge pirate attitude even without the costume.

His eyes were dark with desire. "Come on, love, ride me."

She did, keeping up the rhythm he'd set. He held her hips lightly, urging her on when she moaned. She quickly learned he was like that, praising her for responding to him. His voice, a low, hypnotic sound, registered dimly as sensation clouded her brain. He was a talker, and the words pushed her along as much as his touch. She tightened, felt herself clamp around him, shockingly quick. She shook with it, tried to stop moving to prolong it, but his hands kept her going, moving her up and down his shaft relentlessly.

"Yes," he urged. "Come apart for me."

His hands moved up to cup her breasts, and she moved again on her own, slower now, wanting it to last, but then he pinched her nipples hard, and she exploded, rocking helplessly with it. His hands clamped on her hips, moving her as he liked, filling her impossibly deep each time he slammed her down onto him, over and over, until he groaned and shuddered with his own release.

She collapsed on top of him, her heart thundering, and heard his matching heartbeat. They lay like that for few minutes, catching their breath. Amber let out a deep sigh of satisfaction. He gently rolled her to her side while he took care of the condom. Then he was back, pulling her on top of him again. His hands stroked up and down her back, relaxing her even further. She felt like a limp noodle, and he was so warm, she started feeling sleepy. She must've dozed off for a bit, until he said her name.

"Yes?" she asked, not bothering to lift her head.

"Good, you're awake."

His hand that was stroking her back so warmly kept going, sliding down her back, down her bottom, dipping his fingers lower to slide inside her sex, and hold her like that. She was too relaxed to move or protest.

She felt him harden underneath her.

"I want you again," he growled.

She lifted her head. "Already?"

"I've never wanted anyone like I want you." His eyes gleamed. "Like a craving."

The words turned her on, but she said nothing because her body spoke for her, tightening around his fingers. She moaned and rested her head on his chest, closing her eyes, knowing she was in for more.

"Yes, good," he whispered in her ear as he slid another finger inside her. Her body tightened around him again. His fingers spread wide and a moan escaped. "Let me take you like I read about. Like a werewolf."

She felt suddenly awake. What kind of magazine was he reading? *Hunt and Get Fit* had werewolves?

He released his hold on her only long enough to slide her onto her stomach.

"Werewolf?" she asked, but he was already wrapping an arm around her waist and pulling her into position—head down, tail up. She was beginning to understand. "Doggie style."

"More animalistic." His hands settled on her inner thighs and spread her wide open. She waited, not exactly sure what he meant, but wanting to find out. She heard the rustle of the condom wrapper, a throaty groan, and then he thrust inside her fully, making her breath catch at the sudden invasion. "I want to make you howl like in *Carnal Werewolf*."

Somewhere in the far-off reaches of her brain she knew that title. It didn't sound like a magazine article.

"You'd better prop yourself up on your arms because I'm going to pound you," he said. Her whole body quivered in response. "All fours, love."

She'd no sooner gotten her arms into position than he was making good on his promise, pounding into her, one hand tucked around her center, just holding her, his fingers increasing the pressure with each thrust. Her mind shut down, and there was only heat and incredible pleasure rushing through her. Oh, God, she was close already, like she hadn't come down from the aroused state he'd left her in not long ago. This was too fast, too much. She wanted to slow it down, but couldn't seem to form the words.

"Howl for me," he growled.

She panted. "I'm not a howler."

"You will be."

She hung on, her fingers clutching the sheets, as his fingers began to stroke her center, opening her more. She cried out and bucked, but that only opened her further to him. He groaned and covered her, pushing more fully inside, his fingers opening her folds, stroking, making her wild. But she couldn't move, couldn't slow it or stop it, could only go along for this ride that was fast becoming an overwhelming, unbearable tightening on the edge of release.

"Oh, God," she gasped.

His voice was low in her ear. "Do it for me," he urged. "Howl for me."

She trembled, panting, fighting it as he pushed her with his words and devious fingers and unrelenting thrusts. The pressure built inside her, a wave that threatened to pull her under, even as he held her tight. A soft cry escaped.

"More," he urged.

She quivered beneath him and clamped her mouth shut, only to gasp as his fingers became more demanding, and he plunged deeper.

"No," she moaned even as she felt her insides clenching around him.

"Yes." His fingers gave her a pinch and a twist just as his teeth sank into the side of her neck.

She let out a primal howl as her body racked with wave after wave of pleasure. He joined her a moment later with his own growly howl that she would've found funny if she wasn't so shattered. He held her like that, catching his breath, then finally pulled out. She collapsed, completely boneless.

He rolled her so they were side by side, chest to chest, and tucked her close. "That was fucking awesome."

"You made me howl," she said, staring at him in wonder. "No one has ever made me howl."

He stroked her sweaty hair away from her face. "I'm a lucky man."

"I'm a lucky woman."

He kissed her tenderly. "It's you, Amber. I've never been like this with anyone." His thumb pressed on her lower lip. "You just make me want to…I don't know…"

She nipped his thumb. "Dominate?"

He met her eyes. "I need you to come apart for me the way I come apart for you."

She felt herself throb. "Omigod, you're getting me hot again."

He gave her a slow, sexy smile. "Give me ten minutes."

She groaned. "I need a little longer than that."

He pulled her leg over his hip and tucked his hand on her bottom, slipping his fingers inside her again, holding her close. And though she thought she was absolutely done, she clenched around his fingers, hot and ready again. She moaned.

"Your body tells a different tale," he said.

"Oh, God. Please," she said, near desperate for what she wasn't sure. More or less? She couldn't think straight. His fingers slipped in and out, and she broke out in a sweat. "Please. Kate could be back any minute."

He smiled devilishly. "I like playing with you."

His fingers did a slow spiral, and she whimpered.

"You're so responsive," he said.

"Please," she said. She couldn't possibly take any more. Not the way he pushed her past what she ever thought her body was capable of feeling. And he couldn't possibly, not after twice—

The front door opened and slammed shut. Her eyes flew to his. She pushed at his chest, but he still held her intimately, a mischievous gleam in his eyes.

She was wild to get free. She wiggled and tried to pull away, gasping at the intense rush of sensation around his fingers. She didn't get very far. He chuckled.

"Amber?" Kate called loudly. "I'm ho-ome!"

She slapped at him frantically, and he finally let her go.

She dressed quickly before he could get his hands on her again. "Coming!" she called.

He chuckled again. She threw his shirt at him. "Get dressed," she hissed.

He pulled his shirt on. "I can't wait to have you again," he said in a low voice.

The throbbing between her legs shocked her. That voice. The words.

"I know what you like," he added.

She smoothed out her hair with shaking fingers.

"You like when I'm in command." He pulled up his breeches. "You like when I'm demanding. You like when I talk dirty."

She opened her mouth to say…what, she didn't know. It was startling how well he read her so quickly. He crossed to her, pulling her in for a hard kiss, and she sank against him. He released her and smiled down at her. "I told you I could be whatever you want. That works for me too. I love watching you lose control."

She swallowed hard. "What if I said I didn't like that? Would you be sweet and gentle and let me be in charge?"

He tipped her chin up and kissed her gently.

"Yes." He leaned down to whisper in her ear. "But we both know what you really want."

She was suddenly desperate to talk about anything else. This conversation was only making her hotter, and her sister was in the next room. She stood over by the door, needing some space between them. "You want to watch some *Zombie Bonanza?*"

"Actually, I don't like zombies." He sat on the edge of her bed and pulled his boots on. "In fact, I hate *Zombie Bonanza.*"

She did a double take. "You hate *Zombie Bonanza.* But you've been watching it with me for months!"

"It was the watching with you part I liked," he said with a smile.

She took that in. "Well, what do you like to watch?"

"I like sci-fi. Want to check out *Dinomonsters 2*? It's playing tonight at the theater in Eastman."

Oh. That sounded horrible.

"I think I'd be lost," she said. "You know, watching part two."

He grinned. "No problem. I've got the first one on DVD. This will be great. We'll have a *Dinomonsters* marathon!"

She got a sinking feeling she was in for a lot of creepy sci-fi creatures, but she wanted the watching with you part too.

"Okay, I'll watch," she said.

"That's me girl."

She smiled, and he smiled back. She was Barry

Furnukle's girl. Amber Lewis, artist, club hopper, bartender, sci-fi-nerd-loving Amber Lewis.

He crossed to her and gave her a kiss that started gentle and ended with her against the wall, mouth fused to his, his hand cupping her firmly between her legs.

She tore her mouth from his. "Please, Kate's here," she whispered.

He groaned. "Tonight. Send Kate on an errand, anyplace. She can have my credit card and go shopping just...please. I want you like I've never wanted anyone."

A thrill ran through her at the words. It made her feel so desirable and sexy. "Yes. Tonight."

Amber opened the door, and they stepped into the living room.

Kate was on the sofa, hair down, looking thoroughly tussled.

Amber rushed forward. "Kate, are you okay?"

"I'm fine," her sister slurred.

Amber put her hands on her hips. "What did he do to you? Did Ian get you drunk? Omigod, did you sleep with him? I'll kill him."

She headed for the door.

"Stop, sis, it's fine!" Kate barked. "I just had a couple beers." She fell to her side like a rock.

She studied her sister. "That's it?"

Bare watched them with interest. Kate looked over at Bare and promptly turned red. "Amber, you're embarrassing me in front of our guest."

"He's my boyfriend," Amber said.

Bare's chest puffed out.

"Why can't you hook up with an artist like you?" Kate exclaimed. "Why do you have to go for the one kind of guy I can talk to?"

"Weren't you just talking to Ian?" Amber asked.

Kate sat up and punched the sofa cushion. "We didn't do much talking," she muttered.

"That's it," Amber said. "I'll kill him."

Amber marched to the door, but Bare grabbed her before she could get it open. His hands landed on her shoulders, and he turned her so they both faced Kate.

"Do I need to kick his ass?" Bare asked Kate. "I told him to be on his best behavior."

Kate blushed. "No. I told him I was saving myself, and he said he respects that."

Amber relaxed. "Oh."

"See, love," Bare said to Amber. "It all worked out."

Kate burst into tears.

"I got this," Bare said before striding out of the apartment.

She looked at her weepy sister. Kate hardly ever cried. This could take a while. At least she was temporarily excused from the *Dinomonsters* marathon.

CHAPTER TEN

"Ian," Barry roared the minute he opened his apartment door. "What did you do to that poor girl?"

Ian startled and hit pause on the Sox game. "What poor girl?"

"What do you mean what poor girl? Kate! The innocent we sent over here to the lion's den. I told you to be on your best behavior."

"I was. All we did was talk and watch some of the game."

Barry shoved a hand through his hair. "That's it?"

"Yeah. We had a couple of beers and talked."

"Oh. She looked a little mussed up."

Ian smirked. "That was all her. She got a little horny, I guess, what with the beer and the whole"—he finger quoted—"saving herself thing. She sort of shook out her hair and propositioned me. But no big. I told her no thanks."

Barry sank down on the sofa. "Then why's she crying?"

Ian shrugged. "PMS?"

Barry shook his head. Maybe Amber could figure it out.

Ian elbowed him. "Looks like somebody got lucky. It was the pirate duds, wasn't it?"

"Does it matter?" Bare stood, suddenly irritated.

"Not at all," Ian said. "Long as you're happy."

"I'm very happy," Barry said. He went to his bedroom to change into normal clothes.

He didn't know what he'd do if he couldn't get Amber as himself. He hung up the costume carefully. Hell, who was he kidding? He'd take her any way she let him—in costume, out of costume, and any of the many fantasies he'd racked up from those very informative romance novels his mom had left lying around. Those novels featured guys who took command, exactly like Amber wanted. Exactly how he would be. He'd never dominated that way before, but she responded so beautifully, so fully, it spurred him on. He liked that feeling. He liked finding his inner stud muffin. He smiled to himself at that image. Him, a stud muffin. But that's what he felt like, all thanks to Amber.

~ ~ ~

Amber stroked Kate's hair. "Explain it again, honey. I can't help you if I don't understand why you're upset."

Kate sniffled. "I told you. Ian respects me too much to touch me."

"And you wanted him to…touch you."

"Look at me!" Kate gestured to herself. "How many guys do you think want me?"

"Um…" Kate was pretty when she took the time to do her hair and makeup and wear clothes that weren't wrinkled or stained. She looked cute now anyway. Her shirt was clean. Before she could mention that, her sister went on.

"Zero. That's how many. So I tell everyone I'm saving myself. But I'm really waiting for the first halfway decent guy to help me get rid of this damn virginity. I can't go off to grad school a virgin!" Fresh wails ensued.

Amber sighed.

Kate wiped her nose with the sleeve of her T-shirt. "That's why I was so glad to meet Ian. He looked just like Barry only cuter and younger."

"He's not cuter than Bare."

"Yes, he is and just as smart."

"But—"

"If I can't have Barry, I want Ian." Kate's face crumpled. "But he doesn't want me!"

Amber fetched the tissue box and gave one to her sister. "How do you know? Did you kiss him or something?" She cringed thinking of her virginal sister throwing herself at the full-of-himself player next door.

Kate blew her nose with a loud honk and crumpled the tissue in one hand. "No, I would never be so forward. I just did this." She put her hand on Amber's thigh and slid inward.

Amber grabbed her hand. "Kate! Please! You don't have to show me."

"That's exactly what he did. Grabbed my hand and put it back in my lap." More tears leaked out.

Amber handed her another tissue. "Okay, I totally get where you're coming from, but you don't want to throw yourself at the first guy who comes along. Your first time should be special with someone who really cares about you and will be tender and gentle."

Kate took off her glasses and wiped them clean. "Like Barry."

"Yes, like...no, not like Bare." She went hot remembering the way he pushed her, urged her on, again and again. "Some other guy you meet...down the road. *Not Bare*. And not Ian. No one in the Furnukle family."

Kate's eyes widened. She pushed her glasses back on. "Are there more?"

"He did mention a brother in military intelligence."

Kate perked up. "When can I meet him?"

"Kate! Haven't you heard anything I said? Cool it."

"I can't! I'm hot for Furnukles!"

Dear Lord, what had she unleashed on her poor brainy sister? Of course she couldn't resist the big brain and tender heart of Bare. And she was just projecting that same image onto his undeserving brother.

She took Kate's hand. "Promise me you won't sleep with Ian."

Kate stared at her lap. "It doesn't matter, he doesn't want me."

"Promise me."

"Okay, fine, I promise."

"Good. You want to go shopping for some new grad school outfits? It'll be a fresh start for you."

"Yeah, okay."

Two hours later, sitting with a happy Kate at the mall's food court, Amber worried for the male population of M.I.T. Sure, it still looked like Kate from the neck up, dirty blond hair in that weird half bun, half ponytail, the oversize tortoiseshell glasses, but then it was a halter top, tight skirt, and heels. She'd tried to steer her sister toward less revealing clothes, but Kate was on a mission. One that made her dress more like her sister. Amber knew how to handle unwanted advances; Kate was like Bambi out there. Even worse, her petite sister had been hiding major curves under her baggy T-shirts. She had a perfect hourglass figure with a narrow waist.

Kate looked like a nerdy Marilyn Monroe.

Her sister pushed her glasses up and chomped on a fry dipped in mayo. "Do you think I should get contacts? I'm a little squeamish about touching my eye, but maybe then a guy would touch me so…it would all work out."

"Absolutely not. If you're not comfortable touching your eye, then you should definitely not change that because of some guy."

"Yeah, I guess you're right."

Amber let out a breath of relief and grabbed a fry. Kate without glasses, with normal hair, would make her a knockout, fending off brainy, horny guys left and right. She had to ease into the dating pool. One thing at a time. Her sister was definitely not ready for what that could unleash.

"Can you take me to that place that did your belly-button piercing?" Kate asked.

Amber choked on her fry. She took a drink of iced tea to force the fry down. "No."

"Why not?"

"You're too young, and your mom would kill me."

"How old were you when you got yours?"

She'd been sixteen and had done it behind her dad and stepmother's back, but she wasn't about to admit that. "Twenty-six."

"That's not true. That would mean you've only had it two years. I remember it when I was in elementary school."

"Guys hate it," Amber said. Another lie.

"How about a nose piercing?" Kate asked. "Ooh, a tattoo! I could get a tramp stamp so the guys will know I'm ready."

Amber dropped her head in her hands and groaned. Why did Kate have to suddenly decide to lose her virginity on her watch?

"I'll pay for it," Kate said. "I've got lots of cash from tutoring kids for the SATs."

Amber raised her head and forced a smile. "You are beautiful just like you are. And when the right guy comes along, you'll know it. Okay? Let's not mess with perfection."

Kate's jaw dropped, showing her chewed-up fry. "You think I'm perfection?"

"Absolutely."

Kate snorted then gave her a watery smile. "Thanks, Amber. That means a lot coming from you."

"Well, I mean it. And, can you not wear your new outfits at home? I don't think your mom will approve."

Kate waved that away. "She won't even notice. You know her."

"She'll notice this."

"Okay, fine."

They finished up and headed back to Amber's apartment. Ian was loitering on the steps outside, messing with his cell phone. "Hey, ladies," he called.

"Hey, Ian," Amber said.

Kate rushed past Amber, then slowed her pace, chin up, working those hips.

"Who's your friend?" Ian asked before his eyes bugged out. "Kate?"

"Ian," Kate said over her shoulder before walking up the stairs ahead of them.

Amber turned to see Ian ogling Kate's barely covered ass.

"Don't even think about it," she told him.

"Think about what?" he muttered before following after Kate.

Amber caught up with him. "She's off-limits."

He scowled. "Who are you? Her mother?"

"Worse. I'm the one who'll kick your ass."

"She's legal." He bounded up the stairs. "Kate, wait up!"

Amber followed and heard the door slam to her apartment as Kate slipped inside. Ian stood there, staring at the door. Amber shook her head and went inside.

~ ~ ~

Barry returned to rehearsals on Monday night with an extra spring in his step. He waited on stage to rehearse the act one finale while Toby talked something over with Jasmine and Will. He was so relieved Amber was his girlfriend. His hunger for her was overwhelming. She'd made another of his fantasies come true last night at her place. After she sent Kate grocery shopping, Amber let him tie her up spread-eagled to her bedposts. He got hard again just thinking about her naked, completely open to him. She trusted him, and he rewarded that trust with multiple orgasms until she was begging him to take her. After, she called him a fucking stallion. He loved that. He had her again this morning as soon as she woke up. Every time he saw her, he wanted to be inside her. He'd been afraid he'd push too far, wanting her so much, but she met him each time willingly.

Toby, Jasmine, and Will were deep into discussion. The cast milled around chatting. He tried to think cooling thoughts. *Down, boy.* He glanced backstage where Amber stood, script in hand, at the ready for anyone who forgot a line.

She caught him looking and ran her tongue over her lips slowly, seductively. His cock pulsed against his jeans. He bounded off stage to her side.

"Wench," he said. "You know what you do to me."

She grinned saucily. He kissed that saucy mouth. She rubbed herself against him, making his tenting problem far worse.

He pulled back and smacked her ass. "Vixen."

She smacked him back. "I want you to think about me when you're with all those flirty Major-General's daughters."

"You're all I ever think about."

She beamed.

God, he wanted her. He glanced around backstage. No one else was back here. He grabbed her hand.

"All right, people," Toby called. "From the top."

"Tonight," he told her.

"Yes," she said in a breathy voice that made him question his sanity. How could he not take her right here, right now? The urge to have her was intense, primal, absolutely consuming. He just wanted to grab her by the hair and drive into her. He felt like a fucking caveman consumed with his baser urges. This was what happened when you unleashed your inner stud muffin—he fucking took over. He had to force himself to turn away.

"Where's our Pirate King?" Toby asked.

He bounded back on stage and flew through rehearsal, eager to finish so he could get Amber alone again. Having her watch him made him up his performance, which made the rest of the cast increase their energy to match his. Especially Kevin, his pirate lieutenant who always tried to outsing him in pure volume. Everything was rolling along smoothly, other than the fact he had to strain his voice to be heard over Kevin. All he could think about was finishing rehearsal and getting back to Amber. And then the fight scene happened.

This was their first time working through it with the police wielding plastic clubs and the pirates wielding wooden swords. Jasmine was coaching them along in how to move on stage while fighting. They were getting the hang of it. Barry was enjoying himself, swinging his sword like the Pirate King when a real sword fight broke out between Kevin and Zac.

The two were crashing their wooden swords against each other. Zac swung hard and clipped Kevin on the shoulder, who retaliated with an impressive swing of his sword in a wide loop over his head, finishing with a hit that Zac parried.

One of the pirates, Alan, added sound effects in the background. *Vwo-ow-ow! Vweem. Vweem.*

Barry stifled a laugh. It did look a little like a light saber fight.

"Guys, knock it off!" Jasmine hollered, but she didn't dare step between the pair. The wooden swords had some heft to them and could hurt if they made a direct hit.

Everyone stopped to watch as the men's swords clashed into each other.

Vwo-ow-ow! Alan made his sound effect again. The cast tittered. These two really took their work seriously.

The swords clashed into each other, back and forth, as Kevin and Zac circled each other.

"I know where you want to bury your sword," Kevin spat. "He won't have you."

Zac's sword was forced almost to the ground, but he rallied and swung back so hard that Kevin's sword went flying. "It's none of your business whose sword I polish or bury!"

Kevin somersaulted to get his sword. The cast pushed to the edges of the stage.

Vwo-ow-ow!

Their swords clashed again.

Toby pushed his way to center stage. "What the hell is going on here?"

Zac and Kevin continued their duel.

"Ow!" Zac screamed. "You hit my wrist!" He launched back even fiercer than before.

Vwo-ow-ow. Vwo-ow-ow.

The cast became uneasy, whispering among themselves. Barry heard his name mentioned. The swords clashed over and over as the two men circled each other.

And then a voice rang out: "Help me, Obi-Wan

Kenobi, you're my only hope."

It was Amber. She stepped between the men and held her arms out, separating them. It broke the tension and everyone laughed. Even Zac. Kevin still looked furious.

"Alderaan is peaceful," she said. "Give your weapons to Toby."

Toby's eyes bugged out as Kevin and Zac handed him their swords.

"What the hell was that about?" Toby asked as Kevin stormed off stage.

Amber jabbed a finger into Zac's chest. "He's mine."

Zac glanced at Barry and flounced off stage. Barry stared at Amber, a sci-fi lover's wet dream. He'd never wanted her more. And his heart, which had already been falling, took a complete, irreversible dive into deep love.

CHAPTER ELEVEN

Amber woke on Saturday morning as she did every morning since she'd hooked up with Bare, with him spooning her, his erection pressing into her bottom insistently. His hands were under the Dancing Cow T-shirt she wore as a nightgown with nothing else, trailing over her breasts and belly, tracing the tiny diamond stud piercing, warming her as she slowly awoke. They always stayed at his place because Ian slept like the dead whereas Kate was always trying out new flirty moves on Bare, flouncing around the apartment in Amber's shortie pajamas even in the daytime. Kate's most recent flirt: muttering "expand my polynomial" while walking quickly past Bare, who later claimed with a wink that it meant she wanted a threesome. Ha! Not likely.

Birdsong filled the room as his alarm clock went off. He must've forgotten to shut it off for the weekend. The first morning she'd heard it, she'd commented, "The birds are really loud on this side of the building." He'd thought that was hysterical. Now she was used to it. As used to it as she was to what came next.

He shut off the alarm, lifted her leg up over his, and growled, "Say my name." It was his way of checking that she was fully awake.

"Bare," she whispered, and he slipped inside her. She felt like she was a part of him, like they were always connected in this intimate way, even when they weren't. When he was working or they were at rehearsal, the memory of it stuck with her. It was incredible, this closeness. With few exceptions, most guys took off after their night together. Bare always wanted to be with her again and again. He did indeed have the stamina of a racehorse, and she didn't mind at all. She'd never felt so loved, never felt so close with another person.

Now he urged her on as he always did, with his words, his hands, his devious mouth, his unrelenting thrusting until she broke for him, shattered by the intensity before he took his own release. She was like a limp ragdoll by the time he was done with her. A glowing, satisfied ragdoll.

This was their first Saturday together. They had the whole day off until that night's rehearsal. Even better, Ian was visiting friends in the city.

Bare made her breakfast—an omelet, toast, and coffee—and she had just stood to clear when she caught his hot look across the table. Next thing she knew he had her on the kitchen table, driving into her, making her come from the thrill of it. When they finished, he collapsed on the sofa. She thought for sure he was done with her.

But then he joined her in the shower. After a thoroughly arousing cleaning, they fell into bed together. They lay, side by side, facing each other. He never stopped touching her, stroking her, playing with her, teasing her. She was in a constant state of arousal when he was around.

She curled into his chest. He maneuvered her leg over his hip and pulled her closer. She could feel he wanted her, the shower had been only an invigorating cleaning, but she didn't have the energy to move.

"I want you so bad all the time," he said as his hand curled around her bottom, slipping his fingers inside her, the way he liked to hold her.

"Mmm-hmm," she said, way beyond conversation.

"I want you always willing and open to me." His voice was low in her ear, and her body responded as it always did to his dirty talk, clenching around his fingers, warming to his words.

"I have an insatiable hunger for you." He nipped at her earlobe. "You know what I want?"

"What?" Her voice came out unsteady. She never knew what he'd come up with next. The man had made her *howl*.

His tongue traced her ear, and a hot shiver ran through her.

"What?" she prompted, pulling back to look at him.

"Never mind. It's geeky."

"I don't want to know."

"It's a science experiment."

She grinned. "Sexy."

His fingers stroked inside her, and she moaned, instinctively moving with him. "It could be if you let me test my hypothesis."

He slipped another finger inside, and her brain clouded with sensation. She closed her eyes.

His voice reached her dimly. "Every morning you're ready for me just from talking. I tell you to say my name, right? I barely have to touch you. I hypothesize I can use words to get you ready at other times. If I'm right, I could easily and quickly take you wherever, whenever. I could train you with a conditioned response."

She stiffened, but found it impossible to pull away with the way he held her. "I'm not a dog. You can't train me."

"You want to bet?"

She licked her lips, fully alert now, and met his eyes. They were dark with hunger. He couldn't wait to wager for what he wanted so badly. Her.

"I can't think with your hand like that." Her body throbbed around his fingers, even as her mind rebelled against this crazy idea of his.

His fingers did a slow roll inside her. "I don't want you to think."

"Bare, please," she gasped out, but she wasn't sure what she was asking for.

He released her, and she tried to go back to their

conversation. The bet.

"What do I get if I win?" she asked.

"I'll rent you an art studio for a year."

"That was a quick answer. How long have you been thinking about this?"

"Just since I was waiting for you to wake up this morning. I thought it would be awesome to have you as much as I wanted, and believe me, that is every time I look at you, and you like when I'm in command so…"

He waited, letting her fill in the blanks. Did she want to give him that kind of control? She glanced at him, and he smiled encouragingly. Oh, what was she worried about? This was Bare. She trusted him. Besides, it wouldn't work anyway. She couldn't be trained. And she'd get an art studio. All of her canvases and paints spread out. Now they cluttered up her apartment, but her own space was a dream come true.

She bit her lip. "And what do you get if I…lose."

"You. Anytime. Anywhere." There was no encouraging smile this time, only a smoldering gaze into her eyes. His gaze dropped to her mouth. He leaned in, kissing her gently, tenderly, until she fully relaxed again.

She sighed. He turned, rolled on a condom, and returned to her. Side by side again, he pulled her leg over his hip and pushed inside her just a bit, just enough to make it hard to think.

"Will you take the bet?" he asked, pulling out. "I

promise to always have condoms if you promise to test my hypothesis." They were going through condoms by the dozen. She should probably go on the pill soon.

"Hypothesis," she echoed, unable to think clearly when he teased her with the tip, in and out. Her body contracted involuntarily, trying to hold him.

"That I can train you to take me whenever, wherever," he said. "In a week."

Oh, God, he was making her so hot just talking about it. Even if he was right, there was no way he could do that in a week.

"Yes, test it," she said because she wanted him. She wanted the art studio. She wanted.

He pressed in again, just a bit. "I'm going to say, *Amber, here, now* every time I take you until you hear the words and you're hot and wet and ready for me."

She got hot and wet just hearing that. She nodded.

His hand cupped her bottom, pressing her close. "You have to wear a skirt for me all week."

"Okay, okay."

His eyes burned into hers. "Amber, here, now," he growled before thrusting inside her. She gasped at the intensity of it, the suddenness, and then she was along for the ride, hot and cresting as his fingers reached between them and brought her to the edge and beyond.

Even knowing what he was going to do, the words he used, the wager, she didn't fight it. Just stayed in the moment. Because the moment he said it was always one where she was already hot and ready for him. For the rest of the week, every night, every morning, sometimes twice in a morning, he said the words in his growly voice, "Amber, here, now," just before he entered her.

Still, when she had a moment to think about it— when he was at work, because the rest of the time his hands were all over her—she was pretty sure his hypothesis wasn't working because she was already hot when he said the command. The words just added heat to what was already there. She could already picture the art studio in her mind.

~ ~ ~

Barry threw himself into rehearsal on Friday night feeling every bit the Pirate King with the greatest treasure in the world. Amber was his, absolutely his, and he already knew he wanted to marry her. They just fit—physically, humor-wise, annoying sibling-wise, just everything. He liked who he was with her. He was that guy that took charge and made women beg for more, instead of the guy always being told to hurry up and finish. He'd wait until after the show to propose just to be sure it wasn't the pirate effect swaying her in his direction. He pushed that thought aside. That was stupid. He didn't always act like a pirate with her. He was the stud muffin version of himself, which was fast becoming his true self. It worked very well for both of them.

He wiped the sweat off his brow. Jasmine was working their tails off on this musical number with the police. Most of them had two left feet.

"Take five," Jasmine said before heading over to the piano to talk to Will.

Barry stepped off stage and headed to the band room, where he kept a large water bottle. Amber was off-site at a costume shop with Edith. He should probably tell Amber, sooner or later, that the reason her painting sales had slowed down was because he was too busy to keep checking the website and buying them. She'd mentioned her sales dwindling a few times now. He took a long drink, considering. No, he wouldn't bring it up. Why hurt her when he didn't have to? She was happy painting, so she could just keep doing that. He finished drinking and mopped the sweat off his face with the bottom of his T-shirt.

"Found you!"

He turned and smiled at Amber. She walked right up to him and kissed him. He still couldn't believe she was really into him. It was like a goddess hooking up with a nerdy earthling. But this nerdy earthling was a quick study, and this goddess was his favorite subject.

"I've got a surprise for you." She grabbed his hand and pulled. "Come on."

"I don't have long. Jasmine is going to want me back on stage in a few minutes."

"I just came from there. She and Will are still arguing." She pulled again, and he followed. "It won't take long."

They went down a long hallway and stopped at a small storage area with a wooden wedge holding the door ajar. It was all the costumes. He already had his pirate costume, so he wasn't sure what she—

"Ta-dah!" she said, pulling a costume off the rack.

It was a large cow costume—white with black spots. Just like his old one, but better.

She held the costume up. "Do you like it? I bought it for you when we were at the costume shop." She held it up to him. "It should fit."

He swallowed over the lump in his throat, overwhelmed with emotion. Before, Amber hadn't seemed to like him as a dancing cow. She'd called him a bird-cow man. But this gift said she accepted him. Understood him.

"Amber…" His voice came out in a growl.

She flushed and looked around the small space. "I don't think we have room here."

He shook his head. He hadn't meant that, though it was interesting that just her name was a trigger. He took her hands. "Thank you."

"Oh. You're welcome." She smiled up at him. "Your voice. It sort of had that growl that means…it's time."

He nodded. "It gets like that when I feel a lot. Like the emotion"—he put his hand on his throat—"just gets stuck there."

She thought about that while she stroked her hand up and down his arm. If he wasn't touching her, she was touching him. It was constant contact, and he loved it.

He put the costume back on the rack for later. "I thought you didn't like me being a dancing cow."

Her hand was in his hair now, stroking through the hair at the nape of his neck. "It's your art. You're a performer. I understand."

His heart squeezed. "Amber…" he growled. Her breathing hitched. "I love you."

She didn't reply, just wrapped her arms around him and kissed him. He kissed her back with all the love he was feeling. He wanted to tell her all that he felt, all that he wanted for them, but then she went up on tiptoe, and their bodies lined up exactly where he needed, which made all rational thought disappear.

"There you are!" a voice called.

He pulled away from Amber, but still laced his fingers with hers.

It was Edith. "Toby needs you on stage," she said to him. "Amber, come with me. We need to do some fittings for the Major-General's daughters."

"Duty calls," Amber said.

She left with Edith, and Barry stood there for a few moments, watching Amber go. She hadn't said I love you back. That didn't mean anything, he reassured himself. Her kiss spoke volumes. Nothing to worry about.

But some part of him lingered over that worry until it lodged uncomfortably in his heart.

~ ~ ~

The next morning Barry looked forward to testing his hypothesis. He stretched out in Amber's bed. Kate had gone home for a visit, so they had the apartment to themselves. It had been a thoroughly enjoyable week because Amber was so responsive to him. His coming up with that bet was a stroke of brilliance if he did say so himself. He had a perpetual hard-on whenever he saw Amber, and once he knew the pure joy of making love to her, instead of getting old, he found himself hard even more. He needed relief; he needed Amber. Not that he didn't love foreplay, but there were times he found it hard to wait. He didn't do it to control her, he did it to control him, so he'd always know when he felt desperate to have her again, she would be okay with him, that he wasn't pushing too hard.

He knew the command was working too. He didn't know if she realized it yet, but he always watched her carefully, gauging her responses to what he did so he could heighten what she liked and let go of what she didn't. After just a few days, she more fully responded. Her eyes dilated, her chest flushed, nipples in hard points, her breathing quickened. He fell deeper in love with her every day. Could barely relax until she was in his arms again. He'd never in his life felt like this. Like he'd been waiting all of his life for her.

He listened to her in the shower, forcing himself not to join her. He'd already had her this morning when she woke. He wanted to give her some space so later when he said the words, the effect would be pronounced, a definite victory for both of them. He was so glad her flirty sister wasn't here. Kate was always hitting on him with some muttered physics or math line. Last time she'd actually said, "There are no lines in this electromagnetic field," while pointing to her ass. She meant an attraction, he figured, and the lack of lines, her lack of underwear, which he tried really hard not to notice in the flimsy cotton pajamas she wore all the time. She really had to work on her technique.

He waited until after lunch. Amber was standing at her easel, pondering a blank canvas. She wore a skirt as he'd asked and had stopped wearing a thong on her own. Just knowing she had nothing on under that skirt was enough to have him throbbing uncomfortably against his jeans. He sat on the sofa with the laptop, looking up movies they might see for a matinee. Only he was barely looking at the screen, all he could think about was saying the words. Taking her again. If it didn't work, he'd warm her up the old-fashioned way. Either way, he wanted her like he wanted his next breath.

She caught him looking and smiled.

"Amber," he growled. "Here, now."

She flushed, and her mouth opened in shock.

He crossed to her. He didn't mention winning the bet. Merely lifted her skirt, thrust his hand between her legs, and felt his victory. She panted. He freed himself, rolled on a condom, and lifted her. Then he was inside her, sweet relief, taking her against the wall. Her throaty moans made him crazy. Her body tightened, and she cried out, but he kept going, feeling a deeper pleasure as her body milked him.

"Again," he growled in her ear, knowing she liked it when he drove her on.

She trembled in his arms, and he knew she needed a push. He slipped a hand between them, stroking quickly over her hard nub until she screamed and grabbed him tight; then he took her the way his body demanded, hard and deep, bringing them both to oblivion.

~ ~ ~

Amber forgot about losing the bet as she was so consumed with being with Bare. She never knew when the words would come, but they did and frequently. She gave willingly, wherever and whenever he wanted her. In the backseat of his car, in a bathroom stall at the movie theater, in his walk-in closet while his brother was watching TV in the living room, on his dining room table, in the back room of his shop. There wasn't one room, one space in either of their apartments they hadn't used. Not one place that didn't have a hot memory.

The following weekend Bare asked her to go to the beach with the bird sanctuary at dawn so they could see the latest birds that had come back from the winter. And while birding wasn't exactly her thing, she'd found that going anywhere with him held a new level of excitement. She never knew when he'd say the words that made her hot, but she knew she'd come apart in his arms, leaving her completely boneless and satisfied. He was only temporarily satisfied, but that was thrilling too. Knowing it was only her he'd ever hungered for like this. The man did have a way with words.

"I heard there was a sighting of an American woodcock," he told her on the drive over.

"You're such a dirty talker."

He grinned. "I know. But that is what it's called. It's rare, and I want to see it with you."

"Aww."

"Here, look it up on my app." He handed her his cell. "It's not finished yet, but I've got some basic data. Just key in American woodcock, and you'll see the picture and description."

She did. "Okay. Got it."

They took a run on the beach. And then she followed him through the trails quietly. Bare would stop occasionally and look through the binoculars. When they hadn't seen the bird after an hour, she suggested they return to the beach.

He handed her the binoculars. "Here. Pretend to observe."

"Why do I have to pretend to observe?" she asked, peering through the binoculars. "I know what to look for."

He maneuvered her so her back was against a large tree. The binoculars bobbled as she realized his intent.

He set them on the ground, his hand stroking up her inner thigh as he stood. She wore nothing under her skirt as he well knew. She trembled, knowing what came next, even before he said the words.

He growled in her ear, "Amber, here, now," and took her up against the tree. Her breath caught at the sudden filling of her body. The man was perpetually hard for her. She was no longer truly surprised; she was always primed and ready with the hot look and the words that turned her on. Thank God they went birding at dawn when no one else was around. Her cry of ecstasy a short while later startled the birds from their roosts. His was a guttural groan that vibrated against the side of her neck.

He set her down, straightened her skirt, and zipped his jeans. He grinned. "I'm so glad I trained you."

"You didn't train me," she protested hotly. She just liked sex with him. A lot. And his voice and words and stuff.

"No?" He pulled her close and growled in her ear, "Amber."

Her insides clenched. Just her name was all it took. It was that growly voice. It got her every damn time.

She shoved him away. "Don't play with me."

He smiled, his eyes alight with mischief. "I like playing with you."

"You're getting arrogant. I want sweet and tender Bare back."

He studied her and tucked a lock of hair behind

her ear. "I love you. You're like a dream come true for me, and I can't imagine ever being with anyone else."

Her stomach dropped. What this man did to her—physically, emotionally. It was the most wildly intense relationship of her life. She could handle the physical stuff a lot better than the anxiety running through her at his heartfelt words. It was strange. She knew she should feel happy, elated even, but instead she felt panicky. It was too good to be true.

"Say the command," she said, looping her arms around his neck. "Take me again."

Instead he wrapped his arms around her and sighed heavily, his breath parting her hair. "Come on. I have something else I want to show you today."

"You have to feed me first."

He pulled back and grinned. "All right."

They stopped for breakfast at a nearby restaurant, and then he drove her to an old Victorian home back in Clover Park. It had a row of doorbells by the front door like it was divided into apartments.

"What are we doing here?" she asked.

He squeezed her hand. "It's a surprise."

He led her up the back stairs and unlocked a door to a studio apartment in the attic of the old house. The place was empty and clean. It was huge with hardwood floors and lots of light streaming through large windows at either end.

He handed her the keys. "This is your new art studio. You've got a whole year in this place."

She stared at the keys. Looked back to him in

confusion. "But I lost the bet."

One corner of his mouth kicked up. "I think we both won. Don't you?"

She grinned. "Wow."

She walked around, taking in the space. There was a small bathroom tucked in one corner of what might have formerly been a closet. A small kitchenette on the other side. The rest was wide open. And the ceilings, while not high, were fine for her needs. The ceiling cleared Bare's head by an inch.

"Open the refrigerator," he said.

She opened the small fridge and found it stocked with all her favorite cheeses. She smiled.

"Crackers are in the cabinet."

She pulled open the small cabinet above the sink and found boxes of her favorite crackers all lined up. She suddenly felt uneasy, like it was too much. How could she accept this gift? Who knew if they'd be together a year from now? He'd be stuck paying the rent on this unused place.

"Bare, I don't know what to say."

He took her hand. "Do you like it?"

"I love it, but I can't accept this. It's…you shouldn't have done this."

"Why?"

She shook her head, and he wrapped his hands around her waist.

"I wanted to. You deserve a studio space. Now you can spread out. Maybe do bigger canvases." He searched her face. "What's wrong?"

She pulled away. "A year is a long time to pay rent on a space," she said quietly, avoiding his eyes. "You don't even know if we'll be together that long."

"Why wouldn't we be? Things are great. I love you."

She wished she could easily say the words back to him. She hadn't said I love you to anyone since her mother said them to her along with goodbye. It was like they were forever tied in her brain, even though she knew that was wrong, somehow I love you meant goodbye. She did have feelings for Bare, strong feelings, but…would their relationship last? None of her relationships before had lasted.

"Amber," he snapped.

Her eyes flew to his, startled at his tone.

"Why aren't you saying anything? What are you thinking?"

"I can't accept this gift," she said firmly.

"Too bad." He put his hands on his hips and glared at her. "I signed the lease, and you're stuck with it."

"Bare…" She didn't know what to say. He was mad, and she didn't know how to fix it. She crossed to him and rubbed her hand up and down his tense arm.

He stared at her hand. "Don't you want to be with me long term?" he asked quietly. "I want that for us. Am I still not cool enough for you?"

A laugh escaped. "You're very cool."

"You think this is funny? I'm putting my heart out here, Amber. Where's your heart?"

"I don't know what you want me to say. I'm sorry. I'll…" She swallowed hard. "Thank you for the art studio."

He narrowed his eyes, and she squirmed under his scrutiny. "Just tell me right now if you don't see a future for us. Just say it."

"I-I don't know."

He ground his teeth. She touched his cheek, and he jerked away from her hand.

"Please don't be mad," she said. "How can I know?" She raised her palms. "How can anyone know? We can't predict the future."

He pinned her with a hard look. "Do you love me?"

Her throat clogged up. She dropped her gaze to the floor. How could you really know if you loved someone? At what point did lust turn to love? When did like a lot turn to love? How could you ever feel safe enough to put your heart in someone else's hands?

He tipped her chin up. "Look at me. I know you must feel something."

"I do. Something." Her eyes welled up. She was screwing things up again.

He cradled her face with both hands. "I feel like I've been waiting my whole life for you. I want to marry you."

Her stomach dropped. "Don't say things like that."

"Why?"

"Because you don't know. You can't be sure. You've only known me a few months."

He dropped his hands. "Three and a half months. That's long enough to know what I feel for you."

She looked at the ground. He took a step back. A long, uncomfortable silence stretched between them.

"Nothing to say?" he finally asked.

"Bare, I'm screwed up. I have…issues. I'm not so good with this heart stuff. Not like you."

He jammed a hand in his hair. "Everyone has issues. Everyone's screwed up. Just tell me I'm not alone in this. Tell me you feel the same way about me that I feel about you."

Marriage, forever, love that never ended. She'd never thought they were possible for her. Never truly believed anyone would want to stick around that long.

"I don't know," she said helplessly. "Please don't be mad. I'm trying. I just don't know."

He swallowed visibly. "Maybe we should take a break. Maybe I'm pushing you for too much."

"Bare, no."

"I got carried away," he muttered. "I'll see you later. The place is yours for the year."

And then he left. She sank on shaking legs to the floor. He said he loved her, and then he left. No good ever followed those words.

CHAPTER TWELVE

Barry didn't stop by Amber's place on Sunday like he normally would have. He was torn. He wanted her, wanted to be with her, but he was starting to think maybe he'd built up what they had in his mind to more than it really was. He always did that. Whenever he got into something, he went overboard.

Or maybe she only wanted him for his body. He snorted to himself. That couldn't be it. He set out the possibilities.

A) He loved her, and she loved him, but lost her voice whenever she tried to say the words.

B) He loved her, and she didn't love him.

C) He loved her, and she wasn't sure if she loved him yet.

What were the odds? The likely probabilities? He didn't know, but the more he thought about it, the more he realized it didn't matter. Every possibility led to one inevitable conclusion—he loved her. He stopped by her place on Monday before work, but she wasn't home. He stopped by after work, still not home. Kate didn't know where she was, or so she claimed. He hoped he'd see her at rehearsal.

She wasn't there either. He rocked on his heels, waiting on stage for the music to start. What did she do, skip town because he'd gotten her an art studio and declared his love? The answer hit him suddenly between scenes. She was at the art studio. He should've checked there. Of course she'd want to paint. Painting was her soul.

"Pay attention, Bare!" Toby barked from the audience.

He shook his head. "Sorry," he called. The music had started, and he hadn't moved. "Go ahead, Will."

Will started the music again. Barry jumped in on cue, faking enthusiasm for the performance, anxious to finish and check the art studio.

"Next scene is 'The paradox,'" Toby said. "Delilah, you're up with Zac and Bare."

Delilah rose slowly from her seat in the auditorium and met them on stage. Jasmine and Will got louder, arguing over by the piano, both leaning forward, hands on hips.

"What's got into them?" Zac asked.

"Lovers' quarrel," Delilah answered.

"Those two?" Barry asked. "They've done nothing but fight since rehearsals began."

"Love, hate, same deal," Delilah responded.

After several minutes where Jasmine's voice got

higher in volume, which seemed to trigger Will's voice to get lower, Delilah finally put an end to it.

"Excuse me!" she said dramatically. "I am a professional. That means the show must go on!"

Will returned to the piano. Jasmine turned on her heel and approached the stage.

"Sorry about that," Jasmine bit out. "I think you guys know what to do in this scene. Bare, if we could maybe get a little more kick-up-your-heels gleefulness into the scene. Maybe a few more of these lunging kneels." She demonstrated, going from one knee, then moving forward onto the other knee. "Yeah?"

"Sure," Barry said. "Exactly where in the song do I add that?"

"Let's run through the song," Jasmine said. "I'll move along with you." She turned. "Will, play 'A Paradox' if it's not too much trouble."

"No trouble at all," Will said. "I can play it multiple times, and they will all sound exactly as the composer intended."

"God forbid you get creative," Jasmine muttered.

The music started, and they ran through the song. Amber took a seat in the auditorium, and Barry amped up the energy. She was here, and that meant she wasn't done with him. He hadn't pushed her away. He was the swashbuckling Pirate King, and she was his to plunder anytime, anywhere. A heady notion. A magnificent fact. He would claim her body as he always did, and one day, he'd claim her heart too. She just needed time. He was so relieved, he didn't care how much time it took. He'd wait her out, just as long as they were together.

The song ended. Jasmine, Toby, Edith, and Amber clapped.

"Very nice, Bare," Jasmine said. "The best I've seen from you. Zac, Delilah, you both were great too. I don't think we need another run-through. Moving on!"

Edith went to call for the cast who were in the next scene. It would be Mabel and the police brigade. He stepped backstage and met Amber on her way in. He gave her a dip and a kiss with some heat behind it.

"Yo-ho-ho," she said.

God, he loved this woman.

"I perform better when you're here," he said.

"Oh, do you?" Zac said flirtatiously. "Don't like a solo performance? Of course it's always better with another person or two. If you ever need a third—"

"We don't," Barry said quickly just as Kevin came up behind Zac and gave Barry a murderous look.

Kevin pulled Zac out of the wings to the hallway.

"That was a little weird, wasn't it?" Amber asked.

"Little bit." He couldn't resist kissing her again. Her lips were soft and yielding. He pulled back. "Where've you been? I missed you."

"At the art studio," she said. "I painted the largest canvas I've ever done."

He smiled. "I can't wait to see it."

She blinked rapidly. "So you're not mad at me anymore?"

"No."

She threw her arms around him, and he held her tight.

"I'm so glad," she sighed. "Just…be patient with me, okay?"

He stroked her hair, so relieved to have her back in his arms. "Okay."

~ ~ ~

Amber loved her new art studio. Last weekend, she'd moved all her supplies in. It was glorious. She quickly got into a routine of painting all day, having dinner with Bare, and then going to rehearsal. Bare never wanted to interrupt her art, so he asked her to text him when she was done and they'd arrange to meet for dinner and go to rehearsal together. She didn't let herself think about the year lease on the place because that only made her anxious. She focused on the moment, and that let her be creative, filling her with joy.

Today, Friday, she was putting the finishing touches on the largest canvas she'd painted so far. It was an abstract, her favorite kind, with red, blue, green, and gold. Almost a tie-dyed effect. She stopped with a laugh. It looked a little like Bare's rainbow tie-dyed boxers. She added some purple so she wouldn't always be thinking boxers. She'd never sell this piece. She wanted to hang it right here. It was warm, bright, and cheerful, and it would inspire her further.

She hadn't sold much art over the past month or so. Maybe it was time to get another portfolio together and hit up some galleries. She hated doing that, though. She always felt so pathetic as they scrutinized her art and handed it back to her. Some part of her wanted that gallery showing desperately. If only to show her mother that you could be recognized as an artist without throwing away everyone that mattered in your life. When Amber had graduated from art school, her mother had sent a hand-painted graduation card. Inside the card was an invitation to see her mother's gallery showing in Paris. Amber had torn it to bits. But the memory, her mother's loopy handwriting, her cheerfully scrawled, "I made it!" across the fancy French announcement was burned in Amber's brain.

She pushed her mother out of her mind. Nothing killed the creative spark like thinking about her mother. She went back to painting. The work flowed without interruption, and she hummed along to the music on the small speaker dock she'd bought.

A while later, the timer on her cell chimed that it was close to dinnertime. She picked up her cell and texted Bare about dinner. He texted back: I'm growling.

He didn't mean his stomach. She smiled and texted back: Here, now.

She met him at the door naked. They never made it to dinner.

~ ~ ~

Amber helped with costume changes backstage while the cast ran through a final dress rehearsal. She couldn't believe the weeks had passed so quickly. The show was tomorrow. She was so glad she'd joined the crew. It was magical watching the show come together, everyone working together, getting the timing of the dialogue down, the singing, the dancing, and the movements on stage. Not to mention the lighting, sound, and music. Even Toby, as cranky as that man was, seemed satisfied. But best of all was watching Bare shine every night as he more fully inhabited the role of the Pirate King. She liked to think their time together helped put some of that swagger into his step. The man was insatiable. He wanted her morning, noon, and night. And she was happy to oblige.

She still had to beat the ladies off Bare with a stick after rehearsals, and the lead guy, Zac, had become more flirtatious of late, but between her and Steph, they were able to keep hands off her man. Who would've thought the dancing cow guy would turn heads like that?

Bare turned, right in the middle of a song, sought her out in the wings and threw her a wink and a smile. Even in the middle of a performance, he paid attention to her. No guy had ever cared that much about her. She was beginning to think maybe, just maybe, she was in love. Bare hadn't said the words to her again, but somehow she felt them with every look, every touch. Did that mean they had a future? Her heart raced just thinking about it. She forced her thoughts back to the moment. It was the only thing that kept her calm. Moment by moment. Now was good. She'd deal with the future when it came.

Kate had sat in the back row watching dress rehearsals all week and fallen deeply in lust with Zac. A losing proposition there, but her sister was swayed by his handsome face. She slipped out to join Kate in the auditorium for a few minutes while Zac sang his heart out to Mabel, declaring his love.

"Do you think Zac ever sleeps with women?" Kate whispered when Amber sat down.

"No," she whispered back.

Kate couldn't tear her eyes away from him. "He's so good with Mabel. It looks so real."

"He's acting."

"You think he would act with me?"

"No."

"Barry is amazing."

"No."

"I didn't ask a question."

"I'm not sharing."

Kate snorted. "You know how you kick me out sometimes so you can hook up?"

Amber didn't reply. She wouldn't have to kick out Kate if her sister ever actually went anywhere or did anything.

"Last time I hung out with Ian," Kate said. "We heard you scream."

Omigod.

Kate went on. "Ian said that means full-tilt boogie orgasm. Was it?"

Omigod. Amber stared straight ahead.

"I told Ian I wasn't saving myself anymore, but he didn't believe me."

"Good."

"He said if I saved myself this long, I must be pretty serious about it and that was between me and my future husband."

"Good for him."

"I'm starting to hate him."

Amber laughed. The song ended, and the few people in the audience clapped.

"I can't wait for Saturday night," Kate said.

"Yeah, that's usually the best performance. Friday night works out the nerves. Saturday night really shines."

"Plus the cast party." Kate smiled widely. "I can't wait to party with Zac."

"Forget Zac. Talk to some of the guys in the police brigade."

"But they're not as cute."

"Forget cute. They're nice. Like you."

"You don't think I'm cute," Kate pouted. "You said I look slutty."

"That's because you stopped wearing underwear, and you keep trotting around in my summer pajamas, which are practically see-through. You do have new outfits." Amber stood. "I've got to help out backstage."

"I'm a twenty-one-year-old virgin," Kate said. "I may perish from a lack of male stimulation."

Amber barked out a laugh. "You won't perish."

"Sure, you can laugh. You're getting the full-tilt boogie treatment."

Amber shook her head and left. She really hoped Kate ended up with the right guy when it finally happened for her. Her sister's single-minded determination to end her virginal situation could end in disaster.

~ ~ ~

After rehearsal, Amber helped the cast out of costume and worked with Edith to hang everything in its place on a rack in the band room. Steph was in great spirits as she handed over her dress.

"I've been doing this for years," Steph said, "and I think this is the best production we've ever put on."

Edith turned. "I think so too." She lowered her voice. "Bare brought everyone up a notch. He's a wonderful Pirate King."

Amber's heart filled with pride for her guy.

Edith spoke louder now as more of the cast filtered into the room. "The whole cast is so professional. It's sure to be a hit."

"You ladies want to join us at Garner's?" Zac asked, handing over his costume. "One last hurrah before the show?"

Bare came up and wrapped an arm around

Amber's waist, his hand spanning her bare midriff. "Sure."

"We'll be there," Amber said.

"Excellent," Zac said with a quick brow raise to Bare before strutting out of the room.

"He never gives up, does he?" Amber asked. She took Bare's costume and hung it with the others.

"He can't resist the Pirate King." She could hear the smile in his voice.

She turned. "Me either."

She went up on tiptoe to kiss him. His hand cupped the back of her head, and the kiss ignited.

Edith cleared her throat. "I'll finish up here. You guys move along. *Please.*"

"Seriously, guys," Steph said. "There's a rumor you got down and dirty backstage behind one of the pillars from Daddy Warbucks' mansion."

"That's ridiculous," Amber said even as she felt herself flush. It was behind the newsstand from *Guys and Dolls*. The cast had taken a fifteen-minute break, hitting the vending machines in the cafeteria, while Bare hit on her backstage in a fierce, urgent coupling that ended with his hand clamped over her mouth to muffle her scream as she came.

Bare's hand trailed down her back as he leaned down to growl in her ear, "Maybe we should skip the bar."

"Come on, Bare," someone called.

"Your public awaits," Amber said.

They exchanged a hot look that made her throb,

knowing they'd come together again soon.

The bar scene was hopping on a Thursday night. Their group huddled together in one corner of the room.

"You guys, this has been fantastic," Toby said, making a rare after-rehearsal appearance. "I just want to thank every one of you for really giving it your all. You should be proud of yourselves."

"Aw, thanks, Toby," Zac said.

"Hear, hear," Bare said, raising his beer bottle.

He had her on his lap, one hand resting on her upper thigh. She was loose from the beer, enjoying being with everyone, but still eagerly awaiting his growled command.

"And I want to see you all next summer when we do *Grease*," Toby said. "We haven't done it in seven years, and the audience loves it."

Everyone was in high spirits, much of the cast had grown close over the past six weeks. The Major-General's daughters were feeding French fries to the police brigade. The pirates were stealing kisses. Except her Pirate King, who only kissed other women when required on stage. She didn't mind the quick pecks he gave the other girls. How could she when he was all over her every night? And every morning. She fidgeted on his lap, restless for that urgent coming together she'd grown to crave.

"Soon, love," he whispered in her ear. "Just a little longer."

She wasn't surprised he read her correctly. They'd

grown incredibly in-tune to each other's bodies. He gave her thigh a gentle squeeze and turned to talk to the Major-General, who was happy to regale them with tales of his time off-Broadway decades ago.

She slid onto the barstool next to Bare, unable to sit on his lap without wanting more. His hand laced with hers, keeping their connection, as they chatted with the cast. Zoe chimed in with stories of her singing gigs in the city. Zoe was still hoping to make it big with her singing career, but hadn't yet gotten her big break. In the meantime, she worked as a waitress at Garner's, where Daisy had gotten her a job.

It seemed everyone had a tale of some brush with greatness in New York City. Not Bare. He didn't have that driving ambition for it. His performance was for the joy of it. She understood because that's how her painting had been for a very long time, for the joy of it. Until she'd tried to make some money at it. That had taken the joy right out of it, feeling like a failure because she couldn't sell. And then suddenly she did. She had that one collector that made her feel like she was a success. She hadn't sold much lately, but it hadn't fazed her. She had her art studio, she had Bare, and the creative joy was back.

Toby stood. "I gotta go. Don't party too hard. Big night tomorrow."

They waved him off. She watched Bare as he talked to Zac—his easygoing smile with the laugh lines around his eyes, the stubble he'd let grow for the show that gave him an edgier look, his shaggy, unruly hair that looked awesome with a pirate bandana wrapped around it. That mouth. What he did to her.

He turned, caught her looking, and his gaze heated. He stood. "Amber looks tired. We're going to head out."

"Yes," Amber said with a measure of relief. "And you all don't stay out too late either."

"We know, we know," Steph said with a laugh. "Get lost. We know you just want to do it."

Everyone laughed. Amber gave Steph a hug. "Thanks for convincing me to join the show. It's been amazing."

"You're welcome," Steph said. "Maybe next summer I'll get a boyfriend out of it."

"Not everyone gets to be with the king," Zac said in a mock state of outrage.

"The king is dead," Kevin declared before wheeling back and socking Bare in the face.

Bare staggered back. "What the hell?"

"Kevin!" Zac screeched.

Kevin threw Bare to the ground and got in another punch before the guys in the cast pulled Kevin off him.

"I should've been the Pirate King!" Kevin hollered. "Now I will be. You can't go onstage with two black eyes."

"What is wrong with you?" Zac demanded.

Amber rushed over to where Bare was still on the ground. His eye was going to have a shiner. The second punch had left a red mark high on his cheek, but not as bad. "Are you okay?"

He sat up and winced, touching his cheek. "Yeah, I'm okay. Let's just go."

"Kevin, you're out," Jasmine said. "I'm calling Toby right now."

"But I'm the pirate's lieutenant!" Kevin whined. "I have my own song!"

"Alan will take your place," Jasmine said, stepping away to make the phone call.

"Alan can't sing tenor!" Kevin wailed.

"Zac, get him out of here," Amber said.

Zac pulled the still-protesting Kevin out the front door.

A few moments later, after some sympathy from the rest of the cast, Amber headed out the door with Bare. When they got to his place, she joined him on the sofa, holding ice on his cheek where it was swelling.

Ian took one look at his brother and shook his head. "I never knew theater was so dangerous. I'll get some Tylenol."

He headed for the bathroom medicine cabinet.

"I'm a sorry excuse for a man," Bare said. "I should've punched back."

"No, you did the right thing. I'm glad you didn't stoop to his level."

Bare smiled and winced at the effort. "You think Kevin's right? That I can't go on stage like this?"

"Of course not. I'll fix you up with makeup. Hell, a Pirate King can have a bruise or two. We'll just switch the eye patch to cover the black eye."

He wrapped an arm around her and let out a sigh. "I'm beat. I'm heading to bed."

She stood to go with him.

He smiled and winced again. "I can't sleep with you. I'll want you too much, and I really need to actually sleep."

"All right," she said, giving him a soft kiss. "Sweet dreams."

He left, and she let out a sigh. She went back to her place. Her bed felt cold and empty. Her heart ached for his pain.

~ ~ ~

Barry woke the next morning to the sound of a woman giggling. Damn, his face hurt. He heard the giggle again. To his fuzzy brain it sounded like Amber. He groped blindly through the covers. Had she joined him last night? He opened his eyes. Nope. He was alone. He hadn't wanted Amber to see him like that. The nerdy guy who got his ass kicked, who didn't fight like a man.

He heard that feminine giggle, so familiar, and his heart kicked up. He yanked on a pair of jeans over his boxers and grabbed a T-shirt. What was Amber doing here? Ian wouldn't do that to him. Amber wouldn't.

He strode to the living room and found the blanket moving over two people on the sofa. He ripped the blanket away from their heads.

"Kate!" he exclaimed.

Kate threw the blanket back over her head. "Don't tell Amber."

"Ian," he growled.

"Go away, bro. Geez."

Bare headed across the hall and knocked on Amber's door.

She answered the door, eyes wide. "Omigod, your face."

He winced. He knew he must look like hell because that's how he felt.

"Have you seen Kate?" she asked. "I don't think she came home last night."

He groaned. "Don't freak out."

"I'm already freaked out."

"She's with Ian."

"No!"

She rushed toward his apartment, but he grabbed her before she could knock. "You do *not* want to go over there right now."

She clapped a hand over her mouth. "Omigod."

"Yeah."

"Bare, she's a virgin."

They heard a loud moan. Female.

He grimaced.

"Omigod," Amber said again.

"Let's go to your place."

She turned and let him in. "This is so bad."

Another moan drifted from across the hall.

"Put on the TV so we don't have to hear them,"

he said.

She rushed over and turned on the TV.

They sat on the sofa, took one look at each other, and cracked up.

He put his hand on his cheek. "Ow, my face hurts when I smile."

"I'll get ice."

He leaned his head back. She came back with an ice pack, Tylenol, and some water. He downed the Tylenol.

Amber straddled his lap and put the ice pack on his cheek gently. "I missed you last night."

"Mmm..." he murmured. He couldn't face her then. Didn't feel like he deserved her now. He had a good thirty pounds on Kevin and still the guy had taken him down.

She peered behind the ice pack. "I can fix this." She put the pack back. "We'll ice it off and on all day."

He didn't respond. He hated her seeing him like this.

"I know how to get your mind off this," she purred.

"I can't."

Not even Amber straddling his lap in her tiny pajama shorts was doing it for him today.

She leaned forward, chest to chest, and looked up at him. "Kevin ambushed you. That wasn't fair. Then he attacked when you were down. It wasn't your fault."

"But I shouldn't have been down. I'm bigger. I

should've socked him right back with that first punch."

"You were the bigger man," she said.

"That's why I should've taken him down."

"I mean the bigger man for not hurting him. That was much harder to do."

He grunted. He still felt like a wimp.

She bit his earlobe and growled out, "Bare, here, now."

"That only works on you."

She sat up. He wished he could do what she wanted, but he was stuck back in that place where he was the guy who got picked on, the victim, and he'd looked like that in front of the one person he most wanted to impress. Before he had his growth spurt at sixteen, he'd taken his share of punches in school, after school, anywhere the bullies could corner him. He was about to push her off his lap when she surprised him by asking, "Do you remember when you took me like a werewolf?"

He'd never forget it. "Yeah."

"You made me howl."

"Yeah." That had been awesome.

"And when I told you no one had ever made me howl before, what did you say?"

He smiled a little. "I said I was a lucky man."

She slid down his lap and went to her knees in front of him. "You're about to get very lucky…man."

She undid the button on his jeans. He felt himself get hard despite his foul mood. She slowly pulled down the zipper.

He sucked in a breath. "I've never asked you to do that."

She smiled and licked her lips, which made his cock pulse against his boxers. He'd never asked for this because he always wanted to give to her, had felt it selfish to ask her to give to him. It was enough that she let him be with her so much.

She took him in hand, and he hissed out a breath. "You don't have to—"

"That's exactly why I'm happy to," she said before she took him fully in her mouth.

His eyes rolled back in his head as she had her way with him. He was indeed a very lucky man.

CHAPTER THIRTEEN

Amber had just sent a very satisfied Bare back to his apartment when Kate returned wearing Amber's pink satin robe.

"Well, you were wrong!" Kate announced cheerfully. "I didn't have to do my hair, or wear makeup, or wear non-wrinkly clothes or any clothes at all."

Amber cringed.

"All I had to do was walk across the hall wearing this robe and nothing else, and it was all systems go, full thrusters ahead."

Amber stared at her. "You wore my favorite robe naked."

"Oh, sorry. You want it back." She started to untie the belt.

"No! You keep it!"

"Good. I think it's my secret weapon. If you'll excuse me, I didn't get much sleep last night." She headed toward Amber's bedroom.

"Wait, so are you okay? Are you and Ian together

now?"

Kate stopped and turned. "I'm fine and no. I told him it was a one-time thing." She giggled. "Well, two times. I'm much too young to be tied down. Besides I don't want to be hydrogen."

Amber stared at her in confusion.

"Only one electron orbiting me," Kate explained.

"Oh. Goodnight, Kate."

"Night." Kate disappeared into the bedroom. She popped her head back out. "I'd rather be polonium."

"More electrons?" Amber guessed.

"Yes, and also glowing. It's radioactive." Kate pursed her lips, deep in thought. Finally, she confided, "I still haven't had a full-tilt boogie orgasm. Though the second time I did experience a very pleasant—"

"Go to sleep!"

Ai-yi-yi.

Amber decided to wait a little to get her shower so she wouldn't disturb Kate with getting ready. She turned to the huge pile of mail that had stacked up on the half wall separating the kitchen from the living room. She'd been too busy to deal with it and just kept stacking it up there. She flipped through it quickly, looking for bills. A small envelope caught her eye. The loopy handwriting familiar. It was from her mom. She debated for a moment. Her mom had sent a hand-painted card several months ago, inviting Amber to visit. Amber had sent back the card with one word scrawled across the painting in angry red marker, a capital letter response—NO. She hadn't heard from

her since, but she knew from her dad that her mom
had asked him to step in. She'd told her dad to forget
it and mind his own business. He let it drop. Her dad
never involved himself in her life any further than he
had to.

She turned and dropped the envelope in the trash
unopened.

~ ~ ~

"Daze, you made it!" Amber exclaimed. It was
opening night, and Daze was here with her husband,
Trav, holding their son, Bryce.

"Of course I came!" Daze exclaimed. "I've got to
watch Zoe, Steph, and now Barry, and all the great
scenery and props you helped with."

Amber smiled and turned to Trav and Bryce. "Hi,
guys."

"Hey, break a leg tonight," Trav said. "Don't mind
us. If you hear a little guy squeal, it's only because he's
overcome with joy to be watching you." He tickled
Bryce, who squealed and wiggled all around. He tossed
him up in the air. The kid's blond hair flew up and the
look on his face was pure joy.

"He means he'll take him out if he gets too loud,"
Daze whispered. "This is so exciting! So Barry plays a
pirate? How's that?"

"He's amazing. Really. And I'm not just saying that
because I'm in love with him." Amber clapped a hand
over her mouth. She couldn't believe she'd just said

that.

Daze grabbed her arm. "Amber! You didn't tell me that. Wow."

"Seriously? Barry?" Trav asked, tossing Bryce over his shoulder.

"Yes," Amber said, more certain now. She was in love with him. She waited for the anxiety, the panic that usually clutched at her, but felt at peace. She loved him. It felt right. She probably should've told Bare that first. "Watch him tonight. He's changed. He's…" She felt herself blush. "Just watch."

"Cool," Trav said. He turned to Daze. "I'm gonna let him run around outside until it's closer to show time."

"Okay."

"Give mommy a kiss." He leaned Bryce over to Daze. Bryce puckered up and gave Daze a big wet kiss on her cheek.

"My turn," Trav said with a devilish grin. He kissed her on the lips. Daze watched him leave, a contented smile on her face.

Just then Zoe came up to them. "Daisy-chain!"

The two women hugged. Zoe pulled back and stared at Daze's stomach. "That babe has grown since last month. Look at you." She held out Daze's arms to show off her baby bump.

Daze smiled. "I know. I get huge when I'm pregnant. I'm five months now." She looked at both of them and bit her lip. "Can I tell you a secret? Trav wants to keep it quiet, but I'm just busting to tell people."

"What?" Amber asked.

"I had the ultrasound and…" Daze beamed. "It's a boy."

"Woo-eey!" Zoe exclaimed.

"Congratulations," Amber said. "Wow, two boys."

"I know. Trav wants to go for number three, but I said I'm already thirty-five, and I'm tired. I told him he can have the next kid if he wants one so bad."

"I'll bet that went over well," Zoe quipped.

Daze laughed. "He said he would have the next kid if that's what it took." She shook her head. "The man always agrees then works his way around to what he wants. He's sneaky that way."

Kate appeared at Amber's side, back in her ancient jeans, stained T-shirt, and her hair up in its usual messy half bun, half tail. Her glasses had a smudge of toothpaste on one lens. Ian trailed behind her.

"Guys, this is my sister, Kate, and Bare's brother Ian," Amber said. "This is Zoe and Daisy."

"Nice to meet you," Kate said.

Ian smiled. "Hello, ladies. Hey, I remember you, foxy—I mean, pregnant lady."

"It's Daisy," Amber reminded him.

"I gotta run," Zoe said. "I have to do my vocal warm-up."

"I should go too," Amber said.

"My seat is front and center," Kate announced. She turned. "Ian, I will see you later."

"Can't I sit with you?" Ian asked.

"I reserved my seat ahead of time. I'm sure that can't be changed at this late date."

"There's no reserved—" Amber stopped at Kate's sharp look. "Bye."

She heard Kate hiss under her breath, "Stop following me," as Ian trailed after her.

Her sister hadn't yet realized that nothing caught a guy's interest better than not chasing them.

"Break a leg!" Daze called. Amber waved.

Backstage, the cast was in a tizzy of excitement as the auditorium filled with more and more people.

Zac kept reporting back. "Nearly a full house. Center section is filled."

Five minutes later. "Sides are filling in."

Fifteen minutes later. "Guys, we've got a full house." He jumped around, bouncing in a circle. "Energy up."

"We're already up," Kevin said. "You're going to jinx us. Shut up."

Kevin had been demoted to pirate number five. Alan had eagerly taken on the role of the pirate's lieutenant. He was pretty good too.

Amber went to the band room to help with Bare's makeup. She found him applying the beige foundation that would keep him from looking washed-out on stage. He was doing a terrible job blending it in.

"Here, let me," she said, taking the wedge sponge from his hand.

"Hello there, me beauty." He pulled her in and kissed her gently.

"Hello, my Pirate King." She worked on blending the line of foundation from his jawline into his neck.

"Kevin really did a number on my face," he muttered.

She rubbed further down his neck. "It's not that bad. The swelling went down at least." She grabbed a towel to protect his white pirate shirt before blending further.

"I still have a black eye."

She grabbed the eye patch and slid it over his eye. "See, not that bad."

"What about the other eye?"

"I'll fix it." She added some foundation to the sponge and delicately patted around the bruise high up on his cheekbone, blending under his eye.

He grabbed her wrist and kissed the sensitive underside. "I love you," he growled.

Her heart swelled, knowing it was the emotion that made his voice like that. She forced the words past the lump in her throat because she truly meant them, even if it was hard to say. "I love you too."

He released her wrist and stared at her. "Amber," he growled. He cleared his throat. "You do?"

"You know I do." She put her hand over his heart, felt it thumping hard. "You've always known here."

"No, I didn't always know." His eyes searched her face. "Only hoped."

She smoothed the foundation down his cheek over the stubble. "Now you know."

"You still going to love me after the show when

I'm not the Pirate King?"

"Of course. What a thing to say."

"I'm holding you to that."

She continued blending on the other side of his jaw, into the neck. "I fell in love with you, Bare, not the Pirate King."

"Prove it."

She stopped and stared. "Prove it? How?"

"Take a ride with me when the dancing cow magnets are on the car."

"No problem."

"And make it moo."

She swallowed hard. This was getting embarrassing, but if it put his mind at ease. "Okay."

"And then…" His voice lowered, and she waited with a mix of dread and wild anticipation. "I want you…in my cow costume."

"You want me to dress up like a cow?"

"No, I want to make furry love to you when I'm the cow."

"No."

He raised his brows. "Amber," he growled. He knew what that growly voice did to her. "Furry love."

She studied his face looking for one sign that would indicate he was joking. His expression was serious. But then his eyes gave him away, and he smiled, laugh lines forming at the corners of his eyes.

She smacked him on the chest. "You!"

"You were thinking about it, weren't you?"

"No. Not for one minute."

He grabbed her waist and pulled her into his arms. "I'm a lucky man."

She smiled. "You are."

"Ten minutes 'til curtain, people," Toby called.

"That's my cue," Bare said.

She put a hand on his shoulder to keep him in the chair and finished up with the foundation. She gave him a quick kiss. "Break a leg."

"I'd much rather…" He whispered in her ear the deliciously naughty things he wanted to do to her.

And while she ran hot with that vision running through her mind, he slapped her ass and swaggered out.

~ ~ ~

Opening night of the show was amazing. Of course Amber expected nothing less from such a stellar cast. Bare had hired a video recording company to film it since his mother would miss the performance. His mother was helping out her sister who'd recently had surgery. Amber was glad they'd have it recorded so she'd always get to watch her Pirate King. There were a few missteps, like when Kevin purposely didn't say his line and left Bare hanging, but her guy ad libbed, "That's quite a mouthful," and the entire audience roared with laughter. Bare was amazing as usual, bringing all of his energy and heart to the role. She watched from backstage. He regularly looked over to give her a special smile or a wink like they were in on this performance together.

Zoe was fabulous as Mabel. She'd heard her friend sing full-throttle before, but when she had an audience, the woman positively glowed. She watched as Delilah did a convincing Ruth in love with the young, dashing Frederic. Her voice hit one wrong note, but professional that she was, she didn't let that stop her, just corrected course and forged ahead.

Jasmine stood in the orchestra pit, dancing along with them, coaxing smiles on their faces when they were singing. Toby watched from the front row, looking serious. The energy was electric. Amber was going to miss all this. The camaraderie, the late nights at the bar and diner, watching Bare.

This was the second time he'd mentioned her not wanting him when he wasn't the Pirate King. Which was ridiculous. Why would she dump him just because he wasn't a pirate? Was it a pirate she slept with all those nights? All those mornings? Okay, one time she'd played along with a pirate/wench scenario that got down and dirty even in all its dress-up, pirate-talk trappings. She flushed, remembering the rope that bound her wrists, the "flogging" that was more like caressing, until she was begging him to bury his sword to the hilt.

But she knew who he was. A performer. An artist like her. He was still a little goofy, but she saw his tender heart, saw him grow in confidence as he dominated the stage. Dominated her. She went hot just thinking about it.

Bare bounded off stage after his song with

Frederic and Ruth. He was sweating from the hot lights and the exertion of his performance. He took one look at her no doubt lusty expression and grinned. "Thinking of me?"

"No, it's just hot backstage. All the lights." Except there weren't any lights backstage.

He gave her a knowing look and cradled her bottom, pulling her up against his thigh. She was instantly turned on.

He gave her a quick kiss. "How's my makeup?"

She giggled. Her boyfriend was asking about his makeup.

"Can you see the bruise?" he asked urgently.

She stopped smiling. "No, no, it's fine. You look great."

"So do you, beauty," he whispered in her ear. Then he bounded back on stage for his next entrance.

She watched him, watched the cast play off him, heard the audience laugh and applaud. She wanted to hold onto this moment forever. When the curtain went down, it was to a standing ovation. She was so proud of all of them. They took their bows, one at a time, then all together. The audience was still on their feet, clapping. Bare gestured to Will for him to take credit, then to Jasmine in the orchestra pit, to Toby and Edith in the front row, and then Bare surprised her by grabbing her hand and pulling her onstage so she could take a bow with them. She did, and then he dipped her and kissed her like the Pirate King did to all the girls. Except this time it was her turn, all hers. The audience loved it, and so did she.

CHAPTER FOURTEEN

Barry belted out "I am the Pirate King" for what would be his last performance. It was Saturday night, the last night of the show, and the house was packed. He glanced to the wings as he crossed stage right, gave Amber a small smile, and continued. The audience lifted him, made the performance fly in a way he couldn't on his own. It was euphoric, as his mind and body moved without any conscious thought, as he flew through song after song, line after line, dance after dance.

They finished to a standing ovation. He was one of the last of the cast to come forward for his bow, a place of honor, and the applause grew louder. Frederic and Mabel went last. They all joined hands and took a final bow. He gestured to the crew who'd helped them along so they could take their bow. Then he grabbed Amber, pulled her onstage for her bow, and kissed her. The audience ate it up.

Then it was over.

The house lights came up. The audience slowly

exited the building. He felt deflated. He knew what came after this. Goodbye. Everyone moved on. He'd miss everyone. But at least they had tonight to celebrate. And he'd still have Amber. She loved him. He was still marveling over that. A big, nerdy guy like him snagged a beautiful artist like her. He hoped he never woke up from this full-color, sex-drenched, love-filled dream. It was fucking amazing.

"See you all at the party!" he called with a wave. He'd invited everyone to his mom's house. It was large and empty, since she was taking care of his aunt in Maine.

Amber caught up with him in the band room. "My Pirate King."

"My cheeky wench." He gave her a kiss, and she returned it passionately. He already wanted her, the urge so strong he wasn't sure he could wait until after the party. Maybe they could sneak away at the party. There were a few unused bedrooms upstairs.

"Show's over," he said. "Still feel the same way about me? Regular old Barry the dancing cow?"

She smiled, her hand running up and down his arm. "First of all, you're my Bare."

He smiled at the endearment.

"And second of all, you're not just a dancing cow, you're a pirate, and you're a horny dog."

He grabbed her and whispered what he wanted to do to her that involved Nutella in some very interesting places.

She flushed. "How am I supposed to get through

this party thinking about that?"

He trailed his fingers down her spine over the bare skin of her back. "What are you wearing under that dress?"

She had on this flowery halter-top dress that ended mid-thigh. He wanted to rip the thing off her. He wanted to say the words, the ones he knew would get him back where he belonged, buried deep inside her.

"Not much," she teased.

He ran his fingers over her hip, feeling for the thong waistband that...she hadn't worn tonight.

"Amber," he growled in her ear. "Here, now."

He watched as her eyes dilated, and her cheeks flushed. She slapped his hand away. "There's people."

He lunged for her, and she squealed. He caught her around her waist before she could get anywhere.

Steph walked in, hand over her eyes. "Please don't let me see anything rated X. I just want to change and get to the party. I'm not into voyeurism."

"He's just playing around," Amber said.

"Whatever," Steph sang.

Barry slowly shook his head at Amber. He wasn't playing around at all. He was fully prepared to take her in the locker room, in a bathroom stall, the guest bedroom, anywhere that was close and private. He had a perpetual hard-on from the moment they met. That hadn't changed.

"There's some empty bedrooms at my mom's house we could use," he whispered in her ear.

"Bare," Amber said, "please."

Her "please" could mean stop or keep going depending on how hot she was.

"You know the deal," he said in a low voice, going for hot.

Her breathing hitched. He knew he had her, and both triumph and relief surged through him.

She pushed him into a chair. "Let me get this makeup off you."

He sat, but his mind was filled with visions of Amber with the dress bunched up around her waist, her against the wall, him pushing inside—he gripped the sides of the chair so he wouldn't grab her. He could hear Steph putting away the accessories for her costume, rummaging for her clothes. He was about to bust his breeches.

Amber dabbed delicately at his face, washing the makeup off, careful of his bruise. God, he loved her.

She rubbed his arm. "Relax. You feel so tense."

He put his hands on her waist, spanning his fingers to touch more of her. "I'm just thinking of you."

"I'll see you guys at the party," Steph said as she sailed out with her duffel bag.

"We're heading out too," Barry said. "I've got the key."

Steph waved and the door shut behind her. Barry pulled Amber close, unable to resist kissing her before they left. Tasting her spurred him on; he could never get enough of her. She was making these needy little mewls in the back of her throat that made him crazy. He grabbed her hand, intent on getting her to a bed

ASAP.

"Let's go," he said.

She giggled, and they ran out the door.

~ ~ ~

Amber walked into the empty house hand in hand with Bare. Some of the cast were already hanging out on the front yard and followed them in. Soon the party was in full swing, everyone cheerful and congratulating themselves on a job well done. Ian was trying to get Kate's attention while she was busy informing the entire police brigade about the history of *The Pirates of Penzance* as originally conceived by Gilbert and Sullivan in 1879. Zac and Kevin were getting cozy in the corner, arms around each other as they spoke closely together.

"We did it!" Steph said, hugging them both. "Have a drink. Or do you need a smoke?"

"Ha-ha," Amber said. "I brought champagne."

"Awesome. We should all have a toast." Steph called over to their director. "Toby, make a toast for us."

"Come on, everyone," Bare said. "A toast in the kitchen."

Everyone filed in. Bare uncorked the champagne while Amber set out plastic cups. She poured a bit in each cup, sparingly so there'd be enough to go around.

After everyone picked up their cup of champagne, Toby raised his cup. "A toast to the finest cast I've ever had the privilege of working with."

"Aww," Steph said.

"Hear, hear," Zac said.

"To show business!" Delilah said.

"To pirates!" Bare said.

"Let the good times roll!" the Major-General put in, still wearing his pith helmet. What was that guy's name again? They'd been calling him Major-General from day one.

They all laughed and drank. Someone put on some music in the family room. The women started dancing, then Zac and Kevin joined in, and then everyone was dancing. Amber had a brief flashback to Bare's Irish jig the last time they'd danced together. Seeming to know where her thoughts were at, he grinned, and instead did a swashbuckling pirate dance, joining in with the other pirates, who swung arm in arm like they did on their dance number on stage. Steph dragged her into a kick line with the Major-General's daughters. She did a few low kicks, mindful of her lack of underthings.

After several more dances and one too many cups of wine, Amber excused herself, found the downstairs bathroom locked, and headed upstairs in search of another bathroom. As she walked the upstairs hallway, her eye caught on a splash of dark green, red, and lavender on the wall in one of the bedrooms. She stopped. That was strange. It was a dragon. She got closer. It was her dragon. The painting she'd sold on eArt. She stepped into the room and just stared. They were all here. All of her paintings lined up against one wall, stacked up against each other.

Her head spun. Wait. No. Her collector, the woman who bought all her art, was Bare's mom? She thought back to how sales had tapered off when the play rehearsals started, turned on her heel, and raced to Bare. She found him dancing with some of the pirates and the Major-General's daughters.

"How could you?" she hollered over the music.

People nearby stopped dancing to stare.

Bare pulled her out of the room and into a quiet corner of the kitchen. "What's the matter?"

"What's the matter? What's the matter! You bought all my paintings and let me think it was a collector!" Her head hurt. She lowered her voice. "You bought them as your mother, and you never told me. You probably didn't even like them. You just stored them in a room upstairs. I can't believe I fell for it." Tears stung her eyes, and she dashed them away with the back of her hand.

"I do like them," he said. "That's why I bought them."

She swallowed over the lump in her throat. "But you just let me think I was some big success when you were just trying to make me feel better about my little hobby. I thought…" Her voice broke.

He wrapped his arms around her, and she shoved him away, suddenly furious. She'd thrown herself into painting, trying to keep up with her mysterious collector, actually thinking she might have a chance at making a living at her art. And the way she'd confided to Bare about all her great sales. The way he just went along with it.

He reached for her hand, and she shook him off.

"You thought what?" he asked.

"I thought I was a success. I thought I had a future in art. But you were just playing me. How could you? You of all people. I thought I could trust you."

"You can," he said urgently. "You know you can. I love your art, so I bought it. That's all."

"But you didn't buy it as yourself. You bought it as Susan Dancy. What the hell, Bare?"

The tears came now, rushing down her cheeks, and she took off out the back door.

"Amber, wait!"

She kept going.

He caught up with her in the backyard. She stopped and took a few deep breaths. It was dark outside, and she was heading the wrong way for an exit. Besides, he was her ride.

"I'm sorry," he said. "I planned on telling you, but then we were both so busy and things were going so well between us."

"You were afraid I would stop sleeping with you." She wanted to hurt him the way she was hurting. "You and your conditioned response. You ever think it wasn't you, but more of a Pavlovian thing, hmm?"

He cradled her face with one hand. "Amber…"

That voice, that growly voice that meant huge emotion. It got to her every time. She covered her ears. "Just take me home!"

They walked out to the street, where he'd parked his car. He'd removed The Dancing Cow magnets from the sides, and it looked like a normal car, except for the loudspeaker on top. She wanted to grab that loudspeaker and rip it off. She felt like a wretched fraud, and he was the worst—letting her believe in her art, completely ignorant that it was her own boyfriend just making her into a big phony success.

She blew out a breath and got into his car.

He slid into the driver's seat and turned to her. "How can I make it up to you? I'm sorry I waited so long to tell you."

"I don't think we should see each other anymore."

"No, I don't want that."

"Well, I do. I can't trust you."

"You can always trust me."

"You lied to me! You made me believe in myself and my art. The whole time I went on and on about how excited I was to sell all those paintings and you were secretly laughing—"

"I wasn't, I swear. I would never laugh at you."

"And your mother! She must've thought it was crazy, all these paintings being delivered every day. There's at least twenty paintings just sitting in a spare bedroom."

"Am—"

"Don't! Don't say my name. Don't say another fucking word to me."

He shut up.

He pulled the car out into the street. She heard him call Ian, tell him to lock up when everyone left, and stared out the window, unable to stop the tears rolling down her cheeks. She felt like the most pathetic starving artist that ever lived. At least her jerk ex-boyfriend Rick had been honest about how her paintings were a cute little hobby. Bare pretended they were the best thing in the world, cheered her on when she got sales, all the while buying them for his own little game. She'd never, ever felt so betrayed.

~ ~ ~

Bare dropped off an eerily quiet Amber and went to his apartment in a near panic. He couldn't lose Amber over this. He hadn't thought it through. It had all been with the best of intentions, all of it. He just wanted her to be happy. For once his brother wasn't hanging out on his sofa eating all his food. He really could've used someone to talk to and help him figure this thing out.

He took a few deep breaths. *Okay, calm down.* Think rationally, logically. This is a problem, and there is a solution. He sat on the sofa. He'd make a flow chart. Problem, possible paths to solutions, possible outcomes. Yes, flow charts made sense.

He grabbed his laptop and began. Problem: Amber wants to break up because she's upset. Desired outcome: Not to break up.

Path to solution: Stop the upset.

See, already he was a step closer to desired

outcome. He stared at the blinking cursor. How to stop the upset.

A. Apologize.

He deleted that one. He'd already done that, and the upset hadn't stopped.

B. Bring gifts.

Flowers, chocolates, jewelry. Okay, that was a definite possibility and easy enough. He ordered some flowers to be delivered with a small note that said, Love, Bare. He added a small teddy bear to the order because he was her bear. She always called him Bare. He got choked up and shut the laptop.

For the first time in months he found himself utterly alone. No cast and crew surrounding him. No Ian annoying him. No Amber wrapped around him. She'd said that Pavlovian response thing just to hurt him. She never would've responded to his command if she wasn't already into him. That couldn't be trained into an unwilling subject. She'd wanted him just as much as he'd wanted her. Well...he probably wanted her more. He hungered for her in a way that was unnerving, even to him, in its insatiable need. He'd never felt like that with another woman. Like he craved her all the time. It was why he'd thought of that wager. He couldn't stop wanting. He needed her to be ready and willing and, by God, she was.

He closed his eyes and tried to think. His mind was null, void, an empty, aching blank.

Fuck.

What was he going to do now? What would the

Pirate King do? Dammit, this was exactly what he'd feared deep down. Show over, him and Amber over. Only it wasn't because of the pirate effect. It was because of him.

He kicked himself for not telling her about the paintings earlier, before they'd gotten in so deep, before when it would've been a misunderstanding or an awkward conversation, because now it was fucking Armageddon. The end of their world together.

CHAPTER FIFTEEN

Amber couldn't paint. Two weeks and she couldn't move brush to canvas. What was the point? No one wanted her paintings. No one would ever buy them or appreciate them. She avoided the art studio Bare had rented. The place was filled with memories of the times he'd joined her there, the many, many, many times they'd made love. All that time he'd praised her art, knowing he'd sneak off and buy it when he got a chance.

Even at her apartment where she had some art supplies, she still couldn't paint. It was only the first week of August, no rehearsals, no day job, and all of it wasted. All she did was mope around her apartment and annoy her sister with her bitchiness. At first Kate had been sympathetic. Well, as sympathetic as Kate ever got. She made Amber lukewarm chamomile tea whenever she got snippy, or near tears, or angry. Basically all day. Until finally Amber couldn't take even one more cup.

"No more tea!" she told Kate. "It's not calming

me down. I'm still upset. All the time."

Kate let out a stream of obscenities that had Amber's jaw dropping. Her sister never cursed. Kate marched out of the kitchen and stopped in front of Amber, where she was sitting on the sofa watching *Zombie Bonanza*.

Kate blocked out her view of the TV. "That's right. I call bullshit. *Enough*, Amber. I swear I'd rather hang out with puppy-eyed Ian than have to deal with you sniping at me every fucking day."

"He's only puppy-eyed because you won't sleep with him," Amber retorted. "Smart move. I should've followed your example."

Kate rolled her eyes. "You and Barry were like cats in heat. I could barely get out of the apartment fast enough. Don't flatter yourself. There's no way in hell you could've followed my example."

Amber deflated.

Kate shoved her glasses back in place. "I hate to be the one to point out the obvious but, logically, you breaking up with him because he bought your paintings makes no sense."

"I told you he didn't just buy my paintings. He lied about it. He bought them as his mother and had everything hidden at her house. He let me go on and on, thinking I was actually getting somewhere with a real collector who loved my work when it was all him."

"Maybe he just didn't have room at his apartment to store them."

"Argh! That's not the point." She waved her hand toward Kate's laptop. "Never mind about me. Just go back to your prime numbers."

"I'm off that. Now I'm looking into posters for my new grad school apartment." She sat next to Amber and showed her the screen. "What do you think of this one?"

Amber glanced over. Sheldon from *The Big Bang Theory*.

"Perfect," Amber said. "It's like the male version of you."

"I liked you a lot better when you were getting laid," Kate said.

She liked herself a lot better then too.

"Just please go over there and talk to him," Kate said. "Ian and I can't take the two of you anymore."

That really burned. Ian and Kate crashing their apartments and freeloading all summer and *they* couldn't take it?

"You two are lucky we let you stay with us rent-free all summer," Amber sniped.

Kate turned. "I can move out if you'd like."

Amber immediately regretted her words. "No! I'm sorry." She hugged her sister. "I'm just upset. Don't move. You can stay until school starts."

Kate went back to her laptop. "It's only two more weeks."

"I know."

Amber went to her easel, her mind a blank. She waited, hoping for that spark, that tiny inkling of an idea of color or shape. Nothing.

A few minutes later, Kate announced, "I've called an emergency meeting of your friends."

"What?"

"You haven't left the apartment in two weeks. That's not like you. Steph and Daisy are coming over." She set Amber's cell phone back on the coffee table and went back to her laptop. Obviously she'd pulled her contact info from her cell.

Amber bit back a groan. She hadn't called her friends because all she wanted to do was be alone. She was terrible company, and the only reason Kate put up with her was because she was still easier to deal with than Kate moving back home and dealing with her mother.

An hour later, Steph and Daze swooped in.

"Come here, girl," Steph said, wrapping Amber in a hug.

"You guys," Amber said, her voice muffled by the taller woman's chest. "I'm fine."

Steph turned and pushed her toward Daze, who also gave her a hug though not nearly as tight due to the baby belly between them.

"You're lucky we love you," Steph said. "Otherwise your complete noncommunication would really piss us off."

"You need your bitches when your man does you wrong," Daze said.

They cracked up. Amber hadn't laughed in so long it felt strange. They settled on the sofa. Kate brought over wine, with iced tea for Daisy, and sat cross-legged on the floor in front of them.

"So how bad can it be?" Steph said. "This is Bare we're talking about. The man is crazy about you. What in the world could he possibly have done that was so bad?"

Amber was quiet. It was painfully embarrassing. She shot Kate a look. This was all her fault for bringing her friends into this.

"Did he cheat on you?" Daze asked.

"He wouldn't have had the energy for that," Steph said. "He was screwing her every chance he got."

"I can confirm that," Kate said.

Amber flushed and drained half her glass of wine.

"So what's the problem?" Daze asked gently.

At Amber's silence, Kate piped up. "He bought her paintings as a woman."

"Kate!" Amber exclaimed. That sounded all kinds of wrong.

"Are you saying he's a cross-dresser?" Daze asked.

Steph raised her brows. "Theater people *are* strange."

"No, he's not a cross-dresser!" Amber exclaimed. "He bought my paintings under his mother's name, and then he just let me think I was so great selling to some mysterious collector when the whole time it was really him."

"Aw," Daze said. "That's kinda sweet."

Amber turned a murderous look on Daze. "It's not sweet! He was laughing behind my back. He lied to me!"

Steph turned to Daze. "He must really like her paintings." She turned to Amber. "Didn't you sell a couple thousand dollars' worth?"

"Yes, but that's not the point!" Amber drained the rest of her glass. This little chat wasn't making her feel any better. Her friends were supposed to rally around her, not Bare. Wasn't there anyone who'd be on her side? Anyone who'd understand this kind of betrayal?

They got quiet.

"Do you think his mother really did buy your paintings?" Steph asked. "Like maybe he had nothing to do with it?"

Amber shook her head. "No, it was him. I confronted him, and he apologized."

Kate raised a finger. "I told you he apologized."

Steph and Daze looked at Amber sympathetically.

"Honey, you still love him, or you wouldn't be this upset weeks later," Daze said. "Don't let these bad feelings come between you. It just makes things worse."

"You should talk to him," Steph said. "Try to forgive him."

"I can't," Amber said miserably. She reached for the bottle of wine, but Steph snatched it away.

"Give me one good reason why you can't," Steph said.

"Because I'll cave," Amber said, "and I don't want to cave. Bare did it with the best of intentions, right? But that's how he is. He'll just keep doing what he thinks is best for me, all with the best of intentions, and the hell with my feelings or what I want."

The women exchanged an uneasy look.

Amber felt instantly wary. "What?"

"You should talk to him," Daze said.

"What did he do now?" Amber asked.

Daze looked to Steph, who looked to Kate. Kate sighed and went to her laptop.

"Here, see," Kate said. She clicked a few times and brought up an e-vite. "We all got them."

The e-vite read: Please come to an Amber Lewis invitation-only gallery showing at the Moonlight Gallery. Monday at 7 p.m. Refreshments served.

The party was in a little over a week. This was so humiliating. It had to be Bare. Oh, here she was, the wonderful artist who couldn't get a show on her own, who'd never sold a single painting, whose boyfriend had to rent the gallery to get them to agree to show her stuff. She hadn't checked her email since the breakup, or she would've known.

Kate looked closer. "Omigod."

"Now what?" Amber snapped.

Kate turned, eyes wide. "Your mother RSVP'd yes."

Her mother? Amber shot straight off the sofa. How could he do this to her? Go behind her back, embarrass her with delusions of success, involve her mother? She marched across the hall and pounded on Bare's door.

The door swung open. Bare stood there,

unshaven, his hair too long. He looked tired. "Amber," he said in that growly voice.

She didn't care if he was upset about their breakup. She was more upset. She was the one betrayed. Twice.

"How could you?" she hollered as she pushed past him into his apartment.

"Hey, Amber," Ian called from the kitchen.

"Ian," she bit out.

"I'll be sitting on the curb eating worms," Ian said, leaving with a beer and a bag of cheese puffs.

"You got the invitation," Bare said.

"Isn't it enough you made me out to be a fool by buying all my paintings? Now you have to humiliate me in front of everyone with a fake gallery showing?"

"It's not fake."

"So you showed the gallery my paintings, and they agreed to a showing?"

He jammed a hand in his hair. "Well, no, not exactly."

"Tell me exactly how this happened," she bit out.

"I rented the space. It's a party in your honor. To show your work."

"To show my-my," she sputtered, so furious she could barely speak. "Again you go behind my back! Again you're trying to build me up like I'm some great artist. No gallery has ever wanted my work! Argh!"

She paced back and forth in his living room. Her mother was flying in from Paris for Amber's showing. Her mother, who she hadn't seen in fifteen years, finally saw a reason to make an appearance. She would get here, see Amber was a fraud, and leave. Again.

She stopped and turned to him. "How could you invite my mother?" Her voice came out small.

He pulled her to the sofa, and she sank to the cushions, all the fight gone out of her. Her mother, the great artist, who had showings in galleries in Paris, was going to see her daughter was an absolute failure. Bare slipped an arm around her, holding her close, and she breathed in his familiar scent. She would've cried, except she was reaching a near catatonic state of shock. She couldn't believe her mother was actually coming. For this. Her mother thought Amber was finally important enough to bother with. Finally important enough to cross an ocean and visit. But she wasn't. She never would be.

She swallowed hard. "How did you even find her?"

"Your dad gave me her email. He's easy enough to find. You told me where he worked before."

"Why would he do that?" she whispered.

"He said she'd want to be invited."

"Bare, *she left me*." She sat up. "She dropped me off when I was thirteen with the brainiac family and never looked back. No visits, no phone calls, no emails, just a stupid card whenever she got around to it. That means she doesn't get what she wants."

"I'm so sorry. I didn't know the history. I thought since you were both artists...Your dad convinced me it would be a good thing." At her sharp look, he quickly added. "I'll uninvite her."

She felt sick. Absolutely sick. "You can't uninvite her. She probably already bought plane tickets."

She pulled her legs up and wrapped her arms around them, sitting in a tight fetal position. She rested her chin on her knees and stared blankly at the floor.

She spoke softly. "Do you have any idea what it's like to be a thirteen-year-old girl dropped off with her physicist father and his physicist wife with their brainy daughter? I was the black sheep in that family. I could never fit in, never live up to what they expected, never be understood. And my mother never came back. All I got was the occasional card with a 'Hello, having a great time! Love, Mom.'"

His warm hand rubbed her back. She glanced over to find him regarding her with such sympathy that she had to look away before she broke down sobbing. She didn't want sympathy. She felt pathetic enough all on her own.

"Your father was so adamant," he said quietly. "I should've checked with you first."

"My father never thinks about anything as inconsequential as my feelings. My mother wanted to connect, so he made it happen. Perfectly logical. The hell with me and what I feel."

He pulled her into his arms, and she let him, needing that small bit of comfort.

Her voice came out sounding choked. "Did *you* ever once consider my feelings?"

"I was all about your feelings. That's what this

whole thing was about."

"You butt in where you don't belong. Just doing...whatever." She pulled away and stood. "Forget it. Why am I even talking to you about this? I'm not going. You can explain to my mother and everyone else why you've staged a fake gallery showing and send them home."

Yes, that was the right thing to do. She might not have had a say in this whole gallery thing, but she did have a say in going along with the deception, and she wouldn't.

He stood, his eyes pleading with her. "Amber, please. I've got everything planned. A lot planned."

"Enjoy your party," she said in a tight voice. She turned to go.

"Wait!"

She rushed out the door, sailed through her apartment, ignored her friends' questions, and locked herself in her bedroom where she cried big, heaving sobs like she hadn't cried since she was thirteen years old.

CHAPTER SIXTEEN

Barry knew he'd crossed the line, but damn if he was going to cancel everything now. He'd spent more than a week lugging Amber's paintings around to galleries in the city. He'd hand carried five paintings of what he felt were her best work, along with a photo album with pictures of the rest. One by one, the galleries had turned him down. They were idiots not to see the artistic merit. He thought they were fantastic when he'd first seen them, even before he knew he had a chance with her. She was a brilliant artist. But like many brilliant artists, she wasn't yet appreciated.

It was when he finally returned the paintings to the guest room at his mom's house that his mom had given him the solution.

"Why don't you just rent a gallery?" she asked when he sat at the kitchen table to join her for lunch. "Many artists start out with a patron who hosts them."

"They do?"

"Why the hell not?" she asked with a smile.

That's what he loved about his mom. She was a

why-the-hell-not kind of person. That left open all kinds of possibilities in the world. For the first time, he felt hope. He would host a show, let the world see Amber's brilliance, show her that it wasn't just him that liked it. He'd prove he'd never once tried to build her up falsely, only encouraged her because he believed in her. A few phone calls later, he had a space booked. The gallery was normally closed on Mondays, but was willing to rent the space out for special events. And this would be a special event. He went all-out because this wasn't just about her. This was about them. And he had to win her back.

He'd gotten in touch with Kate to collect email addresses for all of Amber's friends, and emailed Amber's dad to collect the family email addresses. Her dad had been very insistent that this was the kind of occasion her mother would want to attend. Bare had agreed. It seemed that having her mother recognize her as an artist could only be a good thing. He hadn't known how bad things were between Amber and her mother. He'd make it up to her. He'd do whatever it took to be with the woman he loved.

He snagged his cell and texted Kate, begging her to get Amber to the party. Kate responded immediately with: I'll get her to the party if you'll get Ian off my back. I'm a single female who wants to stay open to other male possibilities.

He replied: Done.

When his brother ventured back into the apartment, empty beer bottle and half-eaten bag of cheese puffs in hand, Barry told him, "You have to leave Kate alone. I promised her you would."

Ian moaned. "I'm in love with her. How can I leave her alone?"

"I'm sorry, but she's not in love with you."

Ian moaned again. Barry couldn't deal with the moaning. He had enough of his own misery to deal with. He tossed a Dancing Cow coupon at his brother. "Go drown your miseries."

Ian sulked out the door. Barry returned to his laptop, looking up realtor websites. He wanted to buy a house. One with wide open spaces and lots of light to display Amber's paintings. One that had room for an art studio. One he hoped to share with Amber.

~ ~ ~

The next day, Sunday, Barry went to a series of open houses in Eastman, Field Ridge, and Clover Park. Nothing seemed quite right. Some had open spaces, but not enough light. Some had light, but no open spaces, and few had the ideal place for an art studio. But then he got to a renovated colonial in Clover Park that looked from the outside like it had promise. It was well maintained, and the website description said it had been updated and had a detached garage. With some work, he thought, maybe the detached garage could become an art studio.

He walked in the open front door and was startled to see Kevin standing in the entryway wearing a suit.

The same Kevin that had punched him, twice, in an effort to take his part in the play.

"Kevin," he said.

Kevin handed him a brochure. "Hi, Bare. Let me know if you have any questions."

That was it? Hi, let me know if you have any questions?

"Actually, Kevin, yes, I do have a question." Barry wasn't going to just roll over and forget what happened. He hadn't confronted Kevin before because he'd been stuck in that wretched victim mode, but now with no Amber and a whole hell of a lot of misery in his life, he was fully prepared to confront him. He didn't care that there were other people milling about the house.

His voice rose in aggravation. "Why the hell would you ever think it was okay to punch someone over a part in a play?"

Kevin looked around uneasily. "I'm not sure what you mean."

In a rare fit of temper, Barry grabbed the guy by the tie and got in his face. "You know exactly what I mean. You punched me in the face, and I've got a mind to return the favor right here in front of your clients."

"I'm sorry, I'm sorry," Kevin said. "Please."

Barry dropped his hold on him. Kevin straightened his tie.

"You have exactly thirty seconds to come up with a real convincing apology," Barry warned.

"Not here," Kevin said. "Follow me."

Kevin led him outside away from the people milling around. "I'm very sorry, and I know I should've said that a lot sooner. I was jealous because…" He stared at the ground. "Zac was cheating on me. I know it wasn't with you, but every time he flirted with you it just felt so in my face, you know?"

Barry didn't reply. He still didn't think that excused violence.

"Zac always gave me so much attention when I was the lead, and then you were." Kevin blew out a breath. "I know you're the better actor. There's no excuse. I'm so sorry. Me, of all people, should know better. I've taken my share of punches."

Barry pressed his lips in a tight line. Seemed they had that in common.

"Yeah, okay," Barry finally said.

"What can I do for you?" Kevin asked. "You looking to buy a house? I can help you. I find out all the latest listings before they're open to the public. I could get you in early, so you'd avoid a bidding war."

"I don't know if I want you for a realtor," Barry said. "It just doesn't feel right handing over money to the guy that gave me two black eyes."

"You don't have to pay me," Kevin said. "I'll do it for no commission."

"I can't ask you to do that."

"It's the least I can do."

Barry shook his head, turned, and went back in the house. He started walking around, taking in the space.

Lots of large windows. Sunlight streaming in.

Kevin appeared at his side and set about a hard sell, pointing out all of the home's great features. And when Barry mentioned the need for an art studio, Kevin showed him the detached garage that had been used as a woodworking workshop.

"Do you like it?" Kevin asked. "Do you want to check with Amber first?"

"I do need to check in with her," Barry said. *Especially since we're not technically together.*

Kevin handed him his card. "Call me anytime for a second showing with her. No commission. I mean it."

Barry took the card. "All right. Thanks, Kevin." He turned to go.

"Are you going to do *Grease* next year?" Kevin asked.

Barry opened the front door, not bothering to turn around. "Sure am."

"I'll be in the front row cheering you on," Kevin said.

Barry turned. "You'll be on stage, right next to me, where you belong."

Kevin smiled. "Thanks, Bare."

~ ~ ~

Kate was literally driving Amber insane. Her sister spent the entire week bugging her morning, noon, and night about the party. Kate tried to convince her of the merits of such an event, emailed her articles on the benefits of a patron-sponsored art showing, and texted her repeated demands to go, even when they were sitting right next to each other.

Finally Amber had enough. The party was tomorrow, and Kate had reached a fever pitch of harassment.

"Kate, why do you care so much if I go to this stupid party?" she exclaimed.

Kate didn't bother looking up from her laptop. "Because I promised."

"Promised Bare?"

"Yes."

She sat next to her sister. "Why would you do that? Why would you take his side? I'm your sister."

Kate regarded her solemnly. "I want to see you happy. This will make you happy."

"How? My mother will be there."

"Who cares about her? Barry is who will make you happy. You're going."

Amber snorted. "You're going to have to drag me out of this apartment kicking and screaming to go to that party."

Kate raised a brow. "The idea has merit. I'll contact Steph and Daisy."

In the end, it was a note slipped under her door that night that finally got to her. It said: SUM Together (Bare + Amber) > SUM (NOT) Together (Bare + Amber).

Kate took one look at it and cried, "He's so romantic! He means you guys are more together than you are apart. Amber, if you don't go to this party, I swear I will never let you sleep again. I will keep you up every night playing my iBone."

Amber groaned. The iBone was a trombone on Kate's iPhone that she was completely obsessed with. She looked down at the sweet equation and felt her insides melt.

"I have to talk to Bare."

"Yay!" Kate squealed.

Amber took the equation with her across the hall and knocked on his door.

Bare answered looking a lot better than the last time she'd seen him. He'd shaved and had a close, cropped haircut with some spikes on top. She couldn't resist touching the spikes.

"Nice spikes," she said.

He smiled, a lopsided smile that pulled at her heart.

"I got your equation," she said. "Very clever."

"I meant it," he said in that growly voice of his that showed so much emotion.

"I know."

He stepped back. "Come in."

She stepped inside. "Where's Ian?"

"He went out for some food." He gestured to the sofa.

"I'd rather stand," she said, crossing her arms.

He wrapped his arms around her anyway. "Afraid I'll have my way with you?"

She shook her head. "It's just easier to talk if I'm

not, you know, in your lap."

He let her go and sat on the sofa. "Talk to me, love."

"Kate has been driving me insane about this party. Smart move on your part getting her involved."

He inclined his head.

"And while I love the idea of seeing my work in a gallery…" Her throat tightened, and she cleared it. "Bare, you can't just do whatever you think is best for me. I can't be with someone that doesn't give any consideration to my feelings. I don't like you going behind my back. I don't want you making decisions for me. This will only work if we're on the same page. You have to talk to me before you do stuff."

"But you said you liked surprises." His brows scrunched in confusion. "You like when I'm in charge. You respond very well to that."

Her cheeks flushed, and she shook her head. "That's different. Sex is…" She blew out a breath. "Okay, yes, I like when you take charge in the bedroom—"

"Not just the bedroom."

She held up a hand. "I like when you take charge when we're naked, okay?"

He nodded, looking pleased she'd conceded the point.

"And sometimes I like surprises. Little surprises. Like the bouquet of paintbrushes you gave me. Or a visit to the beach. Not you're-having-a-gallery-showing-and-your-estranged-mother-is-showing-up-to-witness-your-humiliation kind of surprise." She suddenly felt like she couldn't force out one more word. This was so hard to talk about. Her eyes welled up.

He stood and folded her in his arms. "It won't be humiliating. It will be a celebration of you and your work."

She sniffled and looked up at him. "You don't understand. She's a great artist who's *invited* to show her work in galleries. She thinks that's what this is, but it's not. It's my boyfriend had to pay the gallery to show my work. It's completely different!"

"No, it isn't. You're still a great artist."

She pulled away. "You just don't get it!"

This had all been a mistake. She thought she could go to the party, but she couldn't because she couldn't face her mother. She was nowhere near her mother's league, and she wasn't going to let her mother witness her failure.

She rushed to the door and yelped when he grabbed her from behind. Her back hit his warm chest just as his hands clamped on her hips. She grabbed his hands and tried to pry them off her. "Bare, knock it off."

His voice, low and close, whispered in her ear. "You said you wanted to talk, but all you're doing is running away. That's the second time you did that. We're going to the bedroom where I'm in charge."

She was so shocked her mind went absolutely blank, which gave him just enough time to sweep her off her feet and carry her into the bedroom.

~ ~ ~

Barry had his hands full of wild, struggling woman, but
he still managed to lock the door of his bedroom
before he set Amber gently on his bed. He'd intended
to pin her there and talk to her before having his way
with her, but she rolled quickly off the bed and stood
on the other side of it.

She jabbed a finger at him, her eyes wide. "I'm
leaving, and you can't stop me."

She was fast, but certainly no match for him in
size. Besides, he could easily block her path to the
door. He was closer to it. "I could stop you."

She grabbed a pillow and threw it at him before
making a break for it. He rounded the bed to block
her path when she suddenly bolted across the bed. He
managed to grab her by the ankles as she went over,
and she landed on the mattress on her belly with a
soft, "Oof." That worked.

"Bare!" she hollered. "Let me go!"

She kicked at him, forcing him to grab both ankles
and hold them pinned together out of self-
preservation.

"Not until we finish talking," he said.

She struggled like crazy, wiggling and getting
nowhere, her curvy ass in shorts tempting him to
touch. Her T-shirt rode up her back, exposing smooth
skin and the dip of her lower back that he wanted to
lick.

"This is ridiculous!" she hollered.

He looked at her wiggling ass. "This is hot."

She stilled. A beat passed. When she didn't move, he released one ankle to cup his hand on her ass. She didn't protest. He nudged her legs apart and slipped a hand between her thighs. She jolted at the touch, always so responsive to him, and he felt how hot she was. He stifled a groan and had a quick battle with himself—talk and then sex. No, sex fixes everything. Yes, sex, sex, sex.

He had to touch her. His instinct won out, and he covered her, resting his weight on his arms as he pinned her beneath him.

"Amber," he growled. "You know I love you."

She turned her face toward his, resting her cheek on the mattress. "I know," she said softly.

"I'm sorry I screwed things up inviting your mother, but I'm not sorry about the gallery party. That wasn't done to hurt you. I did that because of how much I love you. Sometimes I go overboard, I know that. I just...okay, listen—"

"Hard not to listen when you're on top of me."

He rolled off her and pulled her in close so they were side by side facing each other. He wrapped his arms around her, still not sure if she'd make another break for it. She relaxed in his arms, and he let out a breath of relief.

He pushed her hair over her ear and cradled her face. "I'm probably going to screw up again, going overboard, making some elaborate gesture, that's who I am, but I'll try really hard to remember to check in with you. Just don't…" He choked up and crushed her to him. "Don't run away from me," he whispered.

She whispered something back, but he couldn't catch the words with her pressed so close. He loosened his hold.

"What did you say?" he asked.

"I said there's no point in running away from you because you'll just chase me down." She gave him an impish smile.

He couldn't help but smile back as his heart filled with love. "That's right, and I'll take you to my bed every time. Remember that, wench."

She snuggled in closer and wrapped her leg over his hip, a position that drained all the blood from his brain in favor of a more important part. His hand cupped her ass, pushing her closer to where he so desperately needed her.

"I know I'm a chicken," she said, her eyes fixed on some point over his shoulder, "but I can't face seeing my mom. It's just going to ruin the whole night. I'm already queasy just thinking about it."

He wanted to solve this problem as quickly as possible so he could solve his other throbbing problem pronto. He loosened his hold on her, leaving space between their bodies to allow for some brain function. "She's already here in a hotel in the city."

She stared at his chest. "How do you know?"

"She got in touch to see if she could stop by the gallery and drop off some postcards and prints of her own." She stiffened, and he rubbed her arm, trying to soothe her pain. "I told her no, it was your showing, and only one artist would be featured."

She blew out a breath. "Tell her she can't come to the party."

"Do you really think that's a good idea?"

She raised her chin, finally looking him in the eye. "Yes. I don't want her there. You never should've invited her."

"But she came all this way. She really wanted to see you."

Amber went quiet. "It's me or her. We won't both be there."

He understood her reluctance, just as he understood that she needed to face her mother at some point and say whatever she needed to get off her chest. He stroked her hair, studying her, trying to think of the right words.

Her eyes snapped to his. "Don't feel sorry for me. I'm fine. I turned out just fine without her."

"I know you did. And I don't feel sorry for you, well, I do feel bad you didn't have your mom but...what about this? What if you meet her someplace ahead of the party? She'll get to see you. You'll get a chance to talk. And then you tell her not to go to the party."

She dropped her eyes to his chest. "A pre-party preemptive move."

"Yes."

She bit her lip. Tears glistened in her eyes, and his chest ached in sympathy.

She looked up at him, her eyes watery. "Will you come with me?" she asked in a choked voice.

"Yes."

She sniffled. "Can you arrange it?"

"I'll take care of everything."

And then she broke down in tears. He held her through big, heaving sobs until she was all cried out and sleeping peacefully in his arms. He relaxed for the first time in weeks. He'd help her through this, and then at the gallery, he'd make his big move.

~ ~ ~

Amber's stomach was churning the next morning, and she couldn't eat even one bite of food. Kate brought her more lukewarm chamomile tea, which did nothing to ease her nerves. How did one prepare for seeing their mother after fifteen years? She just hoped she was strong enough to get through it.

Bare had called to tell her it was all arranged. Her mother would take the train in to Clover Park. Bare was picking her up, and they'd meet at the park. It was a good plan. Somehow Bare knew, without her saying, that she didn't want her mother at her apartment. And she didn't want to be stuck at some restaurant where there could be an ugly scene. The park was neutral territory.

She drove to the park right off Main Street a little early, hoping sitting in the park would ease her nerves. She sat in the gazebo, their meeting place, and closed her eyes. She could hear kids playing in the small fenced-in playground. Their happy shrieks as they went down the slide, the creaky sound of the swings, the small rocking horses going back and forth. And, in brief moments of quiet, she could hear the birds in the trees. Somehow the birdsong relaxed her like nothing else. Maybe it was because it made her think of Bare.

As much as she might hate it, she still had that one little needy part of her that despite everything wanted to see her mother. Even if it was just to finally say goodbye. She hadn't said goodbye when she was thirteen, hadn't known it was goodbye. She'd been surly and miserable about the forced visit to her dad's house, not knowing it was just the beginning of her misery.

But she wasn't that miserable thirteen-year-old girl anymore. She would say a real goodbye and put the ugliness between her and her mother behind her.

A short while later, she saw Bare, his familiar loping gait walking toward her, a petite woman with red hair by his side. He raised a hand in greeting at her and smiled. She slowly raised her hand, unable to summon a smile. She stood, and then there she was, her mother, right in front of her. She seemed smaller than Amber remembered. Her hair was short and dyed red from its original blond. Her face had lines that hadn't been there before, but she'd still know that face anywhere. She had an artist's eye, inherited from her artist mother.

Her mother smiled tightly. "Hi, Amber. It's good

to see you."

Amber couldn't say the same. She felt Bare squeezing her hand, a show of support, and she managed to say something. "Hi."

Her mom raised her arms, hesitated, then hugged Amber. Amber couldn't hug her back. She backed away and sat on the gazebo bench.

Her mother sat a short distance away. Bare stood uncertainly.

Amber looked to Bare. "You don't have to stay."

He studied her. "I'll be right over there." He pointed to a park bench a short distance away.

She nodded. That lump was back in her throat. She really didn't want to cry in front of her mother. She was twenty-eight years old, an adult that supported herself, she shouldn't need anything from this woman.

"Congratulations on your gallery showing," her mother said.

Amber swallowed. "I don't want you there."

"I see."

Amber turned, seeking out Bare's reassuring presence. He sat at an angle away from them, so he wasn't staring, but could still see her if she signaled to him.

She turned back to her mother. Her mother's head was bowed, and she had her hands gripped tightly in her lap.

"I'm sorry I missed seeing you grow up," her mother said.

"That was your own fault."

"I suppose I owe you some kind of explanation."

"I don't think anything can explain abandoning your only child."

"I sent you cards."

Amber snorted. "Wow. You're still the same old selfish woman I remember. Even your apology is full of how you're not to blame."

Her mother spoke so quietly, Amber had to lean forward to hear. "Your father was suffocating me. He didn't want an artist for a wife, he wanted someone that stood by him, smiling and nodding at stuffy faculty dinners. I was losing myself."

"So you got a divorce. So does half the country. That doesn't mean you move to a different continent."

"I had to test myself, broaden my horizons, remember who I was. He remarried so quickly, and I was still just treading water. I really did intend it to be two weeks in Paris. But then I met someone, a fabulous mentor who saw greatness in me. I had to stay and see how far I could go. I was in a glorious creative period the likes of which I hadn't felt since before you were born. I had to stay. And then I started getting gallery showings. People were buying my work. They loved me over there. How could I leave all that behind?"

"How could you leave me behind?" Amber asked, hating the way her voice came out small. "I could've lived in Paris with you, learned at your side. You knew I loved painting."

"I didn't feel like I could do both. Be a great artist

and a great mother. And your dad and Maxine were doing a good job with Kate. I thought you'd be better off there."

"And no phone calls? No visits? Nothing?"

"I thought it would be confusing for you. You had a new family. I didn't want you to be upset at the end of our visit."

"So you just let me be upset all the time."

"Your dad sent me pictures. You seemed happy."

Tears burned her eyes. "I can smile for a picture without actually feeling happy."

Her mother went quiet. The hard truth was it was convenient for her mother to think her daughter was happy with her new family. Her mother wanted that to be true to absolve her of any responsibility.

Amber listened to the birds and the young kids playing nearby. There was nothing left to say. Her mother didn't have anything near resembling a good excuse for abandoning Amber. No missing limbs, no mental illness, nothing. Just having a great time as an artist in Paris.

Amber stood.

"I would still like to see your art," her mom said.

"I'll send you a picture," Amber said. "I'll even smile next to it. That should make you feel better."

"Okay," her mother said. "I deserve that. And if you really don't want me there, I won't go."

"Thank you. I guess this is goodbye."

Her mother stood. "I'll be staying at a hotel in the city all week if you change your mind about seeing me." She hesitated. "If you like, we could take in the Met or the Museum of Modern Art."

Amber's eyes filled at the invitation because it was far too little, far too late. "Goodbye, Mom."

She walked straight to Bare, who jumped up and folded her into his arms. He leaned down to her ear. "Are you okay?"

She sniffled. "I will be."

He pulled back and studied her face. "What can I do?"

"Just take her back to the train station. I'm going home. I'm exhausted."

"Okay, love," he said, cradling her face, wiping away a tear. "I'll see you tonight for your big debut."

She nodded and hurried away to her car.

~ ~ ~

After another long cry and a nap, Amber felt like she could handle the art gallery party. She might not have any commercial success as an artist, but she was proud of her work. She would walk into that gallery, head held high, and be proud.

Steph and Daisy arrived early, so they could all get ready together. Daze had said she'd drive them all to the city and be their designated driver.

Daze handed her some funky feather earrings to go with her favorite little black dress. Her friend wore a maternity dress with her hair up and a few tendrils hanging down. Steph was attempting to do something with Kate's hair. Even through all of Kate's protests about looking ridiculous while Steph used a curling iron on her hair, Steph kept smiling. Amber was becoming suspicious.

"Steph, stop that insane smiling," Amber said. "You look like one of those creepy clowns."

Steph laughed. "I'm just happy. It's a party in your honor!"

Amber slid some chunky silver bracelets on. "I'm not sure why that makes you smile so much, but okay."

Steph hid another smile.

"I'm gonna smack that smile off your face in a minute," Amber threatened.

Steph ducked behind Kate.

"This was really nice of Barry," Daze said from the bed, where she was now stretched out, lounging on the pillows. "I'll say one thing about him. When he sets his mind to something, he goes big. Did you guys see the crazy tricycle races at last summer's street fair?"

"I missed last summer's street fair," Amber said.

"Me too," Steph said. "What happened?"

Daze's eyes danced with laughter. "Barry took over the lead, led the kids on a merry chase, and nearly knocked over the tent."

Amber could picture that perfectly.

"And his shop," Daze said. "The way he goes all-out as the cow? The way he went all-out as a pirate?"

Amber slowly turned. "I feel like you guys are trying to tell me something. Is Bare going all-out in some way I need to be prepared for?"

"Absolutely not," Kate said. "We would never say that."

"Why wouldn't you say that?" Amber asked. "Did Bare swear you to secrecy?"

Kate stepped away from Steph and fluffed her hair. Only half of it was curled. "Well, I'm all ready. Excuse me while I seek out an appropriate color lipstick for such an event."

Her sister's speech always became more formal when she was nervous. Kate quickly left. Her sister didn't even wear lipstick. Amber narrowed her eyes at Steph and then Daze.

Steph and Daze exchanged a look.

"Tell me," Amber said.

Steph put an arm around her shoulders. "Relax, this is your night. You are the star."

"You're scaring me," Amber said.

Daze sat up and swung her legs over the side of the bed. "You know how Bare was a swashbuckling pirate and dipped you and kissed you in front of everyone?"

"Yeah."

"It's sorta like that," Daze said. "Nothing bad. I promise. And if you don't want to kiss him"—she waved a hand in the air—"just slap him across the face and say 'fresh!'"

Amber giggled. "All right."

A short while later, they headed outside, and Amber stopped short. A black limo was waiting with a uniformed chauffeur.

"Ladies," the man said, opening the back door. "I'm Ken. I'll be your driver this evening."

Kate pushed her forward. "Come on. It's for us."

She couldn't believe Bare had rented them a limo for their ride into the city. "Is Bare in there?"

Kate shook her head. "He and Ian went early to set up."

"Let's go!" Steph said, charging ahead.

They got inside, where champagne was chilling along with a platter of chocolate-covered strawberries. She felt herself melting. He really did go big. And he'd apologized. More than once. And that sweet equation, and the way he'd been there for her with her mom.

"Mmm…" Daze said. "Hand me one of those strawberries. I've got such a craving."

They drank champagne, except for Daisy on account of her pregnancy, and devoured the strawberries. By the time they arrived, Amber was in high spirits.

She stepped into the gallery and gasped. Even knowing it was a party and not an actual showing, the effect of seeing her paintings framed and hanging on the gallery's walls like a real artist's work was amazing. Phenomenal. Dream-come-true life-changing moment.

She felt shaky all of a sudden. "Guys…" She grabbed Steph's arm. "Walk with me. I want to see them all."

"This is amazing," Daze said. "Look at the gorgeous black frames."

And the matting.

And the tuxedoed waiters.

A waiter arrived at their side with a platter full of coconut shrimp. They all took one. Amber glanced around. She saw her father and her stepmother, the cast of *The Pirates of Penzance* huddled together, some friends from work, Ian, but where was Bare? Where was the man behind this crazy event? The man she loved with all her heart. She suddenly wanted to see him desperately.

Her dad and stepmother approached. "Congratulations," Maxine said. "Your father and I are impressed."

"Your work is quite prolific," her dad said, which Amber figured was the best compliment she'd ever get from someone who thought art was a waste of time.

"Thank you," she said.

"Kate, have you been satisfied with your time with Amber?" Maxine asked.

"Yes, Mom," Kate replied.

Amber wasn't sure if they were talking about the visit, her no longer virginal status, or her studies. She always felt confused with her family.

"Your mother wanted to see you," her dad said, sounding almost apologetic.

Amber took a deep breath. "I saw her. I said goodbye. She won't be coming tonight."

"Oh," her dad said. "I guess that's for the best. If that's what you want."

"That's what I want," she said firmly.

"I met your boyfriend," her dad said. "Very nice. Very respectful."

She smiled. "Where is he?"

"He was looking at your paintings," Maxine said. "I'm sure he's still around."

She turned to her friends. "Should we look at the paintings?"

"Lead the way," Steph said.

They walked to the first painting. Her favorite, the dragon. She smiled. She'd missed this painting. She should've kept it on her wall at home.

"I really like this one," Kate said. "Can I buy it?"

"I think I might buy it back," Amber said. "I miss it."

They moved on to the next several paintings. She felt like she was greeting old friends. Hello, red and black abstract. Hello, angsty painting from my past. Hello, flames on clouds. Steph and Daze kept up a steady stream of chatter, complimenting her, making her feel less self-conscious about her gallery showing being arranged by her boyfriend. It was nice to share her art with all of her family and friends. But she still hadn't seen the man behind it all.

She turned to Kate. "Do you see Bare?"

Kate looked all around. "No, but I know he's here. I'm sure we'll see him soon. He was very busy getting set up for this event."

They reached the end of a hallway in front of a series of three paintings. A small white card held the title and artist. It was Elation. The first painting had polka dots exploding, the second bouncing marshmallows, the third a serene sunset. It was very different from her usual work, whimsical and more naturalistic. She remembered painting it right after selling her first painting on eArt. She'd been elated. Ignorantly so, but still. The feeling behind it had been real.

"I don't get it," Kate said.

"It's fun," Daze said.

"I like the sunset," Steph said.

"It perfectly captures emotion," a woman's voice said. Amber turned. It was Delilah.

"Hello, darling," Delilah said, kissing Amber on both cheeks. "How much for the series?"

"Oh, this is a private collection," Amber said. "For display only."

"I'll give you a thousand dollars," Delilah said.

"Sold!" Kate said with a quick jab to Amber's ribs.

Delilah smiled. "Wonderful! I own a small gallery in South Norfolk. I'm going to look around. See what else catches my eye."

Delilah moved on to the next painting, and then the next, with Kate at her side throwing out numbers to her.

Amber watched them go, feeling a little dizzy. Had she actually just sold a painting to a real gallery? She exchanged an amazed look with Steph and Daze. Then Steph squealed, grabbed her, and the three of them did a bouncing hug.

~ ~ ~

Barry hung back, waiting in the wings so to speak, giving Amber a chance to take in all of her work hanging in the gallery space. She had her friends close by, had done a gallery tour, and was now chatting with the cast and crew from the show. She was smiling.

The moment didn't get any better than this. He nodded to Ian, who dimmed the lights. Birdsong played over the speakers. It was the birdsong from his alarm clock. A reminder of their mornings together at his place.

He stepped out, heading toward her. Her cheeks and chest were flushed. Yup, she remembered. He'd worn a suit because this was one damn important occasion.

The effect of being close to her again, knowing she'd forgiven him, was overwhelming. That curve-fitting dress, the heels, the funky jewelry, her scent, a slight hint of roses from her shampoo, those pink streaks in her blond hair. He couldn't resist touching her. He settled his hands on her waist, holding her there.

"Are you enjoying your showing?" he asked.

She grinned. "Delilah just bought a series of my paintings for her gallery."

"She did? I didn't know she had a gallery. That's great! Congratulations!"

She beamed up at him, and he wished he could always see her that happy. He would do his best to make it happen.

"So what's with the birdsong?" she asked.

He raised a hand to stop the music. He turned back to her. "I'm wooing you."

Her brows scrunched in confusion.

Steph giggled nearby. "Woo."

"Shh," Daze said, pulling Steph a short distance away.

He raised a hand for attention. "Everyone, I want to thank you for coming to the first of what I'm sure will be many Amber Lewis art showings. I've just been told we've had a sale!"

Everyone applauded.

He raised a hand. "I'll be keeping some of the paintings on display at the home I hope we will soon buy together as husband and wife."

Amber's hand clutched his arm. "Bare—"

"Just let me say this." He turned to her. "Amber, I've been in love with you since the day we met."

The crowd awwed in chorus.

She shook her head. "I was with Rick then," she said quietly.

"I know. I didn't plan it. It just happened."

He pulled her closer and spoke quietly just for her. "I'm sorry I misled you about the paintings. I won't ever mislead you again."

She blinked rapidly. "Oh, Bare. I could never stay mad at you. You're just too damn loveable."

He grinned. "I am?"

She smiled, and it was like all the birds broke into

song at once. "You are."

"Did you hear that?" he asked the crowd. "She loves me!"

Everyone applauded.

"I found the perfect house for us," he said. "It's in Clover Park. It has these huge windows with lots of light, room for an art studio, lots of wall space to hang your paintings. I can't wait for you to see it."

"I can't wait to see it too. Wait, did you buy it?"

"No. I won't do anything behind your back. I learn from my mistakes." He grabbed her hands. "I can't even tell you how much..." His voice broke and came out in a low growl "I've missed you these past weeks."

She threw herself in his arms. "I missed you too. So, so much."

He held her tight, so relieved she'd forgiven him, so happy she was here for her gallery party.

Kate came over and wrapped her arms around both of them. "You're welcome."

Amber pulled away and laughed. "Thank you, Kate, for your valiant efforts to get me here."

He turned. "Yes, thank you, Kate. Now, if you could just back up a bit. I have a gift for Amber."

Kate stepped back, smiling like crazy. Amber looked a little nervous. He hoped she'd like it. What was he thinking? Of course she would. It was her favorite thing.

He signaled a waiter in the back who stopped in front of Amber with a large wheel of cheese wrapped with a red ribbon.

She stared at it. "You're giving me cheese?"

He bounced on the balls of his feet. "Yes."

She took the offered cheese wheel and staggered under its weight. He reached out to help her balance the load. Everyone was watching and whispering.

"Bare," she said, looking at him across the giant wheel of cheese, "why are you giving me cheese?"

He grinned. "Because I know you like cheese."

She stared at it. "I do like cheddar. Okay. Thank you."

He bit back a laugh. "Eat it soon, okay?"

"Okay."

"Why don't we start right now?"

"Um, okay."

He inclined his head to a nearby table. "C'mon."

She followed him to a table, where he set the wheel of cheese down. "Can you guess what happens when you eat your way to the bottom?"

"I get a stomachache?"

He laughed. "No," he said slowly. He got down on one knee and held the cheese up to her.

She looked at him uncertainly. Then she started to lean down like she was going to take a bite. He flipped the wheel over so she could see the treasure he'd buried there.

"Amber, will you marry me?"

She reached into the small space he'd carved out in the cheese wheel and pulled out her diamond engagement ring.

"My life is never going to be humdrum with you, is

it?" she asked.

He grinned. "No, it isn't."

"What's your answer?" Ian hollered.

"Yes!" Amber slid the ring on her finger. Everyone cheered.

He set the wheel on the table, grabbed her, dipped her, and kissed her. They heard a few catcalls, and he brought her back upright. She threw her arms around him and hugged him tight. He never, ever wanted to let her go. His body went on full alert, urging him to have her again. Soon.

She leaned up on tiptoe and growled in his ear, "Bare, here, now."

He went stock-still, his only response a tightening of his hands on her waist. Then he moved into action. "Amber left a painting in my car. Be right back everyone."

They ran, laughing, to a coatroom way in the back of the gallery, with no coats and no lock on the door, and came together for the first time as future husband and wife.

EPILOGUE

Amber slow danced with Bare at their wedding reception, wearing her pink wedding dress that perfectly matched the pink streaks in her hair. She was now Amber Lewis-Furnukle. Kate was determined to snag her own Furnukle and had been throwing herself at Bare's brother Daniel, a straitlaced military guy, all night. Ian was beside himself, frequently interrupting Kate and Daniel to break up their slow dances. Daniel seemed to find the whole thing amusing.

They married in October because fall was her favorite season. It also gave her time in her art studio in their new home to prepare her wedding gift for him. They'd bought that colonial house in Clover Park with Kevin's help, of all people, for a steal. Kevin had tried to decline a commission, but Bare paid him anyway, no hard feelings. That was how big Bare's heart was. She'd painted a big heart and hung it in their home as her own love poem to him to show what she loved best about him.

But his favorite—as he told her by thanking her

profusely with regular gifts of new paintbrushes, paints, and canvases—was the collection of six birds she painted as a wedding gift. She'd taken pictures of rare finds he was excited about on some of their morning birding excursions and recreated them on canvas. It was his wheel of cheese.

Bare spun her around the dance floor as the song changed to a fast beat and the pink tulle of her wedding gown floated around her. She caught glimpses of their families, friends, the cast from the show that brought them together, and even her mother. Bare had insisted she be invited. He convinced Amber that she didn't have to be best friends with her mother, but it was still important to acknowledge her as family. She'd dragged her feet, but in the end, decided he was right. Her decision was made easier by the fact that she got along so well with Bare's mom, a sweet, affectionate woman, who frequently invited Amber to lunch and shopping. She felt like she'd gained a new mom in the marriage.

Amber hadn't expected her mother to show at the wedding after the way they'd left things, but she had. She was trying. Amber knew she would never feel close to her mother, but what they had was enough. Amber was at peace with it, finally able to let go of all the anger she'd held onto for so long.

Her eye caught on Steph's date, who was doing *The Running Man* while Steph slowly backed away. Dave Olsen was a middle school math teacher Steph had met at a teacher's conference last August. Amber wanted to tell her, *Hang in there. You never know when a guy will go from geek to total stud,* but then Bare spun her around again and, as if he sensed the direction of her thoughts, slid his hands around her waist and pulled her close.

"Amber," he growled, and just that one word had her throbbing. It was the fierce, growly voice, which could mean different things depending on the situation, but *always* meant love. "I love you."

She met his warm brown eyes and beamed. "I love you too."

He pulled her close again and spoke directly in her ear. "Amber," he growled.

This time his voice held a different note. One that indicated he wanted something from her. She tried to pull away, but he had her tight.

She felt herself flush. "Please don't say it."

"Here," he demanded.

"No, there's too many people. It's too embarrassing."

"Come on," he coaxed. "Please. For your husband."

He'd begged her for this ever since they'd planned their wedding. She gave in with a sigh. He knew the moment he won because he released her, stepped back, and smiled.

And then she did an Irish jig for him.

"I love you, wench!" he hollered before joining in.

The crowd separated to clap and cheer them on. She kicked up her heels, surprising him with the move.

He threw back his head and laughed. Then he did the same, kicking up his heels, and took the lead. She stayed at his side, keeping up, thanks to the lessons Jasmine had given her a few weeks ago. Ian joined in, then Kate in an awkward robot fashion, then Zac, spry on his feet. Until everyone was on the dance floor, clapping and dancing along.

Why had she ever thought they were so different?

They were just two hearts at play by day. Two bodies entwined by night. And morning and afternoon.

Two souls mated for life.

~THE END~

Thanks for reading *Almost in Love*. I hope you enjoyed it! The next books in The Clover Park STUDS Series, *Almost Married* and *Almost Over It*, are out now!

Turn the page for a sneak peek at Steph and Dave's story, *Almost Married*, available now!

ALMOST MARRIED

KYLIE GILMORE

Mathlete vs. rock star…?

Stephanie Moore's boyfriend, the adorably geeky math teacher, Dave Olsen, has husband material written all over him. One teensy problem—she's still technically married. When she demands a divorce from the rock star husband she hasn't seen in five years, he shows up on her doorstep wanting a second chance.

Dave is so in love with Steph, he's already researching diamond rings. If only he didn't have to compete with the famous Griffin Huntley. Griffin is going all out to win Steph back, and Dave plans to fight for his woman. A mathlete vs. a rock star? Statistically speaking—oh, the hell with it. Game on!

CHAPTER ONE

Stephanie Moore's boyfriend of six weeks was a perfect gentleman. It was time to fix that.

"You could spend the night tonight," Steph whispered in Dave Olsen's ear as they slow danced at her friend Amber Lewis's (now Lewis-Furnukle) wedding reception. They were in a gorgeous mansion owned by the town of Clover Park, Connecticut, that was frequently rented out for special events.

Dave startled at her words, veering right suddenly and stomping on her foot.

"Ow!"

"Sorry!"

Steph cringed and stepped out of the danger zone. The man was a solid six foot two, and her poor toes couldn't take much more "dancing" with him.

"Could you get me more champagne?" she asked. "No, make it vodka."

"No problem," he said, pushing up his black-rimmed glasses. "Be right back." He stopped suddenly and kissed her cheek. "Sorry about all the toe crunching."

She waved that away. "No worries."

He left to get her drink. Steph took a seat with a sigh, smoothed out her lavender bridesmaid dress, and watched Amber and Bare slow dancing. No toe crunching there. They moved beautifully together. Bare whispered something in Amber's ear, and she giggled. Steph wondered what it would take to get Dave to step it up a notch in the sex department, as in, maybe they could have some. At thirty-two, Steph was way past playing hard-to-get, and Dave, at thirty, really should've taken the hint by now. Subtlety seemed to be lost on him. She'd resorted to cleavage-revealing tops and multiple (casual) peek-a-boo bend-overs both for the frontal and rear views, with no effect. And when she'd grabbed his ass a few times during some marathon makeout sessions, he'd merely chuckled. Not exactly the effect she'd been going for.

Dave returned to her side with a glass of champagne and a vodka with lime. Thank God. She downed the vodka.

"Is that for you?" she asked, pointing to the champagne.

"I wasn't sure which one you wanted, so I got both." He took the seat next to her. "I'm not having anything since I'm driving."

Steph downed the champagne too. Unfortunately, while it did help her forget about her poor crushed toes stuffed into silver Louboutin stilettos, it also had the effect of making her horny. She looked at Dave, who returned her gaze steadily. He had beautiful deep blue eyes behind those black-rimmed glasses. He was a middle school math teacher—a sweet, geeky, perfect gentleman. Dave was definitely not her usual type. But when he kissed her, he put heart and soul into it, and it was scorching hot. She'd found that out after their first date. The problem was—his hands never roamed. She would really like them to roam. It had been too long she'd gone untouched. So long she was almost pure again. A virgin in reverse. She giggled to herself.

"Would you like to dance again?" he asked. "I'm better at the slow songs."

"That's not saying much," she blurted. *Inhibitions down, honesty up.*

He frowned, and she kissed that frowny face. "Let's do the no-pants boogie," she said.

At his confused expression, she made a small poke-the-finger-in-the-hole-multiple-times gesture at him. Still confused. The hell with subtlety. "Let's do it."

His eyes widened behind his glasses. "You mean like…" His face flushed, and he glanced around at the people dancing nearby. "Like, right now?"

She smiled at him dreamily, running her fingers through the silky dark brown hair at the nape of his neck. "Yes."

He tugged on his tie. "But wouldn't you be more comfortable in a bed?"

Dave was so sweet, thinking of her comfort. She nipped his earlobe, and he jolted.

"After the reception, okay?" she whispered in his ear before she licked his earlobe and blew lightly across it. He held himself very still, and she wasn't sure if she'd pushed him away or reeled him in. "A bed sounds great," she added.

"That would be acceptable to me as well," he said in a strained voice.

Just then the reception got rowdy as a disco ball spun and the DJ blasted "Saturday Night Fever" by the Bee Gees. She laughed, watching Bare's antics with his John Travolta imitation. The man was a natural performer. He grabbed Amber and spun her onto the dance floor with him. Everyone flocked to join them.

"Come on," she said, slipping off her heels.

Dave followed her onto the dance floor, giving her lots of space as she danced with one finger pointing up and down in the air. He smiled, just watching her. She boogied all around him, using him much like a stripper pole. *This works much better,* she thought, *less toe crunching.* One disco song followed another and Dave made an excellent pole—sturdy, steady, warm. She was all over him, spinning around him, leaning into him, hanging off him, wrapping her leg around his and swaying. But then "YMCA" by The Village People played, and she had to stop working the pole to do the hand motions.

She'd just gotten to the "A" when he took her hands in his, bringing them down from over her head to the front of her. "Steph, meeting you was the best thing that ever happened to me."

She smiled and kept dancing. "Thanks, Dave!" she

hollered over the music. She did the Y again and the M, missed the C, and jumped in again with the A.

"I really mean that." A lock of hair fell over his forehead.

She smiled and pushed his hair back into its side part just as the song hit the chorus. The crowd joined in, singing at the top of their lungs, drowning out Dave's next words.

"What? I can't hear you!" Steph shouted above the crowd.

"I said I love you!" he shouted.

"Oh!" She stopped dancing in her surprise. Before she could reply, he kissed her. His hands cradled her face as his mouth claimed hers in that slow, thorough way of his. The rowdy music and dancing faded away as heat flooded her. His tongue mated with hers, and she fisted her hands in his hair, wishing fervently his hands would move to other very interested parts of her body.

He released her, and she gazed at him—at his side part, his sweet turned-on face, right down to his navy suit with the New Balance sneakers. Through the haze of champagne and vodka and lust, it hit her with the same shock as her evil cat, Loki, leaping on her head in the middle of the night. Dave was a keeper. She loved him.

She opened her mouth to tell him so. He put his finger to her lips. "You don't have to say anything. I don't expect you to say it just because I did. I just wanted you to know."

She bit his finger.

"Ow!"

"I love you too, you big dork." That earned her another kiss.

Dave pulled back, and they gazed into each other's eyes. She beamed at him.

He grinned. "Fantastic."

"Yes!" Then she danced some more, using him as her personal stripper pole again. She was five foot ten and loved that she could actually look up at him without the heels. It made her feel less Amazon-like. He watched her with half-hooded eyes. She couldn't wait for after the reception. She was sure Dave would be just as slow and thorough in bed as he was when he kissed her. That could be very, very good. Many disco songs and a lot of champagne later, she left the reception hand-in-hand with Dave.

She floated on a happy cloud as Dave pulled her along to his car, practically running. Boy, someone was in a hurry. She giggled to herself. Something was nagging at her brain. Like a hornet circling her head, waiting to sting. Something she needed to tell Dave.

She frowned. Griffin. She needed to tell him about Griffin.

Dave opened the car door for her, but before she could get in, he pressed her against the side of the car and gave her a scorching kiss that made her want to rip his suit off and muss up his neat hair. Just when she was wrapping her leg around his, he broke the kiss.

She put her leg down. "I like your enthusiasm,"

she told him, planting a smacking kiss on his clean-shaven cheek. He turned, meeting her lips for another scorching kiss, and she forgot all about Griffin.

He stepped back, and she wobbled a bit.

His eyebrows scrunched down adorably. "How much have you had to drink?"

She'd lost count. This lovely tuxedoed waiter had been hovering around the dance floor. He always seemed to be there when her glass was empty. "Mostly champagne. I'm fine. Let's go back to my place. It's time you saw the inside." She giggled over her little joke. Dave would see the inside of her apartment and her. Yay!

He nodded slowly, looking a little too serious for her giddy state. He loved her! She loved him! Tonight was the night!

They drove the few blocks to an old Victorian in Clover Park that had been converted into apartments. She grabbed his hand and led him to her upstairs apartment. Once inside, she launched herself into his arms. "Take me, Dave, I'm yours."

~ ~ ~

Dave groaned as he wrapped his arms around Steph and wished he didn't have a conscience. He'd been hard from the moment he'd seen Steph in this curve-fitting dress with the stiletto heels. His eyes had done multiple tours of her ample cleavage, her narrow waist, and the curve of her hips leading down to those long legs in stilettos. Honestly, he'd been hard from the very first moment they met at that teachers' conference. Steph taught fifth grade and had attended his workshop on preparing fifth graders for middle school with the new math standards. Steph was gorgeous—long, silky brown hair, hazel eyes, full pouty lips, and that body. Any guy would want her. But the biggest turn-on for him was her brain. Steph had graduated *summa cum laude* from Columbia, which meant an SAT score above 2100. Their children would be beautiful and smart.

But he'd taken things slow because, after a few encounters in his past that left him feeling unsatisfied, he'd decided he would only sleep with a woman if they loved each other. Not like when he'd slept with Sherri after two dates, only to discover her divorce was actually a separation that her husband was unaware they were having. And definitely not like when he'd been the rebound guy for Lisa, which he'd discovered after a hot all-night marathon of sex. She'd informed him in a note on his nightstand that he'd been the perfect antidote to her ex's sleaziness, and her faith in men had been restored. *Nice guy strikes again*, he thought wryly. He'd restored her faith so well that she'd left him and ventured back into the dating pool.

In any case, waiting for a meaningful encounter hadn't been too difficult. He tended to collect more women friends than girlfriends because he was the guy women confided in but didn't feel *that way* about. Tonight, to his delight, he'd discovered that what he'd hoped for between him and Steph was, in fact, true.

She was smiling up at him, waiting he supposed for him to "take" her, but her eyes weren't focused, and her speech earlier had been slightly slurred. He stroked her hair and let himself imagine for a moment her hair spread out on a pillow as he drove into her. He clamped down on that thought. *Ice bath, infinite snowballs heading his way, parent-teacher conferences.* That worked. He loved his job, even loved the rowdy middle school students, but dealing with the parents, especially those that didn't understand why Bobby couldn't get an A without turning in any homework, were the worst part of his job.

Gently, he set Steph a foot away from him. He looked around her apartment for the first time. He'd declined Steph's previous invitations to come up for a cup of coffee, which always followed a goodnight kiss while she squeezed his ass, because he wanted to be sure it was more than a one-time hookup. Finally, they were on the same page. If only Steph wasn't sloshed when he'd discovered she loved him too. Steph's apartment looked like those Pottery Barn catalogs his sister was forever poring over—wood coffee table with a silver bowl full of fake oranges, a red velvet blanket thrown over one side of a beige sofa.

He reached down to stroke a gray tabby cat that was rubbing against his leg. Steph's dress hit the floor. He jerked upright.

She was killing him. She looked like a lingerie model—light purple strapless bra with matching lace panties, still wearing the heels that screamed *I am very fuckable*. Her words rang through his head, *Take me, take me, take me.*

He grabbed the blanket from the sofa and covered her with it, wishing with every fiber of his being that he'd taken the opportunity to get her into bed before. He mentally slapped himself. What had he been thinking? Who cared about meaningful sex when a guy like him had a chance with a stunning (and smart) woman like her? For a smart guy, that had been a really stupid move.

"Da-aa-ave, I'm too hot for a blanket," she said as he guided her toward a half-open door that he figured was her bedroom.

"I know."

Ice and snow, ice and snow.

He gently pushed her onto the bed. The blanket parted in front, and he focused on her feet. Those slender feet in heels.

"I love you, David Olsen," Steph said in a soft breathy voice that made him break out in a sweat.

Maybe he could sober her up with coffee. He berated himself for bringing her that vodka when she'd asked. He glanced up at her face. Her eyes were already closing.

"I love you too," he said in a husky voice.

He pulled off the heels and stroked the top of her feet, feeling guilty about the red marks from the toe-stepping he'd done on the dance floor. She stretched out those long legs and sighed. He bit back a groan.

"I have to tell you about…" She curled up on her side, giving him an eyeful of curvy ass in lace panties. Just kill him now.

He yanked the comforter over her. "About what? Steph?"

She was sound asleep.

It sucked to be a gentleman.

Get Almost Married now!

Also by Kylie Gilmore

The Clover Park Series

THE OPPOSITE OF WILD (Book 1)
DAISY DOES IT ALL (Book 2)
BAD TASTE IN MEN (Book 3)
KISSING SANTA (Book 4)
RESTLESS HARMONY (Book 5)
NOT MY ROMEO (Book 6)
REV ME UP (Book 7)

The Clover Park STUDS Series

ALMOST IN LOVE (Book 1)
ALMOST MARRIED (Book 2)
ALMOST OVER IT (Book 3)

Acknowledgments

Embracing our differences is what this series is all about, and I thank my family, friends, and readers for embracing mine! Especially my hubby, who knows me at my most geeky and is right there with me. Mwah! Thanks to Big Guy, who told me I had to have a fro-yo guy way back in *Bad Taste in Men*. I'm so glad Barry came to life! Thanks as always to Tessa, Pauline, Mimi, Shannon, Kim, Maura, and Jenn for all you do. Special thanks to *The Big Bang Theory* for making geeks so very cool and loveable.

Special thanks and virtual hugs to my readers. I couldn't do any of this without you!

About the Author

Kylie Gilmore is the *USA Today* bestselling romance author of the Clover Park series and the Clover Park STUDS series. She writes quirky, tender romance with a solid dose of humor.

Kylie lives in New York with her family, two cats, and a nutso dog. When she's not writing, wrangling kids, or dutifully taking notes at writing conferences, you can find her flexing her muscles all the way to the high cabinet for her secret chocolate stash.

Praise for Kylie Gilmore

THE OPPOSITE OF WILD

"This book is everything a reader hopes for. Funny. Hot. Sweet."

—New York Times Bestselling Author, Mimi Jean Pamfiloff

"Ms. Gilmore's writing style draws the reader in and does not let go until the very end of the story and leaves you wanting more."

—Romance Bookworm

"Every aspect of this novel touched me and left me unable to put it down. I pulled an all-nighter, staying up until after 3 am to get to the last page."

—Luv Books Galore

DAISY DOES IT ALL

"The characters in this book are downright hilarious sometimes. I mean, when you start a book off with a fake life and immediately follow it by a rejected proposal, you know that you are in for a fun ride."
—The Little Black Book Blog

"Daisy Does It All is a sweet book with a hint of sizzle. The characters are all very real and I found myself laughing along with them and also having my heart ripped in two for them."
—A is for Alpha, B is for Book

BAD TASTE IN MEN

"I gotta dig a friends to lovers story, and Ms. Gilmore's 3rd book in the Clover Park Series hits the spot. A great dash of humor, a few pinches of steam, and a whole lotta love…Gilmore has won me over with everything I've read and she's on my auto buy list…she's on my top list of new authors for 2014."
—Storm Goddess Book Reviews

"The chemistry between the two characters is so real and so intense, it will have you turning the pages into the midnight hour. Throw in a bit of comedy – a dancing cow, a sprained ankle, and a bit of jealousy and Gilmore has a recipe for great success."
—Underneath the Covers blog

KISSING SANTA

"I love that Samantha and Rico are set up by none other than their mothers. And the journey they go on is really hilarious!! I laughed out loud so many times, my kids asked me what was wrong with me."
—Amazeballs Book Addicts

"I absolutely adored this read. It was quick, funny, sexy and got me in the Christmas spirit. Samantha and Rico are a great couple that keep one another all riled up in more ways than one, and their sexual tension is super hot."
—Read, Tweet, Repeat

Thanks!

Thanks for reading *Almost in Love*. I hope you enjoyed it. Would you like to know about new releases? You can sign up for my new release email list at Eepurl.com/KLQSX. I promise not to clog your inbox! Only new release info and some fun giveaways. You can also sign up by scanning this QR code:

I love to hear from readers! You can find me at:
kyliegilmore.com
Facebook.com/KylieGilmoreToo
Twitter @KylieGilmoreToo

If you liked Barry and Amber's story, please leave a review on your favorite retailer's website or Goodreads. Thank you!

Made in the USA
Middletown, DE
05 August 2015